Praise for Christy Award finalist

SUSAN MAY
WARREN
and her novels

"Warren's fantastic book combines humor, romance
and superb spiritual insight. The first-person narrative
allows the reader to really know Josey and experience
life right alongside her. Filled with life lessons, this
book is not to be missed."
—*Romantic Times BOOKreviews* on
Everything's Coming Up Josey

"Warren presents a likable heroine who learns about
the compromises and joys of married life
and impending motherhood while adjusting
to living in a foreign culture."
—*Library Journal* on *Chill Out, Josey!*

"Susie writes a delightful story... A few hours
of reading doesn't get better."
—Dee Henderson, CBA bestselling author
of the O'Malley series

"Susan's characters deliver love and laughter
and a solid story with every book."
—Lori Copeland, bestselling author of
Bluebonnet Belle

For your glory, Lord

Get Cozy, Josey!

SUSAN MAY WARREN

Steeple
Hill
Café

Published by Steeple Hill Books™

STEEPLE HILL BOOKS

ISBN-13: 978-0-373-78626-8
ISBN-10:   0-373-78626-3

GET COZY, JOSEY!

Printed in U.S.A.

Acknowledgment

What fun I had in writing this story! Remembering the rich cast of friends and family who helped ours survive the frozen world of Far East Russia brought back delicious memories. I have many to thank for this story. Thank you to Krista Stroever and Joan Marlow Golan who let Josey tell her story. Thank you for that gift. Ellen Tarver, my "first eyes" who read the rough story and with me remembered all the things I'd left out. (She, better than nearly anyone, remembers what it's like to live in Siberia!) To my friends in Russia: Vadeem and Sveta Warrenov, who let me stay in their home and introduced me to the intricacies of life with an outhouse. Gene and Luda Khakhaleva, who taught me how to cook and layer my children in fur. To Costa, my friend in heaven, the itinerant pastor who would show up on my doorstep for food and shelter. To my friends in FER who shared my life: Cindy, Patty, Kathy, Melanie, Jennifer, Debby, Robin, Bertha, Lori, Sharon and many, many other women who, like me, learned how to make cookies with foreign ingredients. And to the rest of my fellow Far East Russia missionaries, former and current, Navigator and SEND, who endured and rejoiced and learned with me—thank you for sharing our lives. I hope this book can make you laugh, even in the cold.

Chapter One

My Evil Plot

It's on account of the jellyfish that I ended up in Siberia. That, and a can of Pringles, a volleyball and two very sloppy *plumbere* vanilla ice-cream cones that ended up down the front of my Tasmanian-devil pajama top.

But probably I should tell the entire story of how Chase not only talked me into moving to the backside of the world—where the snow crests off the tundra like whirling dervishes, where a person can literally freeze the nose off her face, and where people eat pig fat for snacks—but how it made me reach deep inside myself to find more of me than I'd ever dreamed.

Definitely more than Chase ever dreamed. But we'll get to that.

I need to state for the record that I, Josey Berglund Anderson, never liked camping. At least, not my husband's definition of camping, which I've discovered is vastly different from mine. But that, in part, is what marriage is all about—discovering the definitions of our personal vocabulary.

Case in point: To me, camping is smores over a crackling fire after a day of hiking some well-used trail along a northern river while the sun sets above a perfect, rose-gilded lake, fireflies twinkling in the indigo twilight. It's watching the moon rise and heating up coffee in a tin camping cup as the night settles in around us. That much I believe Chase and I can agree on. However, it is here where our definitions diverge and trek off into opposite accommodations. I retire to a cabin with indoor plumbing, screens and something to sleep on that is padded and well away from the creepy-crawlies that live in the dirt. In short, when I camp, I want to just add water. This, however, is not Chase's definition. Chase likes to camp from scratch.

I should have known that Chase's interpretation of camping might be different from mine. After all, as an anthropologist—or former anthropologist—his greatest dreams are along the lines of living among the Nepalese, trekking up the sides of mountains clad only in felt moccasins, sleeping in clay-covered huts and eating boiled *dal-bhat* while playing the *sarangi*.

I know, because he has a fifty-pound textbook on the subject. My Chase likes doing things like bathing in a glacial river and wearing the same natty attire for two weeks.

And you ask, I know, how we ended up together. Alas, the differences in our definitions of camping didn't surface until long after our wedding day, and even after the birth of our twins, Chloe and Justin. Perhaps Chase snowed me with his black motorcycle and the way he filled out a football-letter jacket. Perhaps it was the way he chased me across the planet to get my attention and win my heart.

Or maybe, as usual, it was the way he backed me into a corner, one hand propped over my shoulder as he leaned into my neck to plant a kiss and whispered, "C'mon, GI, it'll be fun."

The use of my GI-Josey nickname should have been my first warning. As I've discovered, that word—fun—has vastly different definitions. For example, I do not think it is *fun* to pack into backpacks everything we own—including buckets for hauling water (aka the kitchen sink), swim gear, sleeping bags, clothes, pots and pans, plates, cups, silverware, tents, blankets, a shovel and enough food for ten days—spend two days on a train from Moscow to Simferopol, Ukraine, spend four more hours on a bus and then hike across a treeless steppe to a cliff that drops a hundred meters or so of sure death to the sea where we have to erect our own shelter like nomads, all the while carrying two munchkins (who have their own backpacks, I might add).

I should have realized as we stood on the high cliffs overlooking the Black Sea, watching the waves crashing across a pebbled, not-so-sandy beach and against the boulders below, that setting up camp in a still-rustic yet sturdy cabin hadn't even registered on Chase's list of expectations.

Which led to panic and a softly breathed question. "Where are the bathrooms?"

"Outhouses." Chase pointed to the shovel attached to his pack. "Do it yourself."

Of course.

I stood there a moment, taking in the view, trying to make it all better by focusing on the aqua-green bay under a cloudless sky, on the way the beach curved as if cupping the water, rimmed by rugged, orange, lichen-covered cliffs and lush, green brush. Scattered along the beach like so many shells were tents of all size, shape and color, evidence that Chase is not the only adventurer in Russia. A road wound down to this Chasonian paradise from the cliff, and with a grin, Chase headed for it.

Justin and Chloe ran after him, as if he were the Pied Piper of Hamlin.

I sacrificed three things the day I gave birth to my twins:

1. My waistline. I must have offended it with one too many peanut-butter cookies because it hasn't been back, something my maternity clothes are oh-too-happy to embrace. Chase says two children are enough, especially living in a high-rise, two-bedroom flat in the center of Russia, but I've been holding on to my painfully acquired pregnancy wardrobe (yoga pants and all of Chase's extra-large shirts) just in case. At least that's the story I'm sticking to.

2. My sense of romantic adventure. Take our arrival at the Black Sea, for instance. Instead of running down the beach, the Ray Conniff Singers crooning "Love Story" in my head, rushing toward the crashing waves without a care in the world, I descended the cliff and saw with my maternal eye broken glass, jagged beer cans and old cigarette butts hidden in the sand like land mines. Three-year-old Justin rushed into the water up to his knees, laughing and splashing. I stepped close to grab him in case he went under.

I'll probably never enjoy water again.

3. My bladder. Which has decided that when it wants attention, it gets it. Immediately.

Chase dropped our gear on an empty patch of dirty sand and dug out the shovel. I looked at it, looked at Chase and tried not to cry.

I've come to expect a few inconveniences while living in Russia over the past four-plus years. For example, I don't really expect the electricity to stay on the entire time I'm cooking the Thanksgiving turkey. I know that the hot water will be shut off from May until November, and that if I want a warm bath, I need to prepare at least twelve hours in advance. I have every public bathroom in Moscow plotted out in my mind and have rated them on a scale of "worth walking to" to "I'm desperate." Moreover, I know that when Chase latches on to a new idea, it's much like body surfing. Catch the idea at the right time and you're on top of the wave, enjoying the view. Catch it too late and the wave crests over your head, salt-water up your nose. You land choking and gasping and even a little roughed up by the sand and shells.

I've been wondering—at what point does a girl get to stand in the surf, let the wave crash against her knees and say *Nyet?*

Clearly, I'm not there yet. Which is why, now, I find myself one outpost in a sea of tents facing Russia and Ukraine's idea of paradise, smack in the middle of Chase's definition of a vacation. He's been planning said vacation since we arrived in Russia, and I figure it's his well-earned bonus for four years of dedication to WorldMar, his NGO (non-government organization) in Moscow. Over the past four years, he's launched and managed an entrepreneurial peanut-butter company that's created a new love for creamy spreads—as well as lots of jobs—all the way down the Yalta.

Here's where I admit to my evil master plan, the real reason I agreed to set up camp at the edge of the world. The project has ended, and we've got two choices on the horizon.

Choice One: Head back to Gull Lake, Minnesota, buy a house, and enroll the kids in soccer and ballet lessons. Chase will work for my dad until a teaching position at the school opens up, and we'll finally get to live someplace where the backyard isn't a hazardous-waste zone. (This is obviously my vote.)

Choice Two: Another NGO project, this time working with local, private, chicken farmers.

Can you believe Chase is actually considering it? Not that I have anything against chickens. Rather, I'm thinking that maybe I did my time, and it's my turn.

So, my master plan is, give the man a camping trip, he'll give me Gull Lake. Because, well, four years into marriage I'm learning fast how to bargain. All that time in the market haggling over potatoes has made me a master.

Hence, this last adventure to the south of Ukraine. As far as the eye can see, tents—blue, orange, brown—dot the coast. Russia and Ukraine, in fact all of Eastern Europe, take a vacation in August, most people heading to the sea, where some make, uh, *reservations* and stay at a *resort* (which, by the way, has been my family's livelihood back home in Minnesota for nearly forty years), and others find a space of land and set up a homestead. With kitchens (portable stoves and campfires) and laundry facilities (buckets and clotheslines) and living rooms (tarps staked over cars and paddles and other makeshift walls). Kids run naked to the sea and back—my preschoolers are overdressed in their pull-ups, T-shirts, and sunhats. The smell of fish and smoke taint the fresh air. Someone has decided to run the battery down on their boom box and picked up a radio station. I recognize a Machina Vremina song.

About fifty paces behind all this chaos is another village—of outhouses. Most are made of driftwood or scrap lumber shoved into the ground and covered on three sides (some of them poorly) with an old sheet. The backside is open to face, uh, nature. Not ours, however. The American outhouse is made of four rebars and a dark sheet secured on three sides, with a hanging door for privacy. It's quite sturdy, and I have a feeling it could survive a typhoon.

The fact that there is no chance my backside will flash the world—even in the most dramatic of weather—is my one consolation for having to spend every waking moment sweeping out the tent, making sure our children don't kick off their beach shoes or disappear forever into the sea, cooking another pot of potatoes and lathering on another layer of sunblock.

Yeah, I'm having fun. I love camping.

Gull Lake, think Gull Lake. Three-bedroom home. Swing set.

Dog. A black Lab, or maybe a collie—

"Josey, look what our neighbors Nastia and Vadeem gave us." Chase comes tromping across the sand, all grins. Of course Chase is on a first-name basis with the "neighbors." Another day, and they'll adopt him.

Okay, yes, I have some attitude issues. Although I came to Russia *first,* over five years ago, learned to speak Russian *first,* learned how to negotiate the Moscow subway *first,* Chase was born to live in Russia. He even looks Russian, and he speaks it so well after four years that someone even asked him how he, as a Russian, managed to nab me, an American wife. That particular day, I didn't have an answer for that.

Today I might. Because he's looking tan and toned, his dark-blond needs-a-cut hair curly on his neck and shiny in the sun. He smiles at me, his blue eyes alight with mischief. Wearing a red handkerchief he's tied on his head, a T-shirt with the arms cut off and a pair of swim trunks (the American kind, not the Russian-favored Speedo style), he crouches where I'm sitting, accidentally kicking sand and pebbles onto my towel. I have an eye on Chloe, who is standing just at the edge of the water with a plastic shovel, perhaps contemplating how long it might take to fill the hole she's just dug with water. Her blond hair is nearly white, curling out under her hat like Chase's. Justin is napping in the tent behind me, his lips askew, a fine bead of sweat along his brow. He's going to be a charmer, just like his dad.

Someday his wife will ask me why she agreed to live three billion miles away from her family and home, in a country whose word for "hello" sounds like someone clearing their throat of phlegm. *Zhdrast-vyootya?* Please.

I'll just smile at her and say I have no idea. But of course I will. "What?" I ask Chase.

Chase plunks down a blue bucket—my blue bucket, formerly used to wash preschooler underwear in. "Flounder!"

I stare at the bucket, and my stomach responds before I do. Because the shiny, smelly *thing* is staring at me with both glassy eyes, his fins still twitching. "Both eyes are on the same side of his head," I say, not sure what Chase wants me to do with it.

"That's because he lies on the bottom of the sea, hiding in the sand, waiting to surprise his prey."

Creepy. "Is he a pet?"

Chase laughs. "We're invited to Vadeem and Nastia's place for dinner. We just have to clean it."

Not I, said the little red hen.

But before I can refuse, I'm distracted by a cry from Chloe. She's wandered into the water and has picked up a bag, dripping, see-through—

"That's a jellyfish!" I am on my feet, running toward Chloe, who's laughing and flinging the fish around like it's her teddy bear.

Jellyfish abound in the Black Sea, so much so that

the first time I waded out into the water, I felt as if I were swimming through Jell-O. "They won't sting," Chase—the jellyfish expert—had assured me, as I made a face and cleared a path back to shore.

Sure. Because they like me and want to be my friend?

I grab the jellyfish and fling it out of Chloe's hand. She's startled and starts to cry. I sweep her up. Glare at Chase.

"I'll clean the fish," he says.

Ya think?

I dig into my supply bag and hand Chloe a cookie. She takes it in her grubby little hands, grinning up at me through her tears. Yeah, I have her number. I take one, too.

The Black Sea at dusk is nearly magical, with the colors of autumn streaked like watercolors across the western sky, slowly vanishing into a perfect, diamond-studded canvas that seems so close I feel I could reach out and wrap my fingers around a star. The wind off the sea is cool and smells of the world, of the places it's traveled. Sitting before the fire, as Nastia fries fish on her portable stove, listening to Chase converse with Vadeem, I'm reminded so much of Gull Lake and magical moments back home, that melancholy finds me and moistens my eyes. I love Gull Lake, the small town where I can walk down the street and know the names, even the secrets, of everyone I meet. Where the Fourth of July parade circles the town twice and still only takes ten minutes. Where the most exciting article in the paper is the Annual Walleye Fishing Contest results. I miss fresh-brewed coffee and kringle, and my sister Jasmine, who just had baby number two. And H, my punk, now married, lead-singer friend, who just cut her second album.

I am on the other side of the planet, eating creepy fish, drowning it down with watery orange *sok,* praying my children don't pick up tuberculosis.

"Hey there," a voice says in English.

I look up, startled. Above me stands a dark-haired man, brown eyes, nice smile, wearing dark shorts and a white "Vote for Pedro" T-shirt, holding a tube of Pringles. (Who is Pedro, and what is he running for?) My gaze latches on to the Pringles.

Pringle Man sits next to me. "Want one?"

I am a Minnesotan. I long for a Pringle with everything inside me, but you'll have to offer three times. That was only once.

"No, thanks."

He shrugs. "You look hungry."

I glance around for Justin. Chloe is sitting tucked into Chase's lap, playing with his hat tassels. Justin is crouched by the water, a tiny dark outline against the indigo prairie.

"Justin, honey, come to Mommy." I see him stand, look back and start to toddle toward me.

"I met your husband earlier today," Mysterious Pringle Man says. He crunches another Pringle. "He's an interesting guy."

I glance at Chase. He's in animated conversation. "He keeps me on my toes."

"You're a good wife to let him drag you out here."

Now he has my attention. I smile. Yeah, I am, I know. Mrs. Proverbs 31. "Thanks. We're headed stateside after this. He needed one last adventure."

Mr. Pringles crunches another one. "My name's Marc." He wipes his hand off on his T-shirt. "I'm with Voices International. We represent the Fourth World, researching their cultures. Are you sure you don't want a Pringle?"

That's two. My mouth is salivating. "No, thanks," I say. "What is the Fourth World? I'm only aware of one." I laugh at my joke. He doesn't. Uh-oh, the Pringles might be in jeopardy.

"The Fourth World refers to the LDC, or least developed countries, usually within First or Third World nations. Namely, the indigenous groups who have been largely obliterated by the country in power. Currently, we're working with the Russian Ministry of Indigenous People out of Moscow to study their various people groups. Like the Nanais of Siberia. There are over thirty different indigenous groups in

Russia, and the government is starting to realize they need to figure out ways to help preserve their culture, rather than assimilate it."

"You make the Russians sound like the Borg."

He takes another chip. "It's not unlike what we did to our First Nations people in Canada, making them speak English, sending their children to residential schools, obliterating their culture."

"We did that in America, too."

Marc nods. He digs a little well into the pebbly beach, setting the Pringles can inside. "Where're you from?"

"Minnesota—a little town right in the middle."

"My backyard, eh? I'm from Winnipeg." He smiles at me, and the firelight reveals a twinkle in those brown eyes. Not only is that look aimed at still-pregnant-weight me, but I'm married, and I don't see too many of those zingers these days.

I don't know quite what to do. Is he…flirting with me? Gulp.

No, he can't be. I glance again toward Chase, who looks at me and grins. I grin back. See, happily married, Mr. Pringles.

Marc seems to have followed my gaze, because he waves to Chase. Grins.

Maybe I imagined all that. For sure I imagined it.

"I can't finish these. Are you sure you won't have one?"

That's three. Phew, I was starting to worry. I take the can and smile. If you insist, Mr. Pringles. "Thanks."

Heaven, in one perfectly formed oval chip. I crunch it with my tongue, letting the salt fill my mouth.

Marc's eyes are on me as I enjoy my moment of Pringle bliss, and he's smiling with one side of his mouth. "Methinks someone is missing home."

"Where did you find these?"

He lifts a shoulder. "Spotted them in a kiosk in Simferopol. Bought all eight cans."

My eyes widen, and he laughs. "Yes, I have more."

"Oh, no, that's not—"

"I'll bring you a can tomorrow."

"No, I couldn't." But I could, I could!

I shouldn't.

I shouldn't.

But it tastes so good, so salty, so…home. And I want more.

"Are you on vacation?" I ask, taking another chip.

He nods. "I'm with a group of other researchers. Taking a few days off before we head to an international conference in Kazakhstan." He stands up, dusting off his hands. "I came over to invite Chase to join us in a game of volleyball at our camp tomorrow. We have at least two Americans, and—" he winks "—lots of Pringles. Come with him."

I shamelessly shake the chip crumbs out of the can

and into my hand. I look up at him. He smiles again,
all white teeth and dark, friendly eyes.

I find myself saying, "What time?"

Chapter Two

Just Like Camping

My hometown of Gull Lake, Minnesota, population 2,500, thrives on sports. During a January basketball game, our small high-school gym is hotter than a Finnish sauna, and our cheerleaders can dance in hockey skates. We are a multi-sport town, and our trophy case has been reinforced three times to hold the weight of the embossed accolades. I mention this only to say that I, Josey Berglund Anderson, have my name on a trophy in said case.

Girls Volleyball, 1996, State Champs, "A" division. We were the stars of the Christmas parade that year, and I made the front page of the *Gull Lake Gazette*—displaying the "Josey spike"—three times that season.

I lived and breathed volleyball. Pringle Marc has no idea what he's in for. More than that, Chase, being a football jock, rarely saw me play. I'm feeling seventeen all over again as I pull on my Tasmanian-devil pajamas—and after a moment of long hesitation where I contemplate the sacrifices one must make for competition—I tear off the already ratty arms and tie the hem into a knot just below my waist.

"What are you doing?" Chase traps Justin under one arm, tickling him as Chloe climbs his back, fire in her three-year-old blue eyes. She's such a knock off the old block (meaning me). It's World Wide Wrestling hour in our tent, although I feel as if Jesse "The Bod" Ventura and I already did a few rounds due to Justin and Chloe's propensity to sleep with their feet in my face. Who, again, thought it was a good idea to go camping with two preschoolers who are barely potty-trained?

"I got invited to play beach volleyball with you today," I say, pulling on a pair of shorts. Okay, yoga-pant cutoffs, but with my baggy Taz top, they look more like biking shorts, without the firm sheen (and you know what I mean). I'm wearing my swimsuit underneath, and I grab Chase's crazy bandana hat, untying it for a headband.

"*You're* playing volleyball?" Chase asks, pulling Chloe forward over his shoulder and tickling her belly. She shrieks in delight.

I glare at him. Just because I've spent the past three years wiping snotty noses and cutting food into tiny pieces doesn't mean that the Josey inside—the one who came to Russia when hot dogs were still a delicacy, who gave birth in a Russian hospital, who helped her high-school sweetheart become a peanut-butter mogul—has lost her stride. I can still bump and spike. In fact, them sound like fightin' words.

"Did you think I forgot how?"

Chase gets that deer-in-the-headlights look on his face. Yeah, you're in trouble, pal. He deflects with a smile while Justin shoves his hand into his dad's mouth. "No," he says between little fingers. "I jush thought—"

"I wanna play. I haven't played beach volleyball for years."

Chase pulls Justin's fingers away. "Of course."

"Can you help keep an eye on the twins?" Of course, in principle, I shouldn't have to ask the *father of our children* to watch the twins, but the reality is, my man stepped outta line when the "equal responsibility" gene got handed out. Not that Chase is a bad father. For all his angst before the twins were born, he has plowed through midnight feedings, diaper changes and pre-potty-training in stellar form. But— and I say this with love as he holds down both kids and tickles their feet—he's sort of like a giant inter-active toy.

I married a twelve-year-old. With great shoulders.

He flips Chloe over his shoulder as she slaps his back. "Sure. In fact, I'll sit it out and get them some ice cream. I saw a guy peddling some cones yesterday up the shore. It's almost lunchtime, anyway."

Ice cream for lunch. See, I told you: twelve. But I lean over and give him a kiss because, well, he does have those shoulders.

The sun is hot, and the beach is warm through my rubber swim shoes as we walk to Pringle Marc's camp. No one with all their faculties intact would walk barefoot on the beach in Russia, not unless their tetanus shot is updated. The sea is deep turquoise and so translucent, I spot the darkened underwater shoals where Chase went snorkeling yesterday. He brought us back a bag of clams and mussels. And then proceeded to clean them. And cook them.

I've lost about ten pounds on this trip.

Our neighbor Vadeem lifts his hand to wave—he's playing a card game called *Durok* (literal translation: Fool) with his wife, mother-in-law and two naked daughters, ages six months and eighteen months (one year apart has to be nearly as fun as twins). They've been here for a month now, all five of them sleeping in a tent made for four. I count my blessings as we weave our way through other camps, some constructed of brown Russian-army tents, others of giant nylon tarps. Russians on vacation are a friendly lot, and most of them smile at us. A few toast us with half-full glasses of warm vodka.

I spy the volleyball court. My team is warming up.

Oh, boy. Clearly, I'm the only woman in the group. Which, when surrounded by ten or so shirt-less, tan, just-sweaty-enough male volleyball players, isn't the worst situation in the world. I glance at Chase and smile.

He's wearing a frown. "I don't see the ice-cream man."

I'll just bet that's what he was thinking. But he hides it as he answers Marc's greeting with a hand-shake. "I brought you my secret weapon." He glances at me and winks. "Killer."

Oh, Chase. See, even though I'm surrounded by *Baywatch,* the man has nothing—not a thing, *nada, nichevo*—to worry about.

"Then she's on my team," Marc says, pulling me into the game. He introduces me around to five Ca-nadians, two Germans, an Italian and two Ameri-cans. I don't catch all their names, because, you know, I'm focused on the *volleyball,* but I think there's a Joe, a Duncan, a Kurt and a Paul on my team.

Their camp, adjacent to the court, is a beautiful array of orange and blue family-size tents, evidence that this group lives in luxury. And apparently they've taken the time to police the beach for glass, cigarettes and other menaces, because most of the guys are barefoot. But I don't want anything to interfere with my game, so I'm keeping my shoes on as I line up in the back row for the serve.

"Let's play!" I say, clapping. Marc shoots me a look.

Where's the team spirit? The ball shoots across the net and I go down for a perfect, beautiful bump. It sets up high for Duncan, who chooses to smash it into the net, instead of setting it up for our spike man, Kurt.

Apparently, my teammates need to get their minds on the game. The next serve comes faster and although I call it, Marc dives for the return and we crash heads.

"Sorry," he says. I force a smile.

"No problem, it's just a game." It's just a game, *it's just a game.*

The third shot is out, and Marc takes the serve. It's a net ball, and I shoot a look at Chase. He gives me a thumbs-up. Justin is digging in the sand and dirt behind him, and Chloe is fighting with the sun hat I double-tied under her chin.

I almost miss the serve, but go to my knees to bump it. This time, Paul sets it for Duncan, who spikes it into the opposing team's court.

Now *that's* what I'm talkin' 'bout.

"Paul, that was an awesome set," I say. "Let's see if we can do that again."

Marc glances at me, and I nod at him, all smiles. All this team needs is a little leadership.

Paul steps up to serve for our team. He's got a wicked overhand serve, and pretty soon I'm covered in sand, we're five points up, and Marc is wagering his Pringles against the win.

"I think I see the ice-cream guy," says Chase somewhere nearby. Yeah, yeah. Marc bumps the service up to me, I set up a beauty of a spike, and Kurt arrows it over. We're a well-oiled machine, we are, and even attracting an audience as we rack up three more points. I see fire in the other team's eyes—they are crouched down, their hands at the ready, poised to volley.

We volley hard until Marc sets it, and I go airborne, feeling my wings, that old juice in my veins as I slam the ball over, hard, fast, just skimming the net and kicking up sand on the other side.

"She's hot now!" Marc says.

I glance at Chase, who has Chloe in his arms. He's wearing a strange look, one I haven't seen in years. The same one he gave me from across the room at Lew Suzlbach's graduation party, right before I went joyriding with two of his football buddies. I remember returning to find him sitting in the front yard, arms dangling over his knees, waiting. He corralled me for a ride on his motorcycle—a long ride that lasted until sunrise.

It wasn't long after that that he told me he was attending college far, far away from Gull Lake.

The look rattles me for a moment, and then he smiles. "I'm going for ice cream!"

Maybe I misread all that.

I wave at him and turn back to the game.

We're up by eight, and although the other team makes a valiant effort, they can't overcome the mighty power of, um, Josey and the Guys.

"Okay, Josey, I'll give you your own can of Pringles if you can bring it home!" Marc tosses me the ball to serve for game point.

I send it over the net with a satisfying *thwack*.

The other team volleys well, spikes it hard, but our team dives deep and rescues with a bump. It's set, and I realize it's all mine. A spike from the back row. I wind up, jump, connect—

A scream right behind me snatches my attention. My maternal instinct kicks in before I land.

I'm already turning, the word *Rebyonka* registering in my adrenaline-laced brain.

Baby.

My baby. In the water, jellyfish wrapped around his little body. He is screaming. He's up to his chest and if he falls…

Please, God.

I am in the water before anyone even moves, thrashing my way to Justin. "It's okay, honey, Mommy's coming." Jellyfish swarm me, wrapping like cellophane around my legs and arms as I scoop

Justin up, pulling the jellyfish from his body. But they cling to me and, apparently agitated, begin to sting.

A thousand needles, into my legs, my arms, across my back. I'm shaking them off even as I run to shore, ignoring the fire that is raging across my skin. Marc is there with a towel for Justin, but I don't hand him off. I just wrap his little preschool body in terry cloth and hold him close. He's crying.

I'm breathing hard. Great gasps of forced air. I…can't…breathe.

I drop to my knees. Let go of Justin. He stands there as I put a hand into the sand, another to my throat. I…can't…

"Josey, are you okay?"

"What's wrong with her?"

I look up, blinking, but the world is starting to fade…

"Josey? Josey?"

I come to in a rush, and Chase is right there above me. His hand is around my neck, and a coldness presses into my chest. I'm lying in the sand, a bed of grit. I feel heavy, groggy. My lips are thick.

"Whaf haffen?"

"You had an allergic reaction to the jellyfish." Chase touches his forehead to mine, and I can feel him tremble. "You really scared us." As he pulls away, I see a crowd standing around me full of Russians wearing their Speedos. That's a sight that'll wake anyone from a sound coma. Thankfully, I see others, in swim trunks. A man is holding a ball in his hands.

A volleyball.

The game.

Justin!

I start to sit up, but Chase pushes me back. "Justin!"

"He's fine." He gestures to a place behind me, and I crane my neck to see Chloe and Justin playing in the sand, aided by Nastia, our Russian neighbor. "He was a little shook up, but he wasn't stung. They don't usually sting—"

I raise my eyebrow.

"—unless provoked."

That's me, the Jellyfish Provoker. I close my eyes, aching from head to toe, feeling the stings. I shiver. "What happened?" My voice sounds tight, raspy, as if choked. My throat hurts.

"Your throat closed up. Good thing Duncan is allergic to bee stings. He carries an EpiPen with him." Chase's eyes begin to glisten.

I shiver again, cold spreading down my chest. No, *running* down my chest, into my armpits. I reach up to touch the sensation. It's sticky. Gooey. "What—?"

Chase is making a face. "Yeah, well, I got sorta carried away. I saw you collapse and forgot I was carrying ice cream, and…"

"You smeared ice cream on me?" I lick my finger. *"Plumbere."*

"Your favorite kind."

Uh, no. *Chase's* favorite kind. Shortly after we moved to Russia, we spent a month deciding what flavor and brand of ice cream Chase liked, which involved visiting every ice-cream vendor in the city. Not that I'm complaining about his methods.

I pull the sodden shirt away from my body. "Yuck."

"I'm so sorry, GI. I thought you knew Justin was still here. You waved at me when I told you I was just taking Chloe."

I stare at him. I don't remember that. Do you remember that?

All I remember is, is…

I sit up, looking past Chase, and zero in on Marc, standing right behind him. "Did we get the point?"

Slowly a smile breaks out across Marc's face.

Then he turns to Chase and utters the words that will change my life. And I know then that Chase is a flounder, two eyes on one side of his head, hiding in the sand on the bottom, awaiting his prey.

"See, I told you she'd do fine in Siberia," says Marc. "She's a trouper. Besides, it's just like camping."

Wait! Did someone say *camping?*

Or—worse yet—Siberia?

Chapter Three

No Pressure or Anything

"**H**e did what?"

I'm so relieved to hear my friend Maggie Calhoun's tone of voice—the slight shrill that betrays I'm not nuts to be on a full-out strike against Chase's methods of mind control—that I'm willing to forgive her for losing all her pregnancy weight and being back down to a size six and wearing the cutest pair of Ann Taylor jeans and a cable-knit sweater. I feel like the hometown bum in my fat jeans and Chase's old Gull Lake sweatshirt.

"He planned it. The entire camping trip, the meeting with Marc, the volleyball game. If I hadn't nearly perished, I would have thought he'd planned the jellyfish, too." I'm at Gorky Park, standing in line for popcorn, watching some lovebirds on the lake in the center of the park in a paddleboat. Chase and I used to paddle this lake.

The thing about paddleboats is that the paddlers have to have rhythm and a commitment to work together. Today, Chase and I would probably sink the boat.

"He wanted me to meet Marc, knowing I'd be swayed by the whole ignored indigenous people line."

"You were, weren't you?" This from Daphne, my very pregnant friend, wife of my pal Caleb and fellow orphanage fund-raiser. She has a cute butterball tummy even at seven months, which she hides under a large long-sleeve Gap shirt and a pair of Caleb's baggy pants. I keep pressing her to travel stateside for the birth, to which she replies, "If you can do it, I can do it."

Yeah, well, if I'd had a choice, I would have had soft lights, soothing music and the E-word. Epidural. But one doesn't get to choose when trapped in Russia, not knowing they're expecting twins, who decide to be born early.

But I don't want to scare the girl.

Daphne, better than anyone, knows how my heart-strings are strummed by the weak and helpless, how Chase played me.

I purse my lips. "Yeah, okay, Marc did wage a convincing argument. Small community on the edge of nowhere, going under economically, trying desperately to hold on to their culture, their way of life. And apparently the research he wants Chase to do might help them figure out ways to thrive."

The cause calls to the hidden Mother Teresa inside me, the one who keeps trying to find a foothold in this country. But what about Gull Lake? And the dog we don't have, Shep?

"The way Marc put it, it felt like Chase was practically daring me to go to Siberia."

"And we all know how you do with dares."

Okay, yes, I do respond to the whole "wimp" taunt. Once, when Chase and I were eight, he double-dog-dared me to touch my tongue to the icy playground slide.

That's a memory I don't want to dredge up.

The short of it is, I'm not good at backing down from a dare. And Chase knows it all too well.

I can't help but be proud of the fact that Chase married me for my ability to keep up and even sometimes forge ahead of his challenges. But it bugs me more than a little that he used it against me, the sneak.

"Mommy—me, corn!" Chloe is jumping up and down beside me, clapping her hands. Maggie's little boy, Steven, about four months younger than my twins, is pulling on his mother's arm, his eyes wide as he gazes at the inflatable cage filled with balls. Justin is driving the Hotwheel car he got for his birthday along the metal railings that edge the pathways of the park. When we're out in public, my eyes are ever riveted to the twins. Russia is riddled with safety hazards—from open manholes to wild drivers. And when I say wild, I mean the kind that drive on sidewalks. Lest you think I jest, let me just say that winter is Chase's favorite season because there are no lines in the road and no sidewalk curbs, thanks to the snow. Hence, he drives anywhere his black Moscovitz decides to go. No-Rules Chase. All I can say is that the government didn't ask *me* before they gave him his driver's license; I would have told them he had an aversion to driving—or living, for that matter—inside the lines.

A guy who lived by the rules would see how out of the question it is to ask his wife to move a billion miles to the east into snow and ice.

Sure, Minnesota has plenty of snow and ice. But we also have SUVs and lots of goose down. And snowmobiles. Betcha there aren't any snowmobiles in Siberia.

"Does that mean he's not going to take over the chicken project?" Maggie asks, giving in to Steven. Maggie's husband, Dalton, is the head of Chase's NGO. And Chase's soon-to-be-former boss.

I give Maggie a wry smile. "I was really hoping we'd be heading back to Gull Lake. I wanted to live in a real house and give my children the life I had growing up."

I hand Chloe the bag of popcorn, steering her to

a bench, while Maggie pays the trampoline vendor and Steven pries off his shoes. He's got the cutest head of black curls and dark eyes just like his father.

Justin spies him and comes running to me. "Me, too! Me, too!"

"Stay here," I command Chloe. She grins at me, mischief in her eyes. Clearly she's inherited that dare-me mentality. Where is the duct tape when I need it? I glance at Daphne. "Can you watch her?"

Daphne reaches for Chloe's hand. Chloe yanks it away and glares at her. That's my girl—don't let anyone hold you back.

I take Justin's hand, which he surrenders easily, and we join the line for the trampoline.

"Tired of living overseas?" Maggie asks. Technically, she's lived in Moscow longer than I have, although I've accumulated an impressive five years of Russia time. (Which should equal about twelve years in any other European country.) Before marrying Dalton, Maggie worked for the State Department.

I pay the vendor and help Justin off with his shoes. "It's not so much overseas as Moscow. The novelty of subway surfing has worn off, and I'd give my left foot for a backyard for the kids." Helping Justin through the trampoline door, I turn back.

Chloe is just disappearing down the path, Daphne waddling after her.

I take off at a run. "Chloe! Stop!"

She looks back at me. And, like the rascal she is, pumps it up to a full-out sprint.

Oh, I love motherhood.

I pass Daph, who's bending over, gripping her knees (which she can still see), breathing hard. For Pete's sake, I hiked all over Moscow while roughly twice the size of Daphne.

But it's not her fault I gave birth to Houdini, Master of the Vanishing Act. Already, Chloe's been lost twice in Gorky Park. One time involved the local police and forty very long, stomach-churning minutes.

I catch up with her and scoop her up. "Chloe, you have to listen to Mommy! It's not safe."

That's an understatement. It's not just the hazardous manholes, it's the fact that with her blond pigtails and American attire (that is, no snowsuit in the middle of summer), Chloe may as well be wearing a Kidnap Me sign.

I rejoin Maggie, who's watching the boys.

"Speedy Gonzales get away again?"

I plop Chloe onto the bench. "More than anything, I long for safety, and, perhaps, quiet."

"Siberia sounds quiet. All that snow sort of muffles everything."

Oh, hardy-har-har. "What's wrong with doing it my way, just for once? Can't we just go home and live a calm, predictable life?"

But even as I say it, I know the answer. Living a normal life would require living with a calm, predictable *man*. And, much of what I love about Chase is his wild, adventurous side.

Maggie lifts a shoulder. "Here's my question—is your way the best way? What's best for you and Chase?"

Daphne rejoins us, easing herself onto the bench. A sweat has broken out on her forehead where she's pulled back her brown hair into two pigtails. She looks about sixteen, not at all like the twenty-six-year-old nurse she is. "Maybe it's just a matter of submitting to your husband."

Maggie's head swivels in Daph's direction. Everything inside me goes still.

"Did you say 'submit'?"

I raise an eyebrow. It's not a secret that Maggie and Daphne hold vastly different views on the role of wives, but I'm usually able to divert us around any philosophical land mines.

"Yes, submit. Wives submit to their hus—"

"Daph—"

But I'm too late. Maggie has fire in her eyes.

"I can't believe that in this day and age, you still think that. There goes sixty years of progress."

"Don't you believe in submission?" Daphne asks, ignoring my efforts to wave her off. What, do I need semaphores? It doesn't take a PhD to figure out that a woman who ran her own department in Moscow and speaks four languages isn't about to submit to anyone. And on the other side, it doesn't take a Strong's Concordance to figure out that a newly married missionary who loves Russia is sure she has this submission thing down pat.

"I believe in respect," Maggie says, and the air turns icy despite the warm September breeze. I know that Maggie, if she had ever been on Chase's side, would now go to the mattresses for my right to return to Gull Lake.

Daphne shoots me a help-me look, but I'm useless. Because even though she and I are Christians, I'm not sure I'm *not* on Maggie's side.

After all, a girl should be able to have *some* say where she lives, right? And how?

"Someone has to give in," Daphne says finally. "Obviously Chase and Josey are on different pages here. And if they want a happy ending to their fairy tale, someone has to make the sacrifice."

I'm narrowing my eyes at her. Hello? If it's a contest, I know who's been making all the sacrifices. Ever try grocery shopping in Russia? Where you have to hit eight different stores because no one store has everything? Where you then have to lug two fifty-pound bags home on the subway and up nine flights of stairs because the elevator is out? Now try it with *two three-year-olds*. Then come talk to me about sacrifice.

But it's more than that. It's that I deserve to go

home. I've been an uncomplaining trouper of a wife. I've lived with the constant fickleness of heat and electricity, shopped with infants strapped to my front and back. Eaten carp.

I even went camping.

"Listen, Chase has a perfectly good job waiting for him back in Gull Lake."

"Teaching?" Daphne is squirming, trying to get comfortable on the bench.

"Uh, no. Helping my dad at Berglund Acres. Dad's getting old and needs the help."

"So Chase is going to run the resort?" Maggie asks.

"Um, well, I mean, Jasmine and Milton are there, and they run the restaurant and the books…"

"So Chase would…?" Daphne finally stands up, folding her hands over her belly.

"Uh…" What *would* Chase do? Mow lawns? Plunge toilets? "I'm not moving to Siberia. That's just too much to ask of any woman."

Maggie nods. Daphne raises an eyebrow.

"Siberia, ladies! Where the snow comes sweeping down the plain. They subsist on stewed caribou and live in igloos—"

"I don't think they live in ig—" Daphne starts.

"I'm going home to Gull Lake. Period. End of sentence, end of paragraph, end of book."

"Mommy, I'm all done!" Justin is leaning against the edge of the net. Steven is already climbing out on his own.

Maggie gets up to retrieve her son. "You stick to your guns, honey."

Daphne rubs her hand over her stomach. "I'll make you a scarf."

<Wildflower>: Siberia? Did you say Siberia? Isn't that where they sent people to the Gulag?

H, my Minnesota high-school friend from Gull Lake is online just when I need her and ready with the appropriate words of horror. Born with the name Heather, she has assumed so many identities over the years—from artist to punk rocker, only her IM identity remains of that earliest incarnation. H might not be a Christian, but she knows me—too well, probably, but enough to hold my hand and offer the appropriate advice to my current Chase meltdown

<GI>: Yes! See, H? I'm not overreacting. And worse, Chase is all, "Whatever you want to do, Josey, we'll do. No pressure." Yeah, right, like he won't blame me for his horrible life when he's plunging toilets and cleaning litter off the beach in Gull Lake.

< Wildflower >: Yeah, but *Siberia*. I mean, if you want to stay in Russia, why don't you stick around Moscow? At least you're assured a supply of bagels.

<GI>: I DON'T WANT TO STAY IN RUSSIA!

<Wildflower>: Calm down. I'm just saying, if you're worried about Chase, maybe there are other options that won't give you frostbite.

<GI>: He got a packet of literature from Voices International. Spent the night reading it. Got out his Nepalese book. You know the one.

<Wildflower>: Listen. Just tell him you're ready for a real life. For fast food. TiVo. Running hot water year round.

<GI>: I'm just ready to be safe.

<Wildflower>: Then don't come back to Gull Lake. Because just last week, Bruce Minson busted a meth operation just outside town. And someone ran their truck into the convenience store and took out the front window and the entire DVD rental section.

<GI>: Yeah, but no one is going to kidnap Justin off Main Street. And Chloe's not going to fall through a manhole and end up at the bottom of the sewer system.

<Wildflower>: No, but she could wade into Gull Lake.

<GI>: What's your problem? I thought you were on my side.

<Wildflower>: I'm just saying, if you're looking for safety, I think you'll have to invest in a bubble home. Or a couple of leashes.

<GI>: Where are you right now?

<Wildflower>: In Hutchison. We have a gig tonight.

<GI> How is your new album selling?

<Wildflower>: I just took on an extra shift at the Wolf. And Rex is working full-time at the paper. We're rolling in cash. Oh, and don't worry— Mildred still says no one can write the police report like you.

<GI>: My calling in life. *Sigh* I'll never write again.

<Wildflower>: What are you doing right now? I'm confused, because wasn't that you who wrote the fund-raising newsletter for your orphanage program the past three years?

<GI>: I just thought by now I'd be back in my groove, maybe be editor of the *Gazette*.

<Wildflower>: So your fear of Siberia is a result of your desire for Mildred's orange chair and view of the Harbor Hotel?

<GI>: My fear of Siberia has to do with a thirty-below wind chill. My *depression* about it has to do with the view. Which, from here, looks like moon boots, snowdrifts and dogsleds. I don't know. It just seems like I've pushed "Pause" on my life, and everyone is passing me by.

<Wildflower>: Who, me? Because Letterman hasn't exactly been burning up my line with voice messages, trying to get me to perform on his show.

<GI>: He will.

<Wildflower>: What happened to the woman who wanted to change the world?

<GI>: She expired due to lack of sleep. I just want to come home.

<Wildflower>: So come home.

<GI>: I don't think it's up to me.

<Wildflower>: Just say no.

<GI>: Thanks, Nancy.

Living in Russia hasn't been a total nightmare. I have a cleaning lady. And for a while I had a chauffeur. Sveta and Thug (aka Igor) who got married (thanks, I'd like to think, to me) right before the twins were born. Now Sveta cleans my house once a week while Igor drives for Dalton and Maggie. Meanwhile, I'm honing my ability to surf the Moscow subway— the skill of balancing unaided, as the train careens down the tracks. In fact, I carry my subway pass with pride.

See? That "dare me" mentality can come back to bite me.

Especially now, as I'm hiking back from the metro. My backpack is bulging with meat, milk, cheese, bread, potatoes and *padushka* (translation: pillows, which are really puffs of cereal filled with chocolate, my reward for stopping at four different stores and chasing Chloe through the fish aisle at the market), and I've got an iron grip on Justin and Chloe. Chloe is fighting me with every step, occasionally doing her I-am-rubber act. Justin, my *good* child, is only concerned about missing *Nu Pagadee,* his favorite Russian cartoon.

The sky is purple, as if bruised from the day, and I totally relate. Two weeks have passed since our camping trip—since I was shanghaied by Marc and Chase, since my grip on Gull Lake began to slide out of my hands—and I feel as if I've been through a sausage press.

And shoot, if Chase isn't being cooperative and

romantic and *submissive* with his, "Whatever you want to do, honey."

Yeah, sure. Whatever I want to do.

We live in a gated community, but that only means we have a guard at the front gate who protects all the Mafia-connected tenants in our nine-story high-rise. It's a sad commentary about life in Russia when Mafia Central is the safest place in town. We live right above the mayor and his wife. Which should raise serious questions about his political connections.

I enter the code into the door, and it squeals open. Chloe wrenches herself free and runs for the elevator, which is just opening. She's too short to hit 9, so she smashes 1. Justin runs in, jumping up and down. "Nu Pagadee! Nu Pagadee!"

I suppose I should be happy my child is learning Russian. Except "Nu Pagadee" means "I'll get you!" His other words are "Ruki Veer!" which, sadly, means, "Hands up!" I guess he fits right into the neighborhood.

We all spill out of the elevator, and I open the three-ton metal door that barricades our flat. Sometimes I feel like I live in a prison, what with the metal door and the bars on the windows. I long for a vista without vertical lines.

Sveta's obviously been here, because the flat smells like lemon, the rug by the door is crumb-free, and the shoes are lined up in neat little rows. Justin wrestles off his sneakers and he and Chloe run for the television in our family room. I am just closing the door when I feel hands on my waist.

I jump, and gulp down a scream.

"Sorry. I didn't mean to startle you." Chase is behind me. I turn, barely stifling another scream.

"What are you wearing?" And I'm not talking about his jeans or his black WorldMar T-shirt, but the rather large, um, *animal* on his head, and the fuzzy sheepskin boots on his feet.

"I'm a Cossack."

"You're a crazy person." I touch the hat, which makes him look like an eighties rock star with fuzzy brownish-blond hair that extends down over his ears, adding a distinctly basset-hound aura.

"I got you one, too." And without warning, he pulls a matching hat out from behind his back and plunks it on my head. It engulfs me and I can't see. "It's red fox. Cool, huh?"

No, actually. Not cool. Sweltering.

"This is your idea of no pressure?" I push the hat up with one finger. But he's grinning at me, working his devastating powers of persuasion.

He lifts a shoulder. "If we don't go, we'll wear them in Gull Lake."

"Where?" At the annual ice-fishing festival? At a three-day dogsled race?

"Maybe when I shovel the driveway." He picks up

the tassel attached to one of my basset ears and tickles my chin with the fuzzy ball at the end.

And right then, I know. I can't doom my man to a life of fixing water heaters all winter and putting in the dock each spring. It might be fine for my father, but Chase was born for adventure. For challenges.

For Siberia.

I close my eyes. Sigh. "Promise you'll find me a house with a backyard?"

He wraps those muscled arms around me and pulls me tight, my head against his chest. He smells good, of soap and shaving cream. "That's my girl," he says softly.

Yeah, I'm his girl. Chase's girl. And his girl isn't going to hold him back.

Which, by the way, isn't the same as submission. Just so we have that straight.

He leans back, lifts my chin with his hand and runs his thumb along my cheek. His gaze wanders over my face, one side of his beautiful mouth lifting into a smile a second before he kisses me.

And let me tell you, Chase knows how to kiss.

This is the right decision. I can feel it in my stomach and all the way down to my bones. Peace.

I wrap my arms around those strong shoulders and deepen our kiss.

When Chase finally pulls away, I've forgotten that we have kids, forgotten that he's practically tricked me into moving to a snowy nowhere, forgotten that I'm still wearing a dead fox on my head.

Until he nuzzles into my neck and whispers, "We're going to have so much fun."

There's that word again.

Chapter Four

"I'm so proud of you, Josey!"

Daphne is sitting on her sofa, bouncing Chloe on what's left of her lap as I clear off the fold-out table from dinner. I hear Chase in the kitchen talking to Daphne's husband, Caleb, his voice bubbling with excitement as they do the dishes, good domestic men that they are. I am still in shock over my impulsive *yes*, and something akin to buyer's remorse has haunted me for a week.

Especially when Chase brought home my own pair of fuzzy, sheepskin-covered Cossack boots. Never in this lifetime, Bub. But he was so thrilled, his eyes dancing as he pulled out mini-boots for Justin and Chloe. What's a girl to do?

I swear, the boots will never leave the house with my feet in them.

Daphne's enthusiasm for our sentence to Siberia has me smiling, though. She looks at life through rose-colored glasses, and it's catching. It helps that summer is giving way to fall in Moscow, and the slight breeze filled with the scent of leaves filters in through her open windows. Outside, the sun is still high, and the sky a turquoise blue over the Volga. It's the kind of sunny Sunday that would have found me, in a previous life, playing touch football outside after dinner with Chase and my younger brother, Buddy.

"It's just for a year, Daph—not even that, really. Just until summer. Voices International only has nine months left of their gig with the Russian Ministry of Indigenous People." I am folding up the golden tablecloth to catch the crumbs. "I can do anything for a year."

Daphne lets a wriggling Chloe down. She promptly runs off to tackle her brother, who is playing sweetly and quietly in the next room. "Still, it's not every woman who would let her husband drag her thousands of miles into the endless tundra just so he can watch people."

Oh, thanks for putting it like that. I wad the tablecloth into a ball and stand up to take down the table. In Russia the kitchens are so small, a group larger than three requires the use of the foldout table in the family room.

Daphne runs her hand over her stomach. "Especially when you want to go home, when you've been looking forward to this for four years."

Only making it worse here, Daph.

"I have to tell you something."

The look on her face has me sitting back down. She doesn't meet my eyes. "Caleb and I are moving stateside."

I wait for more, something like, "to have the baby." Or, "for a year." But nothing follows. I raise my eyebrows, and my voice betrays my surprise. Caleb has lived in Russia longer than anyone I know. I thought for sure they were lifers. "Permanently?"

She looks up, and her eyes are teary. "I guess submission is harder than I thought."

Uh-oh, the bubble has popped. I wisely say nothing (see? I'm learning!).

"Caleb wants our baby to live in America, to be around family." She sighs, and for the first time I realize that we are living each other's lives.

I want to be in America, living around family. She desperately wants to stay in Russia.

I finally get why she's proud of me. I put my hand over hers. "I'm proud of you, too."

She sighs and looks up. I'm thinking she's running our last conversation over in her mind, the one about someone having to compromise to make a marriage work. The expression on her face tells me that words are easier than actions.

Her voice drops. "What if he's wrong?"

I frown at her. My voice also drops. "Wrong about what?"

"What if we're not supposed to go home? What if we're supposed to stay in Russia? What if we're missing the opportunity of a lifetime to change hearts and minds, to help people see that Jesus loves them?"

Okay, see, this is why I should never be Daphne's mentor, even though she once wanted me to. Because she is deeper than me. More committed to the eternal.

My primary worry has been about what I'm going to do for bagels and coffee out in the Siberian wasteland.

I stand up again, folding the legs of the table, lowering down one side, then the other.

"Caleb will move it back to the wall," Daphne says, but I pick up the table, moving it myself.

Then I sit beside her.

"I don't know, Daph. But I have learned that when I leap off the edge of my own understanding into the great unknown of faith, God has a way of catching me."

I'm not sure where that came from, but I believe it.

Please, God, make me believe it.

"You're going to be amazing in Siberia," Daphne says, reaching over to hug me.

I just hope to be warm.

* * *

Russia is a very large place. According to Chase, it's two and one-half times the size of the continental United States. Two and one-half. I know—it was hard for me to grasp, too, until Chase bought a map at the *renock* (read: market) and spread it out on our living-room floor. It barely fits between the black leather couches, even with the duct-taped glass coffee table pushed into the hallway.

I can lie down on this map, spread-eagled, and still not reach from one end to the other.

"Where are we going to live?"

"This is Moscow," Chase says, pointing to a dot on the far left of the map. At the moment, I don't care so much about where we're going but more whom I'm going with—Chase is looking devastating today with his dark-blond curls and two-day beard. He's stretched out on his side, one hand propped under his head, wearing a pair of faded jeans and his brown T-shirt bearing the wreckage from supper. Chloe doesn't love oatmeal.

Hey, oatmeal is a perfectly decent food choice any time of the day.

Chloe and Justin are asleep for the night—or rather, they're in bed. I can still hear Chloe singing to anyone who will listen.

"And we're going here." Chase has to sit up to move his hand to the other end of the map. He peers closely at it, finds a speck the size of a mustard seed, points to it and smiles. "Bursk."

I look back at the Moscow dot. "There's a size difference."

"That's because Bursk is really just a village."

Now when I hear the word *village,* I think of quaint German towns, houses with thatched roofs, outdoor bistros, artists painting on the sidewalk while pigeons coo at their feet. I hear the jingling bells of bicyclists and picture their handlebar baskets filled with crusty bread and a spray of daisies. I can even smell the bread baking from a nearby bakery.

Village means quiet. It means provincial. It means…vacation.

I've been on a Russian vacation. I'm no longer that ignorant girl.

But I am hopeful.

"Where's the nearest town?"

"Two hours by boat."

I narrow my eyes. Did he say *boat?* I sit up and move his hand away from the speck. I read the name of the narrow strip of blue next to it. It's in Russian and I sound it out. "Amore."

"Amur, yes. It connects the village—"

"Stop saying *village.* It raises too many expecta-tions. Let's call it a…small town."

"A very small town."

"How small are we talking?"

"Less than five hundred."

I lie back on the floor, staring at the ceiling. I grew up in a small town and more than anything, I long for my children to know the charm of small-town living. But not an on-the-backside-of-the-world small town.

"Less than five hundred, Chase?"

"The people were once nomadic. Only when the Soviet Union was formed did they settle down in one location. They're still mostly hunters, and they make their living hunting and trapping animals for fur. That's why Voices International wants us to study them. They want to figure out ways for them to survive in today's capitalist Russia without having to compromise their society or culture. Too many of their children are abandoning their heritage and moving to cities like Khabarovsk or Vladivostok or even Irkutsk, and forgetting the family and life they left behind. It's destroying their culture and possibly their future."

I get it. And I agree with Voices International's mission. I do. And I believe he can help.

I believe *we* can help. That old feeling—the one that churned in me right before I took off for a year so long ago to teach English in Russia—burns inside me. We can make a difference, change the landscape from despair to hope for these people.

See, inside me still simmers the idea that I can change my world…their world. Our world.

There's the eternal perspective I've been waiting for. However…

"Is it really in Siberia?" Even the word makes me shiver. Yes, I'm a Minnesota girl and can handle a few snowdrifts, but I also remember in my college days reading something about Stalin sending people east, to the Gulag, to Siberia—and we're going there by choice?

"Everything east of the Urals is Siberia." Chase draws an invisible north-south line down the mountains on the map. The line is a lot closer to Moscow than that little blip in the east.

"How cold do you think it gets?"

"You do remember the fur part, right?" Chase leans over, kissing me quickly. "I'll keep you warm."

Yeah, sure you will. I give him a playful push away. "No, seriously."

"Siberia is actually hotter than people think. They have summer, and the snow does melt, and Bursk isn't any farther north than Moscow."

I'm not appeased. "How far is it from here?"

"By plane or train?"

Oh, no. "Plane, please."

"Nine hours."

Okay, nine hours. That's nearly as far as it is from here to Boston. Not terrible. However, my stomach has knotted. I do *not* want to ask this next question. Most wives wouldn't even have to think about it.

However, most wives aren't married to Adventure Boy. "And by train?"

"Seven days."

"Please don't tell me—"

"We're taking the train." He scoots over on the map, right down the Volga River, to where I'm perched on the border of Ukraine. He's got a twinkle in his eyes, and I know he's cornering me so I can't flee. "Seven days in our own train compartment on the Trans-Siberian Railway, watching Russia drift by."

He tucks his arm around my waist and leans over me.

Oh, Chase. I trace the well between his collar-bones with my finger, trying not to smile. "Why can't we fly?"

"Voices International is on a tight allotment. We either fly with just four suitcases, or we bring our belongings with us on the train."

Four suitcases or a train for a week. Shoes, think of your shoes, Josey. I know that my style standards have plummeted to an all-time low from those days when I wore my leather pants without shame, but here's a fact: feet stay roughly the same size regardless of waist size.

My saving grace. Still, right behind the realization that Chase has opted for more suitcases (catching on, are we, Chase?) is a sinking feeling at his word, "tight."

"Just how 'tight' is this allotment, Chase?"

His face does the math for me. Oh.

"It's just for a year," he says. "We can tap into our savings."

What savings? That $5467.42 we've saved over the past four years? Sure, that'll get us real far.

"C'mon, GI, the train. We've always wanted to take the train."

That sounds a lot like a he-we to me. You know, the *we* that really means *he*.

But nestled here in Chase's strong embrace… "It does sound romantic."

"We can go to the dining car. Read a book. Sleep late—"

"Mommy!" Justin shoots out of the bedroom, his jammies off, of course. He's just in his cloth pull-ups and plastic pants. "Chloe is kicking me!"

Of course she is.

Chase rolls over to his side and scoops up Justin. "C'mon, buddy. We'll go have a talk with Chloe."

Good luck with that.

I watch him throw Justin over his shoulder and tickle him as they disappear into our bedroom. We've been living in a one-bedroom flat for four years now, pulling out the sofa bed every night in the living room just like the Russians do. Chloe and Justin share a double bed in the room where we keep our clothing. It's cramped, their toys shoved up against every wall, and shoes and coats overflowing by the door. Our flat isn't much bigger than one of the cabins back at Berglund Acres in Minnesota.

Please, Lord, I want a house.

They have to have houses in a village, right?

When we first got married, Chase and I (okay, just I) wanted to buy a cute little Cape Cod I'd found in the middle of Gull Lake. This was, however, before Chase lost his job—or rather, before he finally told me he lost his job—and found another in Moscow. I never dreamed I'd spend four years surfing the subway and shopping in the open market in Moscow. But the Josey who still lives under long blond hair that needs a cut and wears faded yoga pants loves the city life, the bustle of Moscow.

A village. It might be quaint.

Please let it be quaint.

I hear Chloe now, laughing. I give it five minutes before I have to go in there and calm everyone down.

But listening to the ruckus makes me smile. Chase can make anyone laugh with his disarming grin and the twinkle in his blue eyes. His charm snuck up on me when we met in kindergarten, and by the time we were in third grade, he and I spent every waking moment racing bicycles, building woodland forts and swimming in Gull Lake. I don't remember life before Chase.

Frankly, I don't want to.

I love that Chase doesn't doubt that I'll move to

the end of the earth with him, that I can keep up with him. Especially that I believe in him.

In us.

We can do this. We can change the future for this little town, this people. We can help them survive, keep their traditions, entice their young people to stay. And a good Minnesota girl knows how to stretch her pennies.

Maybe I'll grow a garden. Learn how to put up beans.

I roll over and trace the length of the map with a finger. Its smooth shiny surface flows under my skin as I travel over the Urals, across steppe, tundra, rivers, forest and finally to tiny Bursk, the village on the Amur River.

Bursk. Sounds an awful lot like *Burrrrr,* doesn't it?

It's just a year.

I can do anything for a year.

Chapter Five

"You're Going to be Fine"

Dear Jasmine,
Thank you for the anniversary card. No, I can't
believe that Chase and I have been married for
four years, and I have to agree that it's conve-
nient Amelia's birthday falls on the same day
as our wedding anniversary. Although you'd
think, then, I'd remember to send her a birthday
card. Her party sounds great! I love it that little
Clay stuck both of his grimy hands in the
cake—that's a one-year-old for you! Good idea
making two cakes. I can just imagine Dad,
Mom, Uncle Bert and Aunt Myrtle standing
around the grill, watching your two little ones
splashing in Gull Lake. I remember those days

of summer, running barefoot, lying out on the beach. Did I mention Chase and I went to the Black Sea just a few weeks ago?

Which brings me to some news. I'm actually writing to you from a Trans-Siberian Railway train compartment. We've decided—well, that's not entirely accurate, Chase decided and I'm a reluctant but willing participant—to take a new job in Siberia. Before you jump up and start accusing me of betrayal (I know you had me signed up for the Gull Lake Community Church book club), let me say that this is going to be good.

Remember that time Chase got injured during his junior year playing football? He got hit in the ribs, right under his pads, and had a bruise on his side that took up half his body? He had to sit out two long games—I know, because I was there in the stands, watching him pout on the bench. I also recall the team losing those two weeks, due to the absence of their starting wide receiver. And remember the night during that time when he snuck over to our house, climbed up on the roof and knocked on our window? Halloween—I'd dressed up as the queen of hearts, complete with tiara and gown. I remember it well because he made me sneak out while I was still in my costume.

Oh, wait, I just remembered you were home

all night, sick with the flu. I should probably tell you now that I never responded to your moaning in the middle of the night because that lump in my bed was actually a wad of pillows. Sorry.

Anyway, Chase and I went out on his motorcycle, and we drove down to the football field. He made me throw him spirals for two hours, just so he could feel the pigskin in his hands. He had this look in his eyes, too—a sort of desperation, like he might forget how to catch it and his life would then unravel before his eyes. You know how much football meant to him, especially after his mom died. He acted like it was the only thing worth living for. Although, if I had a dad like Chase's I might have felt that way, too.

So the point is, I got to thinking about that and decided that for Chase, going home would be like being benched for a whole season. I know, I know—when Mom finds out we're staying for another year (and that's all, really, I promise), she'll probably cry and box up one of her famous lasagnas and FedEx it to Moscow—or rather, Siberia. So you need to be there to help explain it to her.

Cookies, by the way, make it through the mail just fine.

Lest you think I'm losing my mind—and

yes, I'm aware that brain cells diminish with each pregnancy, but outthinking Chloe has me at the top of my game—I did extract some promises from Chase:

1. We will live in a house. Seriously. Do you know how often the elevator dies on us? Just last week, we made it to floor 8 1/2? and waited for an hour before help arrived. I long for a yard, something free of cigarette butts, broken beer bottles and open manholes.

I am going to miss, however, the sunset over the skyline of Moscow, the way the sun flows over the tops of buildings, infusing the twilight above Gorky Park with gorgeous color and turning the walls of the Kremlin to bright crimson. I'll miss the way the winter snow hides Moscow under a blanket of grace and how, as I stare down on it from nine flights, it resembles icing.

Which suddenly makes me miss your kringle. I think that could also ship well.

How are things going at the restaurant? So nice of you to take over Mom's job as head baker. Sounds like Mom and Dad's new place in Arizona is nice, also. I hope we're not leaving you and Milton in too much of a bind running Berglund Acres on your own.

But I digress. Back to the promises.

2. We are going to homeschool. I've already started teaching Chloe and Justin their ABCs. Justin is exceptionally smart. After all, he knows how to dodge Chloe's bite better than I do! How hard can it be, really? I love to read, and Chase has a couple of very large books here, one chronicling the history of the world. My kids will be brilliant!

3. I am buying a car. Seriously. I am tired of lugging home groceries on my back, dragging two toddlers on the subway (well, only one, really, since Justin actually uses his legs for more than just dead weight). I want wheels. Especially since we'll be living in a village. Yes, a village. I'm not even sure what a village is. I'm seeing thatched roofs and busy bakers' daughters, but knowing Russia like I do, that can't be accurate. After four years, I know I have to be ready for anything.

I know you think these may be large requests. But a girl has to put her foot down sometimes.

WorldMar took Chase's decision to turn down the chicken project pretty well. Maggie and Dalton were sad to see us go, but they promised to visit. As for Sveta and Igor— they're expecting! Finally, little Ryslan will have a brother or a sister.

Meanwhile, I spent the past two weeks

packing. Thanks to Aeroflot—which won't allow us to take more than one suitcase per person, weighing twenty kilos (that's roughly forty pounds)—and Chase's fear that anything we put in a container to send east will disappear forever, we decided to take the train.

Yes, I said train. For seven days. Across Russia.

Chase was so enamored of the idea, I actually bought into the romance. I packed a few read-alouds for Justin and Chloe, along with a bag of toys, and even slipped in two— okay, five, but what if I run out of reading material?—books to read.

Nostalgia meets reality. It isn't pretty.

Everyone in Russia takes the train. This fact should, I would think, guarantee some amount of standardized comfort. No such luck. It's true that we took the train from Moscow to Ukraine for our vacation, but I thought we'd just gotten a very old train that didn't represent all Russian trains. Silly me.

Have I mentioned that Russia is caught in the 1940s? Think World War II movies, with long, green train cars, smoke puffing out from under the giant metal wheels and officers dressed in uniform standing on either end of the platform, holding what look like AK-47s.

When Daphne and Caleb came to say goodbye and we were all crying, it really was as if we were being sent off to Gulag. (I can't get this out of my mind!)

Thankfully, Chase reserved us a private compartment. I had whittled our belongings down to fit into eight suitcases, but they still fill the upper bunks of our compartment to the brim. Chloe and Justin have had to share our lower bunks the past two nights. Remember: cloth diapers.

Our bunks are made of cracked brown vinyl, and someone turned the heat up to broil— probably in anticipation of never having heat again once we get to Siberia. Justin and Chloe are stripped to the waist and spending their days leaping from bunk to bunk. Between the bunks is a small table on which we picnic each day.

Lest you think Russia is without comforts, they do serve complimentary tea every morning. However, the buildup of grease on the ceiling above the stove in the dining car made me turn to my stash of bagels and I haven't been back there since. Our saving grace is the food vendors lined up outside on the train platform at every little town we roll through. The train stops for about twenty minutes and Chase darts out and buys roasted potatoes in a bag, cooked *palmeni*, winter salad (think potato salad with cooked carrots, pickles and beets) and fresh bread.

The conductors—who aren't nice, stately gentlemen but plump, angry babushkas who would just as soon throw us from the train as bring us our tea—close the bathrooms during these stops. This annoyed me until I took the time to explore this inconvenience. One look through the escape hatch of the toilet directly onto the tracks, and I understood why. Travel note: Never walk on a railroad track in Russia.

Chase, of course, has made friends with our fellow passengers. Last night our neighbors knocked on the door and invited Chase over for smoked fish and vodka.

Now, don't get excited—Chase hasn't become a drinker in Russia. But the man loves his fish, and three hours later I could hear him leading a round of songs next door.

This just might be the longest week of my life.

Once we get there, we're going to be just fine. I know it's Siberia, but really, how cold can it get?

Don't worry about me. It's only a year. I can do anything for a year.

My love to Milton, and kisses to Amelia and baby Clay.

Josey

* * *

"Chloe!"

They say that all your sins come back to haunt you when you have children. I'm here to tell you that they're right. I gave birth to a child who is constantly paying me back for every dark night I slipped out of the house to hang out with Chase and disappear on the back of his motorcycle.

"Chloe!"

She's dressed in just her underwear and T-shirt since we're traveling in a moving sauna. The compartment doors are open—to circulate the heat, apparently—and I get up, duck my head out the door, and peer down the hallway. The little scamp has made her escape. She's standing in the hallway and at my voice, she looks back at me, gives me a grin and bolts.

Oh, good, it's a game. "Chloe!" I step out into the hall, on the chase.

Outside, the terrain is chapped and brown, foretelling the upcoming winter. When we pass through villages, I see the same tired, scarf-outlined faces staring up at the train, old faces that wear travail and exhaustion in their lines, that look at me with wondering eyes, trying to imagine where I'm going, what I'm doing.

I'm trying to imagine the same things.

I'm numbed by the never-ending landscape of identically forlorn villages—the wisps of black coal smoke from broken chimneys and the blue and green houses, poorly hidden behind lopsided fences.

I'm starting to dread what I'll find in Bursk.

"Chloe!" She weaves in and out of the legs of fellow sojourners who have their elbows propped up on the railing that runs along the windows. Most are dressed in nylon sports pants and sleeveless army T-shirts. They all wear the monotony of our trans-Russian trip on their faces. No one makes a move toward the runaway.

"Chloe, stop!"

I've nearly caught up to her when I see a man turn from the window and crouch, right in her path. "Hey there, tyke," he says, and I just about fall over. English!

He's slowed her enough for me to catch up, and I scoop her into my arms, throwing her wriggling and giggling body over my shoulder. "Thanks."

"I see I'm not the only crazy non-Russian taking the train across the Motherland," he says, standing. "Nathan Blume."

"Thanks, Nathan," I say. "Josey Anderson."

"Oh, a Scandinavian," he says, smiling. He's got dark eyes and dark hair and is wearing a T-shirt, sweatpants and flip-flops. His version of Russian casual.

"From Minnesota," I say, filling in the blanks. I take his hand. He has a firm grip.

"South Dakota," Nathan says. "And who is the runaway?" He nods to my daughter, who I now spin around and prop on my hip. She claps at this acrobatic move.

"This is Chloe."

He takes her hand and gives it a little pump.

"I have a matching male version back in our compartment."

"Twins. Wow. Bet that's fun in Russia." His eyes are twinkling, and from his comment, I realize he's been in Russia long enough to understand that twins in this culture are an oddity, and a collective joy. I can't walk down the street without having babushki stop and make comments about my bookends. Russians have no problem asking personal questions, and the most common is, Where is their babushka? Apparently, they should be with their grandmother because someone my age isn't equipped to raise twins.

I sort of agree with that one, actually. But I smile at Nathan. "Oh, yes, it's been so much fun. And now we're moving to Siberia."

"You and the kids?"

"And my husband, Chase. He's working with Voices International to help create industries in a Nanais village."

"Oh? Where?"

"A little town called Bursk. It's north of Kha… Kha…"

"Khabarovsk. And by the way, technically, it's called Far East Russia. But it feels like Siberia. It can get pretty cold there, even if it is on the Amur River. I hope you brought your *dublonka*."

"My what?"

"It's a thick fur coat. You'll need that and a *shopka*—it's a fur hat."

"I do speak Russian, although lately my vocabulary is limited to child-care and household products." I laugh, but there's a sad irony in the fact that I came to Russia four years ago knowing the language, and now my husband can talk circles around me.

Nathan smiles, and I notice it's a warm, nice smile. "A few grunts and some sign language will get you a long way. The people in Bursk are very nice. They're used to having tourists visit in the summertime on excursions up the Amur River. They take them mushroom picking. And of course, it's on my route."

"Route? Are you a postman?" I'm jesting, of course, and he laughs. I think I like this Nathan.

"I'm a missionary. I visit all the northern villages a couple of times a month."

"Josey?" Chase comes up behind me, puts his hand on my shoulder. Chloe squirms in my arms and reaches out for him.

"This is Nathan," I say, handing off the renegade. She doubles over in shrieks as Chase runs his fingers around her tummy. "He's a missionary from South Dakota. Apparently, he knows where Bursk is. He travels there on his route."

Chase shakes his hand, smiling. "Come by our house when you're in town. We'd be glad to feed you."

Chase means *he'd* be glad to feed him, because our visitor would perish before he found something edible besides chocolate-chip cookies made by my hands. The Berglund iron-chef talents I did not inherit.

But I'm not really thinking about that. I'm relishing the word *house*.

I beam up at Chase. "Yes, stop by the house when you're in town."

Nathan chuckles, shaking his head. "A house, huh? Are you sure that's what you want?"

His amused tone rings on in my ears like the dying dismal sounds of a gong as I look out the window to the shadowed steppe, the train chugging toward my future.

Chase's ability to navigate through a country he's never set foot in before astonishes me. He was born to be on the Travel Channel, or maybe that reality show *The Amazing Race.* We pull up to the train station in Khabarovsk, and he has a fleet of men helping us out of our compartment. (The fish-and-vodka breath clues me in to who they are.) Nathan is there, holding Chloe, keeping her from making another escape. Justin is a man after his father's heart, lugging out a duffel bag about twice his size, aided surreptitiously by, again, Nathan.

I really like Nathan, with his now six-day beard. He carries himself like Chase—confident—and Russian rolls off his tongue like he might be Slavic, although he proves he's from South Dakota by expertly handling the Minnesota three-hour goodbye. He is standing beside us and all our gear while Chase hails a cab.

"Chase tells me that you taught ESL?" Nathan says, letting Justin take a running dive at him from the raised wall of a bone-dry fountain while I attempt to keep Chloe away from the feral cats that roam the sidewalk.

"Kitty! Kitty!" Chloe reaches for one as it hisses at her and scampers away. I spot Chase standing on the curb, his hand in the air making the international sign for "I want a cab." In Russia, however, anyone can be a cabbie—yes, there are official cabbies, but even Chase has been known to pull over, name his discounted price and give the occasional fare a ride across town.

"I taught English once upon a time at Moscow Bible Church," I say, shooing away another cat from Chloe with my foot.

"I had friends there," Nathan says. "Matt and Becky Winneman. But they went stateside quite a few years ago. Probably before you got there."

I smile at him. Because I know more about the Winnemans than is acceptable to discuss in polite conversation. Like how Matthew nearly cheated on his wife with a slinky Russian translator and how Rebecca turned to me for help and tried to teach me to cross-stitch in the process. I glance at Chase, at the way he's now negotiating a ride. I'm fairly sure Chase would never cheat on me—at least, I'm sure right now. But I know how easily it can happen.

Not to me, of course. But others.

"So what is it that you do, exactly, in Bursk?" I hook my foot around one of my bags as I see a woman, dressed in layers of acrylic headscarves and flanked by children who could use a good bath, edge toward us. The first time I saw Gypsies was in Moscow, at the train station. My heart cries out against their poverty, but I've also been told that Gypsies are essentially an organized crime syndicate. I'm not sure what to believe, to be honest.

I pull Chloe up to my hip.

"I'm trying to plant a church there, but so far, I can't get the men to come, and the women don't trust me. So—" he gives a shrug "—I'm trying to talk the local *detski-sod* into letting me teach Bible stories."

Justin launches himself again, and Nathan catches him, throwing him over his shoulder. The move reminds me so much of Chase, I'm wondering if these two were twins separated at birth. It would explain why they hit it off so well. He looks at me. "The kindergarten is going to love having Justin and Chloe."

Uh, no. "I'm going to homeschool them."

Nathan gives me a look I can't interpret, just as Chase returns. "I found us a cab."

I'm eyeing the tiny Lada with concern. It's roughly the size and shape of a Volkswagen Jetta, and I wonder if Chase has noticed how many bags we have, or if perhaps he's trying to pull one of those old how-many-people-can-we-fit-into-a-phonebooth challenges.

My face apparently betrays me.

"I'll go with the bags if you take another cab," he says.

I'm speechless for a moment, because—hello—I have no idea where I'm going. Or, for that matter, where I am.

I know I must be in Siberia, because we've been on a train for way too many days, rumbling across steppe and prairie, through forests and mountains. But Khabarovsk resembles Moscow, minus the subway and towering baroque architecture. Crimson maples and yellow poplars line the center boulevards, and Ladas and Zhigulis—cars from the Cold War era—clog the streets. The requisite statue of Lenin stands outside the train station pointing east. I pinpoint the familiar smell of fried-meat sandwiches and exhaust, and the four-story, faded yellow and blue apartment buildings with the tiny curved metal balconies and ornate moldings look like they've been plucked from Moscow's Pushkin Street. But we're not in Moscow. We're in Siberia. Which reminds me—

"Where are we going?"

"To the port," he says, already throwing our suitcases into the car. Nathan hands Justin over and picks up a bag. Chase turns to me. "I'm so sorry, Josey." He picks up another bag. "I can't find a bigger car. If I come back to get you, there is no one to watch our bags."

Shoes. Think of your shoes. "Of course, Chase, I totally—"

"I'll ride with you," Nathan says, throwing in the last of our bags.

He smiles at me, and I'm, for a moment, speechless at his generosity. I shake it off and focus on the task at hand: getting to the port.

Apparently, we Americans have to stick together.

"Thanks, Nate," Chase says, holding out his hand. "I'll meet you there." He drops a quick kiss on my cheek and jumps into the cab.

I watch him go as Nathan hails another cab.

We climb in, and Justin and Chloe momentarily fight for lap space—on Nathan. But I'm so tired and so grimy, I don't care. I'm wearing dirty yoga pants, a pair of Converse tennis shoes I found at the market (and have long since realized are knockoffs) and a sweatshirt stained with Chloe's chocolate handprint. I just want a warm bath and a change of clothes.

But Chase did look so excited, didn't he? That look on his face makes all this worth it.

Nathan tickles both kids as I try not to think about the lack of seat belts while we weave in and out of traffic.

Apparently the drivers could have been plucked from Moscow, also.

I lean my head back against the seat and close my eyes. I pick up an odor of something stronger than beer emanating from the front seat.

Please, God, let us get there.

"Tired?" Nathan asks.

He has no idea. I merely nod.

"Chase says you're staying with the town elders tonight. Probably Anton Vasillyech and his wife. They're nice folks. In fact, I think you'll like Bursk. It's one of my favorite villages. They have an annual winter carnival, complete with reindeer-pulled sleigh rides and ice sculptures. It's gorgeous."

Gorgeous. Hmm.

"And if you need anything, you can always send me an e-mail and I'll bring it up on my route."

I open an eye. "E-mail? They have Internet?"

He nods. "Dial-up, but only at the city government building."

Close enough. As long as I can write home.

Nathan reaches over and taps my forearm. "You're going to be fine."

I hate how much I need those words. But with Chase dashing off to the port without us, I'm wondering just what I'm getting myself into. We had problems our first year of marriage, the kind that made me wonder if Chase even remembered he had a wife. But we learned. We grew. We got cell phones.

Please, God, I don't want to return to that life.

We ride in silence until the taxi pulls up to the wharf. Sure enough, there's Chase, sitting atop our luggage like some explorer, grinning. Chloe jumps off Nathan and dives into his arms as if she hasn't seen him for a decade.

"Our boat leaves in half an hour," he says, grabbing a bag. I stand guard while he and Nathan shuffle our belongings down a gangplank to what looks like a rusty tugboat with portholes along the sides. Justin can't wait to climb aboard.

"See you in a few weeks," Nathan says after Chase stows the last bag. His eyes find mine, and he smiles. "You're going to be fine," he mouths.

You're going to be fine!

I climb aboard and walk down the steps into the belly of the boat. Our gear is stashed in the back, and I sit on one of the molded vinyl chairs. The water is at eye level, or nearly, and I can't help but plot my escape route should we spring a leak. Or meet a tidal wave. I probably can't fit my body through a porthole, but I could shove Justin through and maybe Chloe if she cooperates and…

Okay, the contingency plan is starting to make

me queasy. I lift my hand in a meager wave to Nathan as we leave shore and head out to sea—okay, river.

"Isn't this fun?" Chase says, pulling Chloe onto his lap. She stands up, puts her nose to the window.

"See water, Daddy. Fishes!"

Poor Justin has his arms around my neck, cutting off my air supply. At least *one* of my children remembers our vacation, and the narrow miss with the jellyfish.

Chase grins at me. "We took the Trans-Siberian Railway, babe. Across Russia."

Yay, us. I can barely contain my joy.

But I give him a smile. Who can be a grump in the face of all that enthusiasm?

Siberia is lush and beautiful. Who'da thunk it? Amethyst and ruby, amber and gold—a potpourri of jewels array the trees that embrace the shoreline, dotted here and there with stately buildings, probably former communist leaders' beach—er, river—homes. Fishermen watch us motor by, and we pass the occasional barge.

As we travel north, my body settles into the rock of the boat, the hum of the engine. We are the only travelers. I'm not sure if this bodes well or not, but it does give us the room to move about the cabin. Justin finally finds his river legs and leaps from seat to seat. Chloe has decided that since she can't have a kitty, she'll become one, and is crawling along the molded seats, purring, her hands tiny paws, swiping at our faces. Chase plays along and pets her. She snuggles into his lap as I give him a dirty look. Guess who's going to have to play Mommy Kitty all day now?

I focus on the sun hovering low over the horizon. I miss my skyline. *You'll like Bursk.* Nathan's words buoy my hopes. Because here, finally, I'll make us a home, one that we can stretch out in. Maybe I'll even build a sandbox for the kids. And get a dog. I'd love a dog—

"We're here!" Chase displaces the kitty and stares out the window. I'm not sure how he knows this because I don't see any Welcome to Bursk signs. But sure enough, we've angled toward shore and a long pier that looks like one good squall would wash it away.

Here?

Chloe makes a run for the stairs, but I grab her. "Not yet, sweetie."

We walk up to the deck together as a family to glimpse our new hometown.

Or…clutch of muddy hovels. You pick, because I see only muddy, rutted streets, rickety fences that border tiny abodes and a trickle of coal smoke darkening the sky. I spy a pack of mangy dogs, ribs corrugating their sides, staring at us from the weedy shore. I sniff the odor of manure.

I hold on to the edge of the boat as we glide in. *You're going to be fine!*

Chapter Six

The Little Lies

My brain can fool me. Not that this is a surprise. We all know that my brain doesn't always communicate with my mouth, which often runs off on its own rampant course without any consideration of the repercussions. However, my brain has recently decided that it has no accountability, and over the past few years I've awakened in Moscow occasionally confused about my whereabouts. The birds are singing and the fragrance from a spray of lilacs on the window ledge fills my nose and I'm suddenly back in Gull Lake, waking to a fresh summer morning. I hear the clatter of dishes—my mother cooking up breakfast at the restaurant next door—and I pull the cotton sheet close to my nose and smell the fresh-from-the-line crispness of the sun.

In that moment, life is good.

Simple.

And doesn't come accompanied by…*Oh, I'm wet!* I open my eyes to reality, and I'm staring at a ceiling with peeling paint, dark walls covered in patterned, brown Turkish-style rugs, and a very damp Chloe, sleeping on top of me.

Soaking me as she snoozes through her early-morning accident.

Where am I?

I ease Chloe off me and onto Chase's side of the bed, which is empty. As I pull the sodden sheet away from me, memory rushes back.

I am in Mayor Anton and his wife Ulia's bedroom. In their three-room house. Located three muddy blocks from the boat dock in the tiny town of Bursk.

In Siberia.

Russia.

Oh, boy.

Sun filters through a flimsy lace curtain and across the brown-painted floor, covered with a worn, red throw rug. Standing now in the middle of the room, I start to shiver. Although it's September, the house, which must be made of cement, collects the chill like a meat freezer. We've left most of our bags in the family room, but I have the one containing my clothes. I change quickly, wishing—oh, wishing— for a shower.

But today we move into our house. *Our* house.
Chase promised.

I change Chloe, who sleeps through the whole
thing, and I tuck her into a warm, dry portion of the
bed. Then I venture out to find my husband.

Chase already has a fan club. Three men sit at the
kitchen table drinking tea with him while he bounces
Justin on his knee. I spot Ulia at the sink. She's a
strong Russian woman with a wide, weathered face
and the hands of a lumberjack. The house has a coal
furnace/stove as big as a Hereford in the kitchen, and
on it she is simmering a pot of what looks like kasha.

"Good morning, GI," Chase says, scooting over
on the bowed bench. "Want some breakfast?"

I notice that his bowl is half-empty and Justin's is
clean. Or maybe Chase is on seconds.

"Pumpkin kasha. You gotta get the recipe."

Oh, sure. Has the man learned nothing since the
day I nearly set the kitchen on fire a week after our
marriage? Do the words "instant oatmeal" mean
anything to him?

He picks up his cup of tea. "These are the town
elders—Misha, Alex, and of course, Anton." They
nod at me without smiling.

I sit beside Chase, and Justin climbs on my lap.
The kitchen bears the markings of age, with a
sagging, formerly white cupboard hanging from the
far wall and a bowed hutch with chipped china behind

us. The room is about as big as my parents' walk-in closet, and with six people at the table, I'm wondering how Ulia manages to breathe, let alone scurry around and ladle me a bowl of the pale-orange kasha.

"*Spaceeba,*" I say in thanks, and she gives me a tight smile. I can understand "go away," clearly in almost any language.

I'm starting to wonder if Voices International neglected to preapprove our visit with the locals.

I dive into the kasha, eyeing the tea, wishing for coffee.

No. I am sacrificing for others. For Chase. I am learning submission.

Coffee is probably the last thing I need, anyway.

The kasha crunches in my mouth, and although I've only eaten pumpkin in pie form, I have to admit the flavor wins me.

I listen to the men talk about people and life in the village. They're telling Chase how they've made their living by hunting fox and trapping mink and beaver for the past fifty million decades. Anton's two children live in Khabarovsk and Misha has a son that moved to Moscow when he was seventeen. He hasn't seen him since. I eye Ulia and notice that she doesn't say a word.

I hope this is a personality quirk and not standard operating procedure.

Submission. Maybe she has the corner on it.

Chloe shuffles into the room in her dry, full-length footie jammies. Her hair sticks straight up, and her eyes are huge, taking in the changes in her world. Yes, well, like mother, like daughter. I pull her onto my lap. "Would you like some yummy kasha for breakfast?" I scoop up a little and aim for her mouth. She turns her head at the last minute and it narrowly misses her hair.

"Chloe!"

"No like kasha! No kasha!" She pushes at the spoon, which goes flying out of my grasp. It hits Alex the Elder, who makes a face that looks uncannily like my daughter's.

"Chloe!" I am trying to figure out who to clean first when Ulia crouches before me and hands Chloe a piece of black bread, buttered and covered in what an un-Moscowed person might think is red jam.

"She's not going to like caviar," I say quietly to Chase as Chloe reaches for it. "What do I do?"

Before Chase can answer, however, Chloe takes the bread and takes a bite. Oh, no, here it comes…

"Mmm. Try, Mommy!" Chloe holds out the bread to me as Ulia stands up, a satisfied smile on her face.

Mommy tries some and smiles. Oh, boy, I thought the days I ate caviar for breakfast were gone. Like, when I was pregnant, which I suppose goes a long way toward explaining Chloe's instant love of the delicacy.

Satisfied, Chloe finishes off the bread and pounds the table for more.

Figures I'd have a diva for a daughter.

"Anton told me he harvests the roe from his own catch," Chase says as he accepts the offer of a caviar-laden piece of black bread from Ulia.

"What kind of fish?"

Chase asks, and it takes a second for him to translate. (Apparently, I need to work on my fishing terms.) "Carp."

Oh, perfect. The last time I had carp—a "delicacy" Chase picked up at the market grill—I was sick for a week. And carp eggs? Oh, even better.

I manage to dodge another caviar sandwich before I'm able to escape with the kids to dress them. Chase joins me in the room moments later, closing the door behind him.

"I have good news and bad news."

See, here's the thing. When a woman lives in Russia, she doesn't need to be told there is bad news accompanying the good news. That's a given. She just wants to know how bad it is. "Lay it on me."

"They found us a house."

A house! I throw myself at Chase, and he's momentarily taken aback, apparent by the startled look in his blue eyes. Hey, someone should remind him that we just spent a week locked in a compartment the size of a Russian kitchen with our two kids. I'm a little on the emotional edge here.

He offers me a flimsy hug, then pulls away.

Long before Chase and I were married, I had the ability to read his mind. Not only was he my best childhood pal, but he practically broadcast his thoughts on his face. (I guess that's not really reading his mind.)

Right now my Chase radar is telling me something very bad is in the headlines.

"You're starting to scare me."

"There's no plumbing."

I am eyeing him, because, well, I'm not sure I've heard him correctly. "No…plumbing? Could you elaborate on that?"

"Well…" He looks away from me, wrapping his hand around his neck. "No one in the town has indoor plumbing."

I'm still struggling here. Does he mean…

"Are you saying that I have to lug my water in from…the river?"

His face brightens. Phew! For a second there, I was seeing "Little House on the Prairie." And we all know I'm not Ma.

"There's a pump. Right there in the house. You just have to, uh, lug the water from the pump to the kitchen sink."

Or, no phew. "So, no running water in the house."

"Right."

I can see I'm still not getting it, because he's staring at me, waiting for something to click.

No running water. No running water to fill the

kitchen sink. Or the bathtub. Or the only-in-my-dreams washing machine.

Or to take…a shower.

"Where do we bathe?"

"Well, at home, with a pot of water." Chase lifts Justin down from where he's jumping on the bed. "Or at the local bathhouse."

Local bathhouse.

"Any chance it's a family bathhouse?"

"Segregated." He smiles, his eyes running over me dramatically. "Unfortunately."

"Please." And then it hits me. No running water for a shower also means no running water to flush the toilet. I touch the wall, because I think my knees might buckle.

Chase wraps his hand around my arm, seeing that I've finally got it.

"I promise I'll build you the best outhouse in Siberia."

I have no doubt it will win awards. But… "Chase, no indoor toilet?"

"Babe, c'mon." He leans in and touches his forehead to mine. "It's just for a year."

That'll be just about enough of that.

I'm still in a daze as we are given a tour of Bursk on our way to our new…what, shack? Hut?

I'm putting it out of my mind, however, trying to

look for the shiny lining to this thundercloud. I'm especially not thinking about the word *outhouse*.

I blame this current fiasco on my waffling over our vacation accommodations. See, I let Chase—and apparently the cosmos at large—believe I might be willing to live without plumbing. Just for the record, that isn't the truth.

The one current benefit of our village is that there is no traffic by which Chloe or Justin might be killed. None. Not a car to be seen. Only carts, pulled by reindeer. And if that isn't enough to make one stop and stare, I don't know what is. Because I'm talking real reindeer here, with the soft, mooselike noses, the big eyes, the tuft of white furry hair on their chests and of course the antlers. I stand on the street corner (aka, the bump between two houses) and watch as a woman who looks like she might have been born at the dawn of time rides a reindeer down the street, her feet dangling in huge felt boots. She wears a worn-thin *shopka* and a wool jacket and looks at me, in jeans and sweatshirt, as if I'm naked and how dare I bring those children out here with just windbreakers? Where are their snowsuits?

Chase has Chloe on his shoulders as he walks with the men. So far, I've counted eight light-blue or -green houses. Each house has two entrances and seems to hold two families. A fence on each side of the house encircles a yard that contains chickens, cows and the occasional goat. And once in a while, a reindeer.

I wonder if I'm going to get a reindeer. Instead of a car, of course.

"A long time ago, they used to herd reindeer, and these animals are the descendants of those herds," Chase says when I ask him about Santa's steeds.

How long ago? I'm wondering. Last week? Since the time of the Mongol horde and Genghis Khan?

"Anton says the market is only open on Saturdays, because that's when they get the shipment of food from Khabarovsk," Chase says over his shoulder. He's been passing on these incidentals the entire tour, like we're in the Smithsonian. He glances at me. "I suppose that'll leave you time to do other things."

Like what? Milk cows?

Attitude, attitude, Josey. *Please, Lord, help me see the good parts. Submission. Joy. I'm proud of you, Josey.* Yeah, Daph, you'd better be.

Anton shows us the town hall—a long green building with saggy steps. "Anton says you can use his office to hook up to the Internet. There are no other phone lines in the village."

Of course there aren't.

Oops. Attitude.

Inside the town hall is a post office. Chase signs us up for a box and hands me a brass key.

At one point, years ago, my good friend H told me that I was a dreamer, looking for a happily-ever-after that didn't exist. Now I'm beginning to wonder if she might be right.

Finally we arrive at our house.

Chase stands outside the gate.

I'm afraid to look.

"It's cute," Chase says, reaching over to wrap his arm around me. I take a breath. Crack open one of my tightly closed eyes.

It *is* cute, in a Siberian sort of way. See, I'm already seeing things with new eyes. It's blue, with giant, ornate white-painted windows. A worn dirt path winds up to the front door. Beyond that, the path continues to the backyard, where I see trampled grass (read: weeds, but we're trying to have a good attitude, aren't we?). Along the back fence, which is painted green, I see a matching outbuilding.

I look away.

"C'mon," Chase says, letting Chloe down to run. She and Justin take off through the yard while Anton hands Chase the key to the house. I hear him say something about bringing our bags over.

I walk to the door, nearly holding my breath. Now I have to admit, when I dreamed of a house, it had two stories and indoor plumbing, but most importantly, potential.

I hear the children's laughter as they race after each other.

Chase hands me the key, and I slowly unlock the door and ease it open. It squeals on its loose hinges.

The door opens to a small foyer that is closed off from the rest of the house. Probably to keep the frost and chill from the warmth of the hearth. I can already smell the musty scent of damp, weathered boards, but at least the former owners were clean. This room's brown linoleum floor has been swept. A row of homemade hooks by the door suggests the frequency of company, and a potato bin bulges with what looks like two sacks of potatoes. Chase gestures to it. "They had their potato delivery last week. Anton ordered us two fifty-pound bags. He told me we'd have to dry them."

Of course we will. Whatever that means.

I nod, though, and push the next door open, the one that leads to the living quarters. Chase calls for Justin and Chloe, who scamper in past me, still laughing.

The house is cool, collecting the brisk Siberian air. A kitchen not much larger than Ulia's is on my right. Next to a tiny electric stove and oven I see a sink, with a bucket over the top.

"You fill the bucket and then lift the latch on the bottom, and it filters into the sink," Chase says, reading my thoughts. Oh, I get it—pretend plumbing. I give him a shaky smile.

"I'll have to learn how to light the coal stove," Chase says, moving past me, opening the door to our own massive Hereford in the middle of the room. I note his use of pronoun. Smart man.

"There's the pump," Chase says, gesturing to…a real pump. Now I'm really feeling like Ma Ingalls, because it's the old-fashioned kind, with the long, pump-by-hand handle and a bucket below the spigot. It's over a wood platform, of sorts, that covers a drain in the floor.

I stare at it as truth sinks its claws in.

"I'm not sure I can do this," I hear my mouth say. For once, it's actually cooperating with my brain.

Chase hooks his arm around my waist. "Misha and Anya moved out to live with his mother so we could have this place. Most of the other residents have to cart a watering can down to the village pump for their water."

Oh. Well. Lucky me.

But I still have no words.

"There are two bedrooms," he says, and I hear the note of panic in his voice. I am nearly numb as he moves me toward the first room, right behind the kitchen. Big enough for two beds, it's bright and has a throw rug that smells freshly washed. And of course, the requisite brown Turkish carpet on the wall—high Moscow fashion has found its way east. Chloe is jumping on what looks like a black-and-white striped prison mattress left behind on the floor. Justin is barking at her to stop jumping. Chloe responds with "No! No! No! No! No!"

For once, I'm siding with my daughter.

The other bedroom is smaller, and is nearly filled by the double bed in the middle of the room. "Where do we put our clothes?"

"In the wardrobe in the family room," Chase answers softly. I can tell that he's scared by my reaction—he's still got a grip around my waist.

I suppose dressing in the family room is better than *sleeping* in the family room. I take a deep breath. Someone has left a glass filled with wilting orange, red and yellow chrysanthemums on the windowsill.

"Well?" Chase says, swallowing hard.

I move past him into the family room. Shadow seeps from the nooks and crannies of the room, so I open the curtains. The windows needs a good cleaning, but the sunlight reveals pink wallpaper, a brown-painted wood floor and ornate crown molding along the ceiling.

And a crucifix over the door.

Chase takes my hand. "I know it's rough, GI. Before you say anything—" he holds up his hand "—I want you to know that I agree we're in over our heads here. In fact, I wouldn't blame you a bit if you wanted to pack up and run. This isn't what you signed up for, and really it isn't what I signed up for, either, although you and I know that I could sleep in a barn and probably be happy— Don't look at me like that, I'm not saying you're not as tough as I am, it's just that I don't need things like running water or— Stop looking at me like that! I know how important a bathroom is! But before you make a judgment, I have to tell you something, something I probably should have mentioned to you before, but now I see as glaringly important."

He takes my other hand, and he interprets my silence to mean, "Please go on."

"Anton and Ulia actually had three children."

I'm not sure why—

"Their oldest son committed suicide about a year ago. Right here in Bursk. He left behind a wife and two little kids."

I think of Justin and Chloe without Chase, and something inside me burns.

"It was the third suicide in less than a month in this town. In fact, the suicide rate has skyrocketed over the past five years. That's one of the reasons Voices sent us here—because the alcoholism and despair have started an epidemic. Only one out of every four children stay in Bursk, and out of those, about a third have committed suicide. They're a culture without a future. You can see it in the eyes of the people, can't you?"

I remember Ulia, her almost reluctant smile at my two sweet babies. And severe Anton. Maybe not so severe. Maybe grieving.

"We need to find out why these men and women who have every bit of ability to improve their lives see suicide as a better alternative to living. We need to help them find a balance between embracing their culture and living in today's world. We need to give them hope." Chase runs his hands up to my forearms. "I know I'm not playing fair here, babe. But what if we can help? What if staying here and studying them and asking questions and maybe offering solutions actually changes—*saves*—lives? What if we can make a difference?"

Oh, no, he's singing my song. I swallow, leaning my head against his warm chest.

I spy the crucifix over the door.

Nobody is playing fair today.

To do:
Rebuild the outhouse
Learn how to pump water

I sit in the kitchen, on the windowsill that is large enough for my backside due to the fact that the walls are roughly a foot thick (I've solved the "Where has all the heat gone?" question—it never got in!) and try to figure out where to start making this house a home. We need some furniture, a coat of paint on the walls and food.

"Mommy! Chloe is petting the big doggy!" Justin

runs in, nearly in tears. Now how did she sneak past me? I thought I had her cornered in her new room, having shoved a couple of duffels up against the door.

Then again, Justin's here, too. Another escapee.

"What doggie?"

"Big one!" He's nearly hysterical now, and I scoop him up and shove him on my hip as I run out to the yard.

I spot Chloe standing stock-still next to the fence separating us from our neighbor, as a rottweiler the size of a buffalo stares her down through a hole where a couple of boards used to be. Only the horizontal beam holds him back. I wonder if he used his head to bust through. *Oh, God, please, please.*

He opens his mouth and I'm about to scream when he slathers my daughter with a sloppy kiss. She giggles and then, to my horror, launches herself through the hole at the animal and throws both arms around its neck.

"Chloe!" I, in turn, launch myself at her, pulling her back. "Shoo!" I say to the dog, while newspaper headlines run through my mind. "Rottweiler Mauls Child…"

"Lydia!" The voice comes from the other side of the fence. I'm now holding Chloe football-style on my other hip, backing away from the dog. I see a woman in a housedress and slippers appear in the hole. She hooks a hand around the dog, pulling him back. "Lydia! *Nyet!*"

Lydia?

I come closer to the fence to get a better look. The woman is wearing a green floral headscarf knotted under her chin, yet I see wisps of black hair stealing around the edges. Down one side of her face, an ugly bruise evidences a fall. Or something. I'm remembering Chase's words about despair and the suicide rate, and a horrible feeling rushes through me. I know that wife beating happens in Russia—just like in America—but I know so little about this culture, and I'm hoping hard that I'm wrong.

"Izvenetye," she says, pulling Lydia the Killer Dog away from the fence. She's apologizing, but she's also eyeing me as if I might be from another planet.

I am. It's called Planet Plumbing.

"Zhdrastvyootya," I say, smiling wide, because I can't hold out my hand due to the bundles of children I'm holding. *"Mnye zavoot* Josey."

She isn't meeting my eyes. "Olya," she responds. My ear easily switches to Russian when she says, "Lydia loves children."

Lydia *does* look like she loves children as she whines and tries to get at mine. I hope that love isn't based on their taste.

"I'm your new neighbor," I say, gesturing toward my house. "My husband and I are from America."

She just blinks at me, but since I feel I'm on a roll here, I point to Chloe. "This is my daughter,

Chloe." And then to Justin. "And this is my son, Justin."

Justin sticks his thumb in his mouth, and I don't want to think about where that thumb has been. But he's so cute I can't help but give him a little kiss on his pudgy, soft cheek.

Olya's face hardens, just slightly, and she purses her lips. "Keep your children away from my dog," she says with a growl. Then, to my shock, she turns and yanks Lydia away, stalking out of view.

Oh. Welcome to the neighborhood, Josey.

Chloe wriggles out of my grasp as I turn toward the house. "Doggie!" She makes for the fence again, but I grab her, shoving Justin behind me.

"No doggie, Chloe. Stay away from the doggie, do you hear me?" She looks as if I've taken away her blankie. Her little lip starts to tremble and tears fill her giant blue eyes.

"Seriously, Chloe, the doggie will hurt you. Bite you." I make a yucky face, but she isn't buying it. The wailing begins. I pick up Chloe again and in a last-ditch attempt, add desperation to my voice. "Mommy loves you and doesn't want the doggie to eat you."

She stops crying and looks at me. I feel like a rotten mommy, but you know, it could happen. A little healthy fear is good for a kid.

"Daddy!" Justin calls out. Chase is back, bread in hand, saving the day.

"Anyone for peanut-butter sandwiches?" He also has some unnamed orange soda and something in a bag that, if I can decipher the hieroglyphics, seems to be crab-flavored potato chips.

"You guys having fun?" he says as we make a picnic on the floor in our family room. Chloe is on his lap and Justin is hanging over my shoulders.

"Big dog!" Justin says.

Chase looks at me, raises an eyebrow.

"Nothing I can't handle," I say, and reach for the chips.

I can see that the little lies I tell myself are going to help me make it through the day.

Chapter Seven

A Matter of Perspective

Directions for pumping water:

Pick handle up so plunger goes down. Pour glass of water on top of piston so seals have good suction. As you push handle down, slowly, it creates pressure below piston. Repeat, increasing speed, until water starts to flow.

I've been spoiled. I admit it. Here I thought that when you opened a spigot, water should simply run out. It shouldn't take faith and a slick sheen of sweat across one's brow or a puddle of rusty orange water at one's feet to obtain clean drinking water.

But I've learned a lot of things in the week we've lived in Burrr, Siberia, like:

1. Coal dust doesn't come out of clothing, regard-

less of how much you scrub it in generic washing powder in a tin bucket of freezing water.

2. The purpose of a chamber pot.

3. I can have my milk hand-delivered, as in, my hand can milk the skinny Jersey cow given us yesterday by the village elders. It's currently eating the yard. Chloe calls it "the Moo." I just want it to go away.

4. A person can take a fairly decent bath in a pot of ankle-deep water. It just takes creativity. And washing one's hair takes teamwork. All these things are a thousand times better than getting naked in front of a group of women at the local bathhouse.

5. We are somewhat of an oddity. Every day someone knocks at my door, delivering canned beans, tomatoes, pickles, eggplant, peppers, berries and cabbage (aka sauerkraut). The visitor then proceeds to plant herself in my kitchen for roughly four hours, observing. Anton's wife, Ulia, brought prune-filled *peroshke*. Well, at least I'm losing weight. Seriously. I wore my largest pair of pre-children jeans yesterday. (There are some things worth dragging across the world.)

6. There are people on earth who don't like chocolate-chip cookies. (I know, it baffles me, also.) Case in point: Crabby Neighbor Olya. After finally unpacking our supplies, which included a mixer I purchased in Moscow, I decided to make war reparations and visit the one person who hasn't visited me. So,

armed with cookies and Justin, I surveyed the battle-field for guards (Lydia the rottweiler) and, seeing an all-clear, crossed the lines of demarcation (the hole in the fence) and rapped on her back door.

As Olya cracked it open, I spied one swollen eye and a haunted look on her sallow face. Her eye seemed to be healing. "Cookies?" I offered, and she opened the door just wide enough for me to hand her the plate.

She looked at the plate, frowned and then shuffled to the table where she dumped the lot into a basket filled with what appeared to be bread crumbs. Then she reached for a plate on her table and put four slices of black bread with cheese on it. Since she hadn't invited us in, Justin and I stood watching her from outside.

I'm used to this system, by the way. My first year in Russia, my neighbor Totyemilla gifted me into a corner until I had to date her grandson, Vovka (looked like a model, kissed like a fish). But despite the fact that Vovka and his designer muscles finally made Chase figure out what he might lose, I've always been wary of the gifting process. Who knows what I might get in return? Pickled herring? Fish heads?

But the cheese looked good. I took the plate with a smile and tried to make small talk.

She closed the door in my face.

O-kay.

I had already confided in Chase my concerns

about Olya—and Chase agreed that abuse loomed large among the other painful issues in their culture. *Please Lord,* I prayed as a walked back to our yard, *give me wisdom and discernment.*

"Want a snack?" I asked Justin as we picked our way back through the fence. I held him off until we reached the house, where Chase and Chloe sat in the kitchen finishing the rest of the cookies.

I plunked the plate down before them, and Chloe's grubby little hand snaked out for a piece. Justin reached for one, too.

"What's this?" Chase asked, eyeing the cheese and bread.

"A cheese-and-bread snack from our neighbor."

I was just taking the first bite when I saw Chase frown as he examined the last slice on the plate.

The truth sunk in as the cheesy something that was not cheese coated my teeth. And then something hard crunched.

Cheese shouldn't crunch, should it? And it lacked flavor except…the overpowering bite of garlic. With a rush of heat, my whole face started to burn. "Ahhh," I said, opening my mouth, not sure what to do. Spit it out? In front of the kids?

"Wha is…?" I managed, not wanting to close my mouth. Help, help!

"*Sala.* Garlic *sala.*" Chase, my hero, grabbed a piece of paper and handed it to me.

"What's *sala?*" I asked, after I cleared my mouth. I could still taste the putty on my teeth.

"Uncooked pig fat, soaked in garlic." Chase said this softly, not looking at me.

Uncooked…pig…fat.

"And that crunch?" I asked, barely whispering.

He reached out for the kids' pieces. "Hair."

But that wasn't the worst of it. Here's the final item on the list of things I've learned this week:

7. Roaches live in wooden houses, too.

I thought I'd left the land of roaches when we departed Moscow. The roach wars rage on in all Moscow apartments, which are built with hidden passageways for the roaches to hide in while their homes (read: nests under wallpaper and behind cupboards) are regularly bombed.

Never did I expect to bring them with me to Siberia.

Or perhaps they were already here, waiting for me. Like an ambush.

Here's a little-known fact about roaches—they hate the light. Which tells you something about their character, doesn't it? Thankfully, Siberian roaches are only, say, an inch long.

But what they lack in size, they make up for in quantity. Every single brother, sister, second cousin once-removed, great-great-aunt and shirttail uncle lives in my kitchen. I know because last night, when Chloe whined for a glass of water, I picked her up

and shuffled out to the darkness where our fridge—
the kind with a freezer the size of an ice-cream box—
hummed. I've noticed the opening getting smaller
and smaller each day as ice builds up. Not sure what
to do about that.

Anyway, I didn't bother turning on the light. I just
opened up the fridge to retrieve the pitcher of water.

And that's when Uncle Spike peered over the top
of the fridge to see who was up at this late hour.

I screamed. He dropped to the floor, next to my
bare feet, and Chloe started to cry.

"Chase, Chase!" I hit the light.

And everything inside me sort of melted into a
puddle of horror. Across my ceiling, thousands of
roaches scurried to safety, some parachuting in from
the light fixture, others running for the border along
the floor, the rest skittering to cracks in the wallpaper, disappearing under it. Have I mentioned how I
love wallpaper?

"Chase!"

I stood frozen, afraid to move, lest I step on one
and wedge it between my toes.

"CHASE!"

"What?" He appeared, panic on his face as if I
might be fending off an army of assailants.

"Roaches! They're everywhere!"

Chase looked around, as if confirming my words.
What, did he think I was lying? I watched the crea-

tures scurry across the coal stove, along the sink, into the cupboards. Over my bare toe.

I screamed again. Why should Chloe have the monopoly on expressing terror?

"Stop screaming!" Chase said, grabbing his shoe and beginning a systematic yet hopeless attempt at mass annihilation.

Oh, no, pal. The screaming has only just begun.

\<Wildflower\>: Have you completely lost your mind?

I'm sitting on a wooden stool in a cold office in the Burr town hall. Chase has arranged with Mayor Anton for us to use the Internet, and I've brought my laptop in, used the mayor's protocol and hooked up. The building is long, made of cement, and echoes like a prison corridor. Like all pre-Soviet towns, it was set up by the government and contains the obligatory post office, police force, mayor's office and, most recently, communications center (aka the mayor's credenza, which he's moved into an empty office for us to use). There's nothing but me, the rickety wooden side table, a drooping bookshelf void of books and a calendar for 1988 on the wall.

I consider it nothing short of a miracle they have Internet, even dial-up. And the fact that I have found H online (my time: 2:00 p.m., naptime; her time: 10:00 p.m., party time) gives me hope that God still cares.

I'm just being dramatic, of course, but at the moment, that belief is wavering a bit. Yes, I've dug out my Bible since our move to Bursk, but I haven't opened it. It's akin to Chloe putting her hands over her ears and humming in protest.

This vacancy is why I'm feeling as if I've been run over by a dogsled, pummeled and forgotten in the land of the sun-never-rises.

I ponder H's question a moment, while the cursor blinks at me. Have I lost my mind?

Let's see. I've got no running water, a cow in my backyard I must learn to milk, a neighbor who gives me pig fat, roaches as pets and, best of all, my very own outhouse. I believe the answer would be yes.

<GI>: I don't know. Maybe it's not that bad. In the past week, Chase and I have stripped all the wallpaper off the walls, repainted, cleaned the windows, built toddler beds and a sandbox, fixed the hole in the fence and learned how to cook like pioneers. (Okay, Chase learned how to cook like a pioneer. I watched.) I'm feeling very Ma Ingalls here. And everyone loves Ma. It's only for a year.

<Wildflower>: If you say "It's only for a year" one more time, I'm coming over there. Let me be the bearer of truth—this is bad, Josey. Very, very bad.

Even Chase should realize that. I know you want to change the world, and yes, you even taught the mayor of Moscow how to make peanut-butter cookies, but this just might be over your head.

Oh, no, that almost sounds like a dare. Don't do it, H!

<Wildflower>: You already showed all of Gull Lake that you were more than just the girl who pulled the fire alarm to get out of her calculus final.

<GI>: They never proved that.

<Wildflower>: Whatever. I get it—you're the Girl Who Doesn't Give Up. But seriously, enough. Come home. No plumbing? The smell alone should hit you upside the head and knock some sense into you. I'd be on the next plane.

<GI>: Boat.

<Wildflower>: See?

<GI>: But we're making progress. And you should see the outhouse Chase made me. He shored up the walls and added a little window on the side to let in light. There's a shelf that holds, among other

things, air-freshening spray. He replaced the toilet seat cover with a brand-new porcelain one and covered the area on either side of the seat with tile. There's a pull light that he rigged to come on when the door is opened and go off when it closes. He even painted the building a lovely light blue and put a bouquet of flowers in a vase he attached to the door outside. It's a sight to behold!

<Wildflower>: I cannot believe you are finding this much joy in an outhouse.

<GI>: But isn't he impressive? He's even been invited to attend the council meeting tonight and is hoping to be invited on a hunt for…something. The Mythical White Tiger, maybe.

<Wildflower>: Yes, Josey, we all know Chase is Captain Amazing.

<GI>: But it's more than that. I'm even seeing opportunities, like my neighbor, who looks like she needs a friend.

<Wildflower>: I am the one who needs a friend. I am the one who needs a shoulder to cry on and a late-night drive out to Bloomquist Mountain where I can unload my list of complaints to a

willing ear and receive, in turn, timely and sage advice. I am the victim here.

<GI>: What do you mean?

<Wildflower>: Rex and I need marriage advice.

<GI>: I'm probably the last person you should ask.

<Wildflower>: Rex wants to break up the Sugar Monkeys.

Now, I've never understood why H named her band the Sugar Monkeys. Yes, it's a punk band. Yes, I understand there's a deeper meaning to the name that I, as a non-songwriter, can't possibly understand. But it's never really made sense to me. However, I can grasp the concept of having a piece of your identity stripped away through no fault of your own. So I'm appropriate in my dismay.

<GI>: What? You've been together for over four years! You and Rex practically ARE the Sugar Monkeys.

<Wildflower>: He wants to go to school for computer programming. And have a family.

<Wildflower>: Are you there? Hello, Jose?

I have to admit, picturing H as a mom pushes my imagination into Never Neverland. H is the last holdout, the woman most likely to cover her body with tattoos. But, hey, if I can go from being a Gull Lake Party Girl to a Missionary in Siberia, then maybe…

<GI>: You should do it. It's time.

<GI>: H? Are you there?

<Wildflower>: I don't know if I can do this.

<GI>: Me, neither. But I keep telling myself I can. Maybe that's what counts.

The cursor blinks and blinks as I wait for a reply, but I get nothing. It takes me about five minutes to realize I've been kicked off the Net.

In the other room, I hear Russian voices, arguing. I rub my hands together and blow on them a bit. Although the temperatures have plummeted to just above freezing at night and a little lower than fifty in the daytime, the heat for the central offices of the village has yet to be turned on. We may be on the backside of the planet, but this little town is heated exactly the same way every other Russian town is—via a central heating source that runs pipes through the village and into public buildings like the tentacles of an octopus. I'm suddenly—and who would have thought it?—thankful for my little coal furnace that Chase keeps chugging away.

Here's a thought. If they can have centralized heating, couldn't they also have indoor plumbing? Isn't that just pipes running through the village? Maybe it's a little more involved, but still. I'm just saying.

I'm already wearing the leather boots—they're just over the ankles—I picked up for a song in the open market in Moscow. I purposely got them big enough to fit my wool socks. I'm also wearing my pea coat, which I rustled up last time we were in Gull Lake.

I am definitely thinner. Probably all those hiking trips to the outhouse.

I hear a knock at the door and turn.

"Vso?" Anton says in his non-cheery voice, asking curtly if I'm done. One would think that, as mayor, Anton would have to be at least moderately friendly.

"Da," I say. Even if I wasn't done, I'd have to be because apparently, I'm getting the boot. *"Spaceeba,"* I add, thinking he'll disappear.

He stands there, watching me, his dark eyes holding a thousand private judgments as I pack up my laptop.

So he's not the warmest coat in the closet. His silent grief demands I give him grace. I smile at him.

"Be careful of your health," he says quietly in

Russian, eyes not leaving mine. I frown at him. Then, abruptly, he turns away.

I was feeling fine until this moment.

Then again, the Nanais talk with a bit of an accent. He might have said, "Be happy you have your health."

Which I am. Very. It just may be the only thing I have at the moment.

I slide my laptop into my bag.

On the walk home, I notice the leaves have already begun to turn to jewels in the scattered poplar and oak, and for a second, I am in Gull Lake.

The homey scent of bread baking drifts from a nearby house, reminding me of Jasmine, and of Mom baking Saturday-morning rolls.

Children, laughing behind a fence, fill me with memories of Chase and me in the sandbox, fighting for Hotwheel track space.

As I step on fallen leaves, the smell of decaying loam from the ground stirs my senses. I expect to see a football.

I lift my collar as the wind finds my ears, digging my chin into the wool for warmth.

Nearing my house, I see a trickle of dark smoke from our chimney against the gray pallor of the afternoon sky. The house next door, home of Lydia the Killer and Olya, is dark and quiet. Not a hint of life.

Not unlike Olya.

Shuffling toward me up the muddy street is a tall, gaunt man. He looks old at first glance, but then I realize he is weathered by environment rather than time. His face is sallow and covered with a grizzled brown beard, and he's wearing a pair of deerskin Cossack boots, a dirty and torn army jacket and a misshapen fur hat, worn so thin that the shiny surface of the hide glints through. He lifts his eyes to me, and even from ten feet away, I see emptiness there.

His shoulders are hunched, and as he draws closer, the odor of alcohol hits me like a two-by-four. I stiffen, and he nods, curtly.

Then, as I pass, he stops. I can't help a glance over my shoulder. I'm ready to swing my computer or maybe just my bag (after all, a laptop is a laptop).

But he's not coming after me. He's opening the gate next to mine. Then, with another glance my direction, he enters, and the gate swings shut behind him.

The wind on my neck raises gooseflesh.

Unless I'm mistaken, I've just met my neighbor.

Olya's husband.

I remember our first year of marriage as a long, dark tunnel, during which I ballooned to twice my body size and eventually gave birth to replicas of the childhood sweethearts I once knew and loved.

Chase remembers this time as the year life slid out from underneath him and he nearly lost me. (Not true.) We've since found our equilibrium, and the last three years have been as smooth as they can be with twins in a one-bedroom flat…

As I sit on our double bed, a cotton duvet tucked around my legs, I listen to the Siberian wind howl over the sound of Chloe singing herself to sleep. I am waiting for Chase to return home from his late-night council meeting and wondering if we are veering off course again.

What are we doing here?

I understand all about the suicide issues—the tidbit of grace I extended toward Olya has expanded exponentially since I saw her husband. I also believe in the divine providence inherent in all of life's less-traveled roads. It's something I learned during my first year in Russia, having made what I thought might have been a rash life decision, only to discover that God knew exactly what He was doing. In fact, He'd planned for me to be doing exactly what I was doing.

Then.

But I'm getting a little panicky now. I mean, after all, I am in *Siberia*.

I pull my Bible from the meager, well-read stack of books I've lugged from Moscow. I've been more or less faithfully plowing through Ephesians. It's only taken me four years, but listen, I have twins— cut me some slack.

As a prisoner for the Lord, then, I urge you to live a life worthy of the calling you have received. Be completely humble and gentle; be patient, bearing with one another in love. Make every effort to keep the unity of the Spirit through the bond of peace.

Did anyone else notice the word *prisoner?* I just have to circle that. A few times.

Maybe I should focus on something else.

Worthy of the calling I've received. What calling? I'm familiar with this word, having grappled with the hidden meaning of it when I first came to Russia, as a missionary. A calling is that soul-deep passion that God puts inside us. A faith that compels us to do what some might call stupid, like moving to the backside of Russia with two preschoolers to change the world.

Apparently, by Paul's standards, a calling is supposed to be a privilege, something I need to be worthy of.

Maybe I'm looking at this thing entirely wrong.

I mean, how many women have the *opportunity* to learn how to kill roaches, milk a cow and cook on a coal stove?

Okay, most of our nation's pioneers and probably two-thirds of the world, so don't answer that. But I'm realizing that it's all perspective, and that perhaps God doesn't send just anyone to Siberia.

So what does it mean to be worthy? When I was a missionary, I purchased a study Bible that came complete with a word-study section. It's helpful. Take, for example the word *humble,* which is in the verse. It also means lowly and comes packaged with phrases like "compassion for the downtrodden."

Can anyone say Olya? I think of her now, in that dark house beside mine. Connected to me, in a way. Part of my world, whether I choose it or not.

Or how about *gentle?* My word study mentions "meekness," and stepping aside to let God fight your battles.

I can't even begin to list my battles. Maybe I should start with p for plumbing.

I think I can figure out *patient,* but when I look it up I find "fortitude." That makes me think of a fortress or a castle. Our home is a castle. Outside, the battle rages. Maybe if I can provide a fortress, instead of a battlefront, Chase will have a place to rest.

Maybe God can use me to protect and nurture Chase as he rests inside our castle.

Yeah, see, I'm really good at this word study! Too bad understanding the words is only the first step in the process.

Peace. "Prosperity. Quietness. Rest."

It strikes me that I've just looked up the attributes of Christ. Humble. Gentle. Patient. *Peace,* as in Prince of Peace.

Is that what it means to be worthy? To be like Christ in this chilly world?

Maybe I *am* here for a reason. Of course I already know that I have a purpose, but it helps to be reminded. Especially when one is waging a constant (and often losing) battle against roaches.

I hear a thumping in the entryway and listen as Chase comes in, closing the door. In a moment he's climbing into bed, snuggling up next to me, his arm around my waist. "Hey, babe," he says, his voice husky and tired.

I reach up and rub his cheek with my hand. It's stubbly, and I hear him sigh.

"How was the meeting?"

He is silent for a long time. Too long. "The council has a request."

I can't pinpoint exactly why, but that sentence makes my jaw tighten. I say nothing.

"They want you to send the twins to *detski-sod*."

Kindergarten. I try—really, I do—to school my tone. "Since when does the council get to decide what's best for my children?"

He tenses, and I know that he's trying to decide if he should run—metaphorically speaking, of course—or stay and fight.

"They're not trying to decide what's best for *our* children. It's just, they think that unless we are in the culture, we can't understand it. And all the kids attend school here by the time they're eighteen months old."

I think that all the time I spend building up my right-arm muscle while pumping water and hiking outside in the wind to use the biffy will help me understand this culture. I don't need to sacrifice my children's education, do I?

"I need to get the people here to trust me, Josey. To see that I share their values. When the Soviets took over, they dismantled centuries of tradition and destroyed the nomadic lifestyle of the Nanais by making it illegal to hunt or fish. Before, the wives partnered with their husbands to find food and take care of the family. But once they built towns, their nomadic mindset began to vanish, leaving a fractured, confused society. All they have left is their traditions, but even those seem to be unraveling."

I understand all about feeling confused. And life unraveling.

Chase's hand closes over mine. It's cold and a little chapped. I interlace my fingers with his, attempting to warm his hand with my touch.

"I need to get involved in their lives and show them that I understand," he continues. "And the first step is letting my children become a part of their society. I think it will be good for them, Jose. And maybe you could meet other mothers through the school. You'd also have more time to spend with our neighbor—she seems like she could use a friend."

What was your first clue, Chase? The big dog with the hungry bark?

Gentle, Josey, gentle.

"But it's your call, GI."

I pull the covers up to my chin. I've finally gotten the smell of mold out of the house after cleaning every last corner. I've picked fresh chrysanthemums and hung them upside down over the window to dry. And the smell from dinner—a pot of potatoes with clumps of onion and dried dill (I'm learning!)—lingers in the carpeted walls.

"I know it's a lot to ask."

Humble. Gentle.

"But maybe it'll make a difference."

As a prisoner for the Lord, then, I urge you to live a life worthy of the calling you have received.

What if I had time to do something, like invite Olya over for tea?

"Half days?"

"That might work." Chase is running his thumb over my hand and I can feel his breathing start to relax.

Patience. Peace.

"Give the cow away, and we have a deal."

He pulls me close, molding his body to mine. The wind rattles the windows, hinting at a coming storm, but I'm warm and dry.

We're going to make it.

I'm only here for a year. For the first time, I'm wondering if it's long enough.

Chapter Eight

Catch Me

I've always been enamored of the whole home-schooling concept. Science projects in cookie-making class and reading epic tales out loud, acting them out later in homemade costumes… I think I was born to be a homeschooler.

So it takes great submission (see that word? Yes, Daphne would be proud) to dress up my children and walk them to the preschool in the middle of town. It's the only building with playground equipment, although that is a questionable name for the rusty, twisted metal in the yard. The merry-go-round is missing all the slats, and the slide has a puddle under-neath that a two-year-old could drown in. The swings are metal and I can picture bruised, pinched fingers as

I hear them squeal on their rusty hinges. As for the monkey bars—why, exactly, do they have monkey bars for three-year-olds that I can walk under? Does anyone besides me think "broken neck"? The only seemingly safe play area looks to be a green and orange painted playhouse with a saggy roof and dirt floor.

However, I remind myself, the Bursk *detski-sod* has not only managed to keep children alive, but it has turned out the likes of Ulia and Anton, Olya and Vasilley. With regard to Vasilley, I'm not sure I find this comforting.

Okay, that was judgmental. But since seeing him, my sympathy for Olya continues to mushroom. So far, I haven't heard yelling from their side of the house, but that bruised eye haunts me.

I have to give the teachers credit for their creativity. Just like the orphanage I worked in outside Moscow, the *detski-sod* is brightly painted, with yellow walls, big blue violets and orange poppies. The room for three-year-olds is spacious, with huge trundle bunks built into the wall and a giant table in the middle with adorable little chairs around it. A Cyrillic alphabet is stenciled on the wall, and an old carpet remnant marks out the play area, where I see a few children playing with dishes, a wooden truck and a naked doll.

A teacher—or should I say overstuffed babushka— sits on a tiny chair with a group of children, reading aloud.

This might work.

I stroll down the halls until I find the office marked Director: Maya Kradenski. I knock on the door.

The woman who opens it scares me. She has shorn-to-the-scalp hair and is wearing a high-necked blouse and a high-waisted wool skirt that make her look like she's come straight from the runways in Milan. Her footwear—a pair of sleek Mary Janes— causes me to consider my hiking boots with some chagrin. (When did I sacrifice fashion for convenience? C'mon, Josey, don't fold!) But what scares me is her eyes. Dark as night, they stare me down as cold as Siberia.

"Da?" she asks. It's not a nice *"da,"* but a why-are-you-bothering-me? *"da."*

"Zhdrastvyootya. My name is Josey Anderson and I, uh, want to enroll my children in your *detski-sod,"* I say, rethinking my words even as they come out of my mouth.

She raises one nicely sculpted eyebrow. *"Ladna,"* she says after a moment, which means roughly "oh, well, I guess so." "I'm Maya." But she doesn't hold out her hand. Instead, she returns to her desk and pulls out a form from her desk drawer.

Oh, yeah, I'm feeling the love.

I take a deep breath, find a smile and pull my beloved children into her office. We sit down on a plush black sofa that I know isn't leather, because I had one just like it in Moscow. I put Chloe on my lap as Maya starts asking questions.

It's a nice office, typically Russian, with a laminated wood desk and a file cabinet, the door of which opens from the top, along one wall. A fake plant stands in the corner and tea accoutrements are laid out on a credenza behind her with a Korean hot-water pot, a used cup and a packet of tea.

Looks like she often drinks alone.

Chloe climbs down and starts to wander around the room. She has kitty paws and is meowing nervously, eyeing me. Justin climbs up on the sofa beside me, but I pull him onto my lap before he can get his muddy feet beneath him.

"They're twins?" Maya asks.

I nod. "Three years old."

She writes that down. "And why do you want them here?"

Why, indeed. "My husband thinks it would be a good idea for them to get to know Russian culture." Okay, that was passing the buck a little, but accurate.

She puts her pen down, folding her hands on top of her paper and regarding me without a smile. "And you?"

And me? I'm submitting, but she doesn't have to know that. In fact, it lessens the impact of the submitting if I announce it to the world, doesn't it? What I want this woman to understand is that these are my precious children, and I'm entrusting her and her staff with their little minds—and furthermore, their lives.

I pet Chloe, who has climbed up my leg, purring.

"I'm a mother," I say, and my smile vanishes. "Please take good care of them."

For a split second that might have only occurred in my imagination, her steely demeanor vanishes, and I glimpse the smallest hint of curiosity. Tenderness, even.

Then it's gone. I'm left holding my breath and praying that my words of faith spoken so long ago to Daphne are true—that when we fling ourselves out there, God catches us.

Dear Josey,

By the time you get this, it will be nearly November, I guess. Do you even get mail in Siberia? I can't believe you moved there—you are so brave! And such a great inspiration to the rest of us. I was just getting used to you living in Moscow. I don't know if I'll ever get used to you living in Siberia!

Guess what? Your sister has finally figured out how to use the Internet! I know you thought I would never learn, but after reading your last letter about sending you kringle, Milton had this bright idea to put my kringle up on eBay, and we're an overnight success! Can you believe it? Go to www.kringlekompany.com. We ship overnight, and we're already talking about buying the old pizza joint in town to turn it into a commercial Kringle Kompany store!

You should see Amelia and Clay in their little kringle aprons. (I've enclosed two for the twins.) Mom has postponed moving permanently to Arizona to watch them every day—in fact, she's even teaching Amelia to read. I know it seems early, but she's four and already is keeping up with Sesame Street and the plethora of early-learning shows. I know I shouldn't let her watch too much television, but today's programming is really quite educational.

Milton says that soon we'll have enough money to add on to the house. I love the cute kitchen in our Cape Cod, but it's getting a little cramped. I'd love to have a granite island and of course, upgrade to stainless-steel appliances. We're also looking into a Subzero fridge—after all, I can't neglect the family! But Milton has been so supportive. He's even sending me and Mom to New York for the Kitchen Expo! I've always wanted to see the Big Apple. We're even staying at the Waldorf!

Oh, I've enclosed a copy of the newspaper. Lew Suzlbach got the job at the high school after the entire town thought we'd be without a football coach this year (too bad Chase didn't want the job). So far, the Gull Lake Gulls are undefeated! It's so fun to watch the games—Milton and I haven't missed one. We love snuggling up together under a blanket in the bleachers. Makes a great date night!

We all miss you. Mom, of course, was saddened by the news that you weren't coming home for another year. I think being around the kids helps a lot, though. I miss you!

Love,

Jasmine

I have heard stories from other mothers about their children who, after being nurtured at home, suffer great anxiety when they are left at preschool for the first time. They throw themselves at their mothers' legs, begging, *pleading* not to be left behind and wailing for hours after their moms leave, only to repeat the trauma the next day—for weeks.

This has not been my experience. Chloe has taken to *detski-sod* like a second home. In her cute pigtails, tights and dresses, she skips to class every day, yanking my arm from my socket in her excitement to get away from me.

Okay, maybe it's not to get away from me, but let's just say a little three-year-old angst would go a long way. Just one temper tantrum, one moment of agonizing goodbye? Justin isn't quite as excited, but when he saw that the children get treats and play games and draw and climb things, he was all in.

I got a tour from Maya and discovered that the *detski-sod* contains a music room, a nap room and, of course, a potty room complete with a long bench with little bowls attached underneath. I guess it's a group event. There are three different classes—Chloe and Justin's is the middle group, with eight adorable kids who are already wearing their snowsuits.

My children are woefully underdressed in wool hats and coats, tights and *valenki*—molded wool boots that Anton sent home with Chase. They resemble a stiff, brown stocking.

I pick the twins up every day at noon, right before naptime, which leaves me three empty hours every morning to do…I'm not sure what.

Maybe it's because my life has been replete with washing dishes and running after Chloe and doing laundry and running after Chloe and grocery shopping and running after Chloe and cleaning the house and running after Chloe that the deafening silence in the house after the kids are gone paralyzes me.

Who thought I'd be the kind of mother who has made her children her entire life?

Then again, isn't that sort of the definition of a mother? Don't ask me! I've never done this before!

I filled up the silences this week by reading a

book. Writing a letter home. Actually purchasing everything on my grocery list.

Wow, I miss my kids.

I am seeing now that I gave birth so that I would have little people to keep me company.

I'm sitting outside in the *detski-sod* yard, on the lead-painted railing, watching as the kids climb on the monkey bars and dig in the sand. Justin is chasing a little boy, playing tag. Chloe has joined a group of girls who have morphed into kitties and they are climbing in and out of the playhouse windows. She probably taught them everything they know.

It's nippy out. The last of the leaves have fallen, a blanket of gold and yellow on the ground. The sun sinks lower earlier each day. I fold Jasmine's letter and shove it into my coat pocket, turning up the collar on my jacket. It smells like Thanksgiving.

I wonder where I can track down a turkey in this town.

And I don't need any wisecracks about looking in the mirror.

The novelty of moving to Siberia has worn off. I look down at my chapped hands and wonder if I can do one more load of laundry in that metal tub. With the cold bite of the fall wind, each item of laundry freezes into a stiff carcass as it dries. I especially love prying myself into a pair of frozen jeans every day.

Chase has interviewed nearly all the men in

town. He has chopped wood, hauled water and even fixed a few roofs with them, trying to unearth the layers of their lives. He keeps asking to go out to check the traplines and visit a nearby mink farm (yes, I said mink), but so far, he hasn't earned the right to witness these sacred rituals. He has, however, earned the right to attend every council meeting and spend long hours at Anton's house eating fish.

How nice for him.

I'm trying not to be negative, but as my hands become more chapped and cracked and as I trot out with a flashlight to use the biffy and I fight my battle against the roaches, I'm feeling like a forgotten soldier.

But we're going to be fine. He's just busy.

And to add to my feelings of defeat, I can't seem to muster the courage to face Olya. What happened to the desire to change lives? The compassion for my neighbor?

I suppose it died when Vasilley about glared at Chase after we offered him the cow. Although he took it, I had to wonder if perhaps we'd offended him.

Then again, had *I* liked being given a cow? We all know how that turned out.

"Mommy!" Justin says, spotting me on the railing. He runs toward me and dives into my arms. I hug him tight, smelling his curly blond hair and smooching him good on his pudgy cheeks.

"Nilzya!" one of the teachers yells. It's the Russian equivalent of "You must never do that again! Never, never, never!" (The Russians can get all that conveniently in one word.) I see that Justin's group is lining up to go inside. She's not smiling at me.

Apparently, picking up my children every day at noon has shaken the status quo. So much for being accepted.

"Go with your group, Justin. Mommy will be inside in a few minutes to collect you." I'm not sure why they demand that I come inside to get him, other than wanting to make a spectacle of his leaving.

Justin makes a face and runs off to join his group.

"Josey?"

I turn, startled by the English, and a streak of warmth goes through me. "Nathan?"

Our American missionary friend is exactly as I remember him—warm brown eyes and a nice smile, although now, he's clean-shaven and wearing a black stocking cap and leather jacket that makes him look more Mafia than missionary. "I thought that was you." He climbs over the fence and sits beside me. "What are you doing here?"

"Waiting for my children to finish with *detski-sod* for the day."

Nathan nods in what looks like approval. "How's that working out?"

I shrug. "The kids seem to like it." Do *I* like it? I don't know. I'm just trying not to need therapy.

"And Chase? How's he doing?"

"Busy. He's trying to get the council to let him go out with the fur trappers, but I guess there's some sort of rule against outsiders, so we're trying to become insiders."

"When in Rome… Sounds like something a missionary might do." Nathan picks up a seed pod and begins to strip it. "So, I suppose you're keeping busy?"

"Uh, let's see. Hauling water. Doing laundry." I look at him. "I got out of milking the cow today."

His eyes are huge, and I laugh when he sees I'm joking. "Please tell me that you aren't milking cows."

"There is nothing wrong with milking a cow, Nathan."

"No, there's not. But you *can* buy milk at the market."

I watch as he peels open the pod. "Chase gave the cow to the neighbors."

Nathan blows the seeds into the wind. "I enjoyed getting to know Chase on the train. He told me you're both Christians."

I nod, although I feel that pinch of guilt in my spirit. Yes, Chase and I attended Moscow Bible Church for the past four years, and yes, we pray at mealtime, but no, we haven't really been on our knees together recently.

Which, perhaps, is why we ended up in Siberia.

No, no. We're not being punished. Not being punished! I ball my chapped hands into fists.

"I saw Chase earlier today and asked him if you would be open to a project. He told me to run it by you."

I eye him, checking my watch. "What kind of project?"

He crumbles the pod in his hand and drops it on the ground. "I'm starting a women's Bible study. I'm wondering if you would lead it."

My eyes widen. "I don't—"

"Listen, I know my limitations, the biggest being that I'm, well—" he lifts a shoulder "—a man. But there are many women in this town who need God's word in their lives. And Chase told me that you were once officially a missionary."

I nod and can't help the niggle of excitement inside me. Oh, I'm so pathetic.

But what if, you know, *this* is why I'm here?

What if God used Chase to get me here and even arranged for my beloved offspring to go to kindergarten so that I could lead hundreds—okay, maybe just a dozen—women to Christ? I now understand the sacrifices. The submission. And I can see the fruit. A group of women are packed into my living room, sitting on the fraying gold-and-brown sofas we inherited from the village elders, eating chocolate-chip cookies and discussing the book of John, the peace of the gospel changing their lives one day at a time.

Maybe I can even find a way to reach Olya.

I take a breath. The wind swirls the leaves at my feet. A tinge of smoke scents the air from the houses surrounding the kindergarten. I love the flow of seasons, the crisp anticipation of knowing things are about to change.

"I'm not sure, Nathan. I've never led a Bible study before." I stand to go inside to get Chloe and Justin.

"I'll help you," Nathan says, and the smile he gives me makes me believe him.

The thought stays with me as I retrieve Justin and Chloe, bundling them up like it's minus thirty out and rejoin Nathan on the street. He takes Chloe's hand and meows to her as we head toward home. She looks at him with adoration in her eyes.

Unabashed loyalty, just because he plays to her kitty routine.

"I have errands to do," he says, "but Chase mentioned letting me bunk with you guys. Will that work?"

"We only have a sofa."

"I'll make dinner," Nathan adds, smiling.

Oh, that rat, Chase. He told Nathan about my cooking abilities. Or lack thereof.

Well, a girl does get hungry.

Bursk has a main street, with four or five rickety side streets, hemmed in by tiny houses that look identical to mine—ornate windows and outhouses in the back, ringed by wobbly fences. The roads taper off to fields and then oak and spruce forests. As in every Russian town, there are two places to shop—the *gastronome* and the corner market, which, in Bursk, is a few rickety kiosks offering vegetables and frozen meats, flanked by rows of people sitting on wooden crates selling jars of *brusnika* berries or sunflower seeds or even cigarettes displayed on old towels. Occasionally, I spot someone trying to unload a pair of shoes or homemade mittens.

Today, as we stroll by, I take in the offerings—dried herring, squares of pumpkin, a spray of chrysanthemums, and...*sala*. With the skin on.

I slow, and sure enough, Olya is hunched over in a ragged wool coat with fraying sleeves and a holey, knitted muffler. She glances up at me and, for a moment, our eyes meet.

And then I see it. A flicker, like a door opening, a peek into darkness.

Hope.

Just like that, it's gone. But I know I saw it; I know it's there.

Please God, let that hope be because she sees You, in me.

I point to the *sala*. "*Pa chom?*" I ask.

She doesn't look at me when she names an amount.

You know, Chase will eat almost anything for a good reason. I fork over the rubles. As she hands over the piece of pig fat rolled up in a grease-dotted piece of paper, she meets my eyes again.

And smiles.

Chapter Nine

The Oddity

The first time I realized I loved Chase—or rather, wanted to let myself love him—we were making pizza in Moscow. Chase is an awesome cook, which is one of the primary reasons we are all still alive and not dead from scurvy. During my first year in Moscow, he not only surprised me with a visit, but made me dinner.

I love to watch a man make dinner.

I realize this as Nathan chops onions and browns some ground beef, using a portion of Olya's *sala*. I'm holding Justin, who has fallen asleep on my lap. Chloe is in her bed, curled up like a kitty. I expected Chase to be home, and I'm waiting for him to appear. But he's probably mending a fence somewhere or building a bridge. Chase already has a number of friends in this town, and I'm proud of him.

I do, however, feel a little strange sitting alone in the house with Nathan. Especially with him singing, making himself at home in my kitchen. He is wearing an apron and a towel hangs over his shoulder.

Darkness fills the windowpanes, and outside, it's started to rain.

"By the way, you're going to have to defrost your fridge soon if you hope to avoid salmonella poisoning," Nathan says.

Oh. "And having never defrosted a fridge before…?" I smooth Justin's hair on his head.

Nathan glances at me and laughs. "How long have you lived in Russia, anyway?"

"Four years. But I had a normal fridge."

He laughs again. "*This* is a normal fridge. And it's easy to defrost. I'll do it tomorrow before I leave."

He drains off grease into a tin can and adds carrots, potatoes, tomato sauce, beets and dill to the pot, along with chicken broth.

My stomach is cheering wildly, but I manage to keep my voice steady. "What are you making?"

"Borscht. I learned it from my landlady in Khabarovsk. She's about eighty and nearly blind, but boy, can she cook." He takes a clove of garlic and grates it into the pot.

"How long have you been here?"

"Three years. I came over for just a year, but once I got involved with the small peoples groups, I couldn't go home."

"Small peoples?"

He takes a spoon from the cup I keep the utensils in on the shelf. Someday I hope to have drawers in my kitchen. "It's the Russian name for the indigenous people groups." He tastes the soup.

"But they're not short."

He nearly chokes and covers his mouth, his shoulders shaking. "No. Small in population, Josey."

He glances over at me, and my face heats.

"But that's cute."

Or stupid. Let's remember, shall we, that I had two kids. At once. There's been a serious drainage of the brain cells.

He turns back to the soup, and I lay my cheek on Justin's downy head. "Isn't it hard to be away from your family?"

"My family will be there when I get home. At least my parents will. My siblings are spread out all over the world. My brother is a cop in Alaska, my sister is a diplomat in London, and my other sister lives in Paris, working on her dissertation on water sources for Third World countries." He adds salt, covers the soup and wipes his hands as he turns to me. "I come from a long line of do-gooders."

"And chefs?"

He nods, and his smile is warm. "But I'm the only one who is doing it full-time, for the Lord."

My brain tells me that Nathan shouldn't be here when Chase is not, but it's nice to have someone to talk to.

Chloe awakens and after a short, disgruntled wail, shuffles out to the kitchen. Her hair is standing on end, her face is hot and red where she slept hard on her pillow and she is dragging the pink blankie my mother quilted for her. She stops just outside the kitchen, ponders me for a moment and moves toward Nathan. She leans against his leg.

He rests his hand on her head. "Hungry, Kitty?"

She nods and makes paws.

I give Nathan a look. He grins at me. Troublemaker.

Justin rouses, and I take him to the outhouse before he has an accident on my lap. Every day, the lack of plumbing bothers me less. Or maybe I'm just like the proverbial poached frog, getting used to the heat.

I'm not sure what to think about that.

By the time we get back, Nathan has ladled out soup, cut bread and put a jar of homemade *smytena* (sour cream, in our language) on the table.

I sit down as Nathan joins me and bows his head. "Lord, thank You for Josey and Chase, and their willingness to be used by You. Please bless their home, and family, and work."

Amen.

He raises his eyes to mine. "Amen."

I smile. "Thanks for the soup."

"How did you and Chase meet?" Nathan asks. I fill him in on our courtship, beginning with the lunchbox fight at the bus stop and ending with Chase proposing to me at a bistro in Moscow.

"Did you always want to live in Siberia?"

Did I always—

"Oh," he says, reading my expression.

"This was Chase's brilliant idea."

"And you agreed because…" He raises an eyebrow.

Right now, sitting in the middle of Siberia, the coal furnace kicking out heat, eating borscht, my husband conspicuously absent, well, I'm not sure. I think it was something to do with a fur hat on my head, overheating my brain.

"Because Chase and I thought we could make a difference." I remember what Chase said about Anton, and think of Ulia. "I *know* we can make a difference."

"I believe you." Only, Nathan doesn't meet my eyes. He is looking at my angry, chapped hands. "Josey, those look bad."

I quickly tuck them into my lap.

"Are you washing clothes by hand?"

I lift a shoulder.

Nathan puts his spoon down. "I had no idea."

"It's okay. We didn't think about a washing machine until we arrived here."

"Chase needs to get you a machine."

"He's been busy. And we're only here for a year, you know."

But the way Nathan is looking at me, I'm thinking that doesn't matter.

"He and I need to have a chat," Nathan says.

I am not sure how to interpret the swell of feelings inside me.

I grew up in the age of dinner parties. My mother, although busy running Berglund Acres, always threw the annual Christmas banquet in the resort dining room, an event open only to our little country church (and occasionally crashed by the other denominations). I have vivid memories of Mom planning the appetizers (including my personal favorite: bacon-wrapped garlic bread with cheese spread), baking breads and marinating the cranberry pork roast. She'd pull out the industrial-size coffeemaker for the buffet, order cheeses from Wisconsin, and once she even asked the organist from the Methodist church to play.

I am not my mother.

But I do know the elements of a great dinner. Food. Ambience. Entertainment.

Oh, and people. And while I'm not inviting the whole town of Bursk just yet, I think entertaining the mayor and his wife merits a nod toward social decorum.

I'm very Martha when I want to be. I found a

white sheet and had the kids trace their hands on it and color the tracings as turkeys. I also cut little square napkins from the ends and hemmed them. Yes, that would be with a needle. And thread.

There might have been blood involved. But it was worth it, because Chase needs to buddy up to Anton if he hopes to find out how to help this village. And I am here to support him.

Chase found a hunk of what might be pork (but could also be beef) at the market, and after lots of washing and seasoning and even some marinating in oil, wine and spices, it's baking in our oven, nestled in a cradle of potatoes. The house smells like Sunday afternoon, and my stomach is alert and on the prowl.

I made—of course—cookies. Sugar cookies. I even rolled them in what some high-brows might call "natural sugar," (known here in Siberia as unbleached, cheap sugar). They look sparkly and festive in the middle of the table.

Then there's the bread I attempted to make. Let's hope that some people like flat bread. (Maybe no one will notice.)

I found two white, slightly bent candles for ambience, and dressed Justin and Chloe up in their best brown-and-green harvest colors. I taught them "Jingle Bells" in case we need a touch of cozy entertainment.

I think my mother would be proud.

The fact is, I miss having friends. I miss Dalton

and Maggie, and Caleb and Daphne. I even miss Jasmine and Milton, although a gal can only be around her former-boyfriend-turned-brother-in-law so long without dropping to her knees to thank God for his goodness. So, I'm hoping that tonight will open the door to further gatherings—maybe even game nights! Besides, I need a girl to talk to other than Chloe, who thinks active listening involves paws and purring.

I hear Chase come in, and a moment later he's in the kitchen, brushing snow off his hair. He looks adorable tonight in a red sweater and black dress pants, his curly blond hair slightly wet. He hands me a bag. "I could only get that orange-flavored soda."

It's better than vodka (which, of course, I wouldn't serve, and hope Anton doesn't expect).

I'm hauling the roast out of the oven when I hear Chase greet our guests in the entryway. I pull the pot holders off my hands and go to the door in time to see him give Ulia a little kiss on each cheek. When did he turn European? But the big shock is Ulia's hair. Where once it was black, it's now…what is that color? Marmalade? Auburn? Burnt pumpkin? I've seen that color before in Moscow, but have never personally known anyone who has chosen it. Oddly enough, it's a good look for Ulia.

Anton double kisses me and then sits down at the table.

Ulia hands me a jar of pickles. "*Spaceeba* for having us," she says. I like Ulia, despite her reserve. She's an orange-haired Morticia Addams tonight, dressed in a black polyester wool skirt and V-neck sweater, her long hair down. She gives me a small smile, and I think she's trying.

I've already served dinner to the kids so I can have them perform (okay, maybe the performance really is just for me), and settle them in their room to play while we eat.

I make a mean roast.

Okay, Chase makes a mean roast. But I carve and serve well. Dinner is delicious, and Anton practically inhales it, cleaning his plate three times.

Ulia, on the other hand, picks at her food.

"How are the kids liking *detski-sod?*" she asks, not looking at me.

Anton shoots her a dark look. She ignores him and lifts her eyes to mine.

My ego is on the line here, but I nod. "They like their teacher. And Maya, the director, seems like she knows what she's doing."

Ulia's lips tighten. She looks back at her food. "Just don't let Chase pick up your kids."

Huh? I'm not sure I heard her right, but apparently Anton has, because he drops his fork. "That's all, Ulia."

But Ulia just looks at me and raises an eyebrow. "Maya lost her husband about two years ago in a fire.

The drunk fell asleep smoking and burned his house down." She wipes her mouth. "So now she thinks she can have her pick of men in town."

I glance at Chase. He's giving Ulia a disapproving look that is reminiscent of the look he gave people dishing dirt on his poor mother in high school.

Ulia, however, doesn't see it. I want to wave flags and warn her off.

"She seemed nice," I offer.

"She's nice until she gets what she wants." Ulia takes a sip of her soda. Anton looks like he wants to strangle her. "Which is Chase."

I glance at Chase, and he's shaking his head. "The kids sure like her." That's my Chase, taking the underdog's side.

"Don't trust her. She has a rock where her heart is."

"Ulia!" Anton says.

She shrugs, picks up her fork again. "Then again, there're a few men she won't touch, like your neighbor, Vasilley." She gives me a smile. "Have you met him yet? The town drunk?"

Anton reaches out and grabs Ulia by the arm. She raises her chin and twists out of his grip. "Josey should know who she lives next to!"

I glance at Anton, remembering his cryptic words about my health. He meets my eyes. "Vasilley has a history of getting drunk and destroying property."

Oh. Like the fence?

"That's why Olya has that big dog, you know. It's not to protect her from the neighbors. It's to protect her from her husband," Ulia adds.

I have lost my appetite.

"Anyone want a cookie?" Chase asks.

It's a long evening, and I find out much, much more about Bursk than I ever wanted to know. Like the fact that Misha and Anya, who moved out of here on our behalf, were actually glad to get away from our loud neighbors.

Seeing as I've heard nary a sound from that side of the house, I have to wonder if their move might really have to do with the roaches.

I also learn about Ulia's daughter-in-law, Sasha, who lost her husband. She doesn't leave her house. Ulia or Anton have to bring food for her and her children.

The fatigue on Anton's face as Ulia shares this tugs at my heart.

I practically collapse at the table after we finally bid them good night. The roast and potatoes are cold, the cookies are gone, and Justin and Chloe are asleep in their good clothes on the sofa.

Chase folds his arms across his chest and leans against the doorjamb. "So maybe they won't be our *best* friends."

* * *

I am the most popular person in town. In my family room twenty women sit hip to hip on my sofa, on every available chair, on the arms of the chairs and on the windowsill. Others are standing. They're all wearing their *shopkas*—a necessity, thanks to the blanket of snow outside. Two weeks ago, winter charged in like a herd of, well, reindeer, on a surge of arctic wind that left the town blanketed in ice and sleet.

Now I live in Siberia.

The positive is that the muddy road is frozen solid, which cuts my laundry by half. The negative—aside from the frost accumulating inside my windows—is that it takes us twice as long to dress the twins for the hike to *detski-sod*.

Now, add the outhouse into the mix, and you get a good picture of my current life.

But I'm popular! And my house smells like brownies. I arrange the plates of chocolate on my kitchen table while Nathan talks to our guests in the next room. He and Chase have visited every family in town, inviting them to this event.

No pressure or anything.

I have to admit, however, that finally my life makes sense. Finally I understand why I'm here. See, what I said to Daphne is true—you fling yourself out there in faith, and God has a way of catching you.

I was born to be a missionary.

I even prepared a three-page Bible study on the opening verses of John. I figure that's the most popular book for investigative Bible study, so we'll spend some time there and then maybe move to Ephesians. (Which would help me finish that book myself.)

Hardly a sound can be heard from the family room. I take a breath, shoot a prayer toward heaven, grab my Bible and enter.

I spot Ulia sitting in the corner, her hands folded on her lap. She's smiling at me, although I have to wonder if she's just hoping to dish more dirt on poor Maya. Still, I'm ashamed to admit that I've made a point of picking up the children alone since our conversation.

As I look around the room, I wonder how many women were commanded to attend my event.

No matter. At least they're here.

Nathan introduces me and then disappears into the kitchen. He and I worked together on the Bible study—he helped me find the right references and write the probing study questions. He's spent a couple of nights a week at our house over the past three weeks, often appearing randomly at my door, usually with the fixin's for dinner.

Like I'm going to turn him away. We Minnesotans don't do that.

He and Chase reunited like old war buddies, and most of the time they stay up late talking after I've put the twins to bed.

I've learned a few things about Nathan from their conversations. Like, he was once engaged. And when the river freezes, he'll take a snowmobile from Khabarovsk to get here. I even heard him talking about the apostle Paul and his singleness, and how he wished everyone could be like Paul.

Everyone? Even Chase?

I sit down on the floor in the middle of the group of women and open my Bible. "Thanks for coming," I say, smiling at the group. I've even practiced what I will say so that it doesn't come out in garbled Russian.

"Today, I'd like to start by studying the Book of John."

One of the women raises her hand like we're in class or something. But at least there's a question. I can hardly wait to get into a deep, penetrating spiritual discussion of life. I smile at her.

She looks briefly at the others and then ducks her head as she asks, "Are all the women in America like you?"

I'm not sure how to take that question. As I'm forming an answer, another woman pipes up. "And is it true that everyone in America has a swimming pool in their backyard?" She leans back, a smile on her lips. "They all have swimming pools on *Santa Barbara.*" She says it like "Sonta Barrrrbarrra."

"Santa Barbara?" I ask.

They come alive as if I've lit a match under them. "I knew Cruz was B.J.'s father!"

"And I can't believe Sawyer killed Frank."

"He deserved it after kidnapping B.J."

"Sawyer didn't do it—it was Reese!" The look on this woman's face scares me. I jump to my feet.

"Ladies! I'm sorry, I have no idea what you're talking about."

Ulia looks up at me with a shake of her head.

"Okay, listen. No, we don't all have swimming pools, and don't believe everything you see on television." Wow, I sound like my mother.

The group falls quiet and looks chagrined. Way to make friends and influence people, Josey. So much for my ability to wow them with my scholarly Bible knowledge. As I look around the room, I see not a single Bible, and I suddenly realize that none of them are here for Bible study.

They're here to view the oddity. At least they didn't bring sauerkraut. I close my Bible and sigh.

Another hand goes up. I feel like a schoolteacher. I quirk an eyebrow.

"Do you know how to make pizza?"

I glance toward the kitchen. "Uh…"

"What's that?" Another woman points to the plate of brownies she can see on the kitchen table.

I'm not sure what to call it. *"Karichnovaya,"* I say, which translates to "brown." I make a face.

"She makes *pechenye*," says a voice behind me. I turn and am surprised to see my neighbor, Olya, who must have snuck in while I wasn't looking. She doesn't look at me, keeps her eyes to the floor. But her presence ignites a hope inside me that catches my breath. I don't look at Ulia, hoping that my conversation with her about Olya and Vasilley isn't written all over my face. See? This is why I shouldn't listen to gossip!

I nod at Olya's words. I *do* make cookies. "Chocolate cookies," I add. (I don't know how to translate "chip.")

"Teach us," says a woman sitting on the arm of my sofa. "We want to learn to make American cookies."

Another woman points to the plate of brownies in the kitchen. Nods and smiles fill the room. Cookies, huh?

Nathan peeks his head around the corner. "Say yes, say yes!"

Well, if cookies will make them listen and show them that I care… Apparently Russian women and American women aren't that different, after all.

"Please," I say, "come into my kitchen."

Chapter Ten

More Than I Expect

"So Olya actually came to your Bible study?"

Chase has brought home a hunk of venison and is pressing it through a grinder he borrowed from Anton. So this is how ground meat becomes ground meat. He adds a little of Olya's *sala* to the mix (minus the hair and skin) to add fat. I know—adding fat? But deer meat is so lean, it will dry out without it.

The things I've learned in Siberia.

The kids are in bed, having eaten their fill of the three hundred thousand cookies I made in front of my captivated audience today. The eagerness of the crowd prompted me to use my entire supply of chocolate chips, and even crack open a jar of peanut butter for a batch of peanut-butter delights.

I figure if Jesus can multiply a few loaves and fish, He can replenish my chocolate-chip supply for the good of His kingdom.

Everyone went away with a doggy bag—a term, I've discovered, that doesn't translate well.

Nathan left, also, catching a boat for his next stop north. I saw him talking quietly to Chase in our entryway before he left. I hope he's not disappointed by my lack of spiritual accomplishment today.

I've never been so full. Yes, I know, I didn't have to eat them, but what's the point of baking them if… Oh, never mind.

"I can't believe Olya was here." I reach out for another cookie, then pull my hand back. Just because they're there… "She acts like she hates me, but she'll smile when I buy *sala* from her, and she sort of defended me today. Go figure."

"I think she does like you—she just doesn't know how to take you." Chase adds salt and pepper to the bowl of ground meat and begins to stir.

"I assume you mean that in the nicest of ways?"

Chase looks up at me, winks. "Of course."

"I just wish I knew what goes on over there." I nod toward the separating wall between our homes. "I never hear any fighting. But she definitely had a black eye." I am clinging to the hope that she banged herself on the outhouse door.

Chase scoops out a hunk of meat and dumps it into

a plastic bag. "Vasilley is a trapper. Although I heard he was trained as a plumber, so who knows."

Plumber? *Plumber?*

"According to Anton, they have a daughter, but she doesn't live with them." Chase twists the bag shut, opens the newly defrosted freezer—thank-you, Nathan—and adds it to the growing pile. "She lives in Moscow with Vasilley's mother."

Okay, I have to have another cookie. They'll just go bad.

"What is she doing there? Going to college?"

Chase gives me an odd look. "Olya's just a little older than we are. Her daughter, Albena, is only five."

"Five? What's she doing in Moscow?"

Chase ladles another portion of meat into a bag. "I guess Vasilley's mother came out here for a visit and asked if Albena could visit her for the summer. That was three years ago, and evidently no one has the money to fly Albena home."

He closes the bag and adds the meat to the freezer.

"She's been gone for three years?" I've lost my appetite. I put the cookie back. "Olya hasn't seen her daughter for three years? Because she can't afford a plane ticket? That's awful." I remember, suddenly, how she looked at Chloe and Justin. My stomach churns. "We have to help her."

Chase is dismantling the grinder. "Vasilley already told the village council that he didn't want their help." He puts the pieces into the sink. "Which is why they're somewhat ostracized from the community."

"Why doesn't he want their help?"

Chase pumps water and puts it on the stove to boil. "Why doesn't *anyone* want help? Pride?"

"Oh, that's stupid."

He raises an eyebrow. "I know a few people who might suffer from the same ailment."

He comes over and kneels before me, taking my hands and running his thumbs over them. They've healed somewhat, but the tips of my fingers are still cracked.

"How come you didn't tell me your hands were getting so chapped?" He looks up, and his blue eyes hold pain. My throat tightens. "No, don't answer that. I should have noticed." He opens them and kisses the palms. "Forgive me?"

Oh, Chase.

I lean forward, wrapping my arms around his neck. "Yes."

He cups his hand against my face, and I lean into it, realizing how long it's been since we've had a quiet kitchen, sleeping children and no company.

Chase's arms can make me forget where I am, make me believe that everything is—and will continue to be—right in the world.

It's a long time before we realize the water has begun to boil.

We do the dishes together—him washing, me drying. "Tell me something," he says, handing me a plate. "Did you come to Siberia because of me?"

I stare at him, not sure exactly what he means. "Do you mean because it was your idea?"

He is scrubbing the grinder, the hot water sending up steam. I'd be crying in pain. "No. Because you thought…well, that you had to."

I eye him. "Isn't that what submission is all about?"

He looks up at me, stricken. His eyes are wide and he's stopped scrubbing.

"What?" I ask. "Isn't that what it says in the Bible?"

He closes his eyes, hanging his head as he leans on the counter with sudsy hands. "I can't believe I got you into this mess."

Yeah, me too!

No! Be humble. Gentle.

"I'm okay, Chase. We're okay."

But he doesn't believe me. "We have no running water. The skin is peeling off your hands. And now our house is covered in ice." He shakes his head. "I guess I was delusional to think that maybe you came here because you believed in the project."

I toss the towel over my shoulder and press my hand to his chest. "Chase. This is a great opportunity for you. That's why I came to Siberia." Because we all know it wasn't on account of my stellar evangelism skills or my ability to make friends.

"I thought you'd find a way to help people—you always do. I would never have made it in Moscow without your brilliance."

Now you're singing my song, bub. Except he smiles on the last word, and I know he's trying to skim over fears lying just below the surface.

I'm having flashbacks of our high-school days, of him tapping on my bedroom window, begging me to take a motorcycle ride just so he could feel my arms around him. I did catch on to that, by the way. It just took a while for me to realize that sometimes a guy wants to know that the girl will hang on, no matter where he takes her.

"I believe in you, Chase. That's why I'm in Siberia."

But Chase's smile dims, and he turns back to the dirty water. "I don't know, GI. Maybe you should have said no."

I think back to the day he came home and plopped a red-fox fur hat on my head that gave my brain an allergic reaction, causing me to say yes. "You're pretty hard to say no to."

He doesn't look up.

"Besides, maybe I'm also here for a reason now."

He's wearing hope on his face as he rinses the grinder, hands it to me.

"Olya. Maybe I'm supposed to help her."

"How?" He's draining the water through the hole in the metal sink. Of course, it drains down into a bucket, which we then lug outside and toss into the outhouse, but still. At least I have a sink.

"Help get her child back from Moscow?"

He bends down, grabs the bucket. "How?"

"I don't know—you're the anthropologist. You figure it out." I snap the towel at him. At least he's smiling.

"How about inviting her to Thanksgiving dinner this weekend?"

Thanksgiving dinner! My face must betray the fact that I've completely forgotten Thanksgiving. C'mon, give me a break. It's not like anyone else in Siberia is celebrating Thanksgiving. It's an American holiday.

Chase just stares at me. "You forgot."

"I…ah…"

Now he's laughing.

"Don't laugh. We don't have a turkey or anything even remotely near it." I haven't seen chicken since Moscow. And even there, it didn't resemble the poultry I'd come to know and love stateside.

"Let me take care of Thanksgiving," Chase said, turning toward the door. Then he stops, leans down and kisses me on the cheek. "The Lord knows I have plenty to be thankful for."

During my first year in Moscow, the fact that Russians don't celebrate Thanksgiving stymied me when the holiday rolled around. While the rest of the city went to work, my fellow Americans and I stopped and gave thanks around a stuffed bird that cost roughly half a month's wages.

I fell for the turkey nostalgia during my first year of marriage, also. It's more ingrained than one might think. But this year, as I stroll through the market noticing the meager meat selection, I realize something.

Siberians don't eat turkey. Lamb, cow and reindeer, yes, but turkey, no. I have trouble scrounging up even a chicken leg.

It's not *what* you eat, but that you eat it *thankfully,* right?

I've always enjoyed shopping at the market—even at Burr's tiny corner market staffed by eight to ten chilly vendors, most of them selling dirty potatoes and bags of ground venison (aka reindeer). They look cold, especially the woman with the fuzzy gray scarf tied under her chin. She's wearing mittens with the fingers cut off, and is stamping her feet and blowing on her hands.

I know Chase said he'd take care of it—and we just ground venison—but I can't help it. My heart says to buy two kilos of venison. They probably had lots of venison at the first Thanksgiving, right?

Although the mercury is well into the minuses, it's clear and sunny as I walk home. It snowed again last night, and a layer of sparkle bedazzles the ring of lush pine that encircles the village. It's a fairy-tale setting along the now-frozen Amur River, the sky a pale blue, the smell of wood-smoke on the breeze. I could be in the middle of a painting, and I find myself singing a Christmas carol.

"O Little Town of Burrrrr, how still we see thee lie…"

Lydia barks, shoving her nose through the slats of the fence as I pass by and enter my yard. I stomp the snow off my boots, hang up my parka and enter my warm house to find Anton sitting at the table enjoying a cup of tea with Chase.

I'm surprised to see them here, given that they left early this morning to do something manly.

"Hey," I say, still humming. I plop the venison on the table. "Thanksgiving dinner."

"Yum," Chase says, then translates for Anton. I'm always amazed (and jealous) at the way Russian rolls off Chase's tongue. I catch about half the words, but I know that Chase is explaining Thanksgiving. Anton is still wearing his dark fur *shopka,* and with those dark eyes and equally dark pants and sweater, he seems more imposing than he is. Or I'd like to think so.

"And about a month after Thanksgiving comes Christmas," I hear Chase say. He's on a roll now, explaining about gifts, Christmas stockings and, finally, the trees we decorate. "Similar to your New Year's tree, but we go out and chop it down at a tree farm every year."

I'm not sure what Chase is referring to, because we haven't chopped down a tree from a tree farm since we were kids. He tagged along one year when our family drove out to Uncle Bert's place for our annual fir. It was the year after his mother died—his first Christmas alone with his father.

I don't correct him because Chase needs all the happy memories he can get to balance out the bad ones.

I set a cup down, fill it with water and add a teabag. If someone loves me, maybe they'll send instant coffee from America for Christmas.

"It's a lucrative business," I say, stirring my tea. "My uncle Bert makes half his income for the year from his trees."

"A farm for trees?" Anton's eyes have begun to shine.

"Bert chops them down and runs a stand in town, too." I sit down, reach for one of my cookies that Chase has pulled from the freezer. I keep a sanity supply, of course. "Most people don't want to go cut their own trees, so he makes a killing."

"I still like chopping down my own tree," Chase, my hunter-gatherer, says quietly as he blows into his cup.

Of course he does. "Maybe we can cut down a tree from around the village."

Chase shakes his head. "Those are owned by the government, we can't—"

"No. The town of Bursk owns those," Anton says. I can practically hear him finish that sentence. *And I own the town of Bursk.*

"I can barely hear you, Maggie!"

I'm in the central phone station, in the room next to the Internet center, holding a phone that looks like it might have been installed under Alexander Graham Bell's direct supervision. I think these are the kind of phones they used in spy movies as lethal weapons.

But I'm thrilled that Maggie has tracked me down, ordering the call to our village the old-fashioned way—a day in advance, requiring the town operator to track me down and schedule the call.

She sounds like she might be phoning from a space station on the moon.

"Daphne had a baby girl!" Maggie yells, and this time it comes through loud and clear.

"When?" I yell back.

"Two weeks ago. In Canton, Ohio. She and Caleb are doing great. They named the baby Isobel."

Oh. For some strange reason I thought that maybe they'd name it after me. Okay, okay, I know, but I *was* her mentor.

"That's great! Tell her I'm thrilled for her!"

"How's Bursk?"

"Cold!" I say. But I don't hear laughter on the other end. Why don't people get my jokes? "It's good. I have an outhouse!"

"A what?"

"An outdoor bathroom. A privy."

Silence.

"Hello?"

"Do you want me to come and get you?"

Was that a joke? "No! I'm fine." Better than fine, really. Because apparently my cookie party was a hit with the women. They've asked to come back. They want to learn to make pizza, and Chase has agreed to guest-star.

In fact, he's been doing a lot of guest-starring around the house recently. He's nearly been a regular.

He even started washing clothes.

"How's Chase's new venture? Is he making headway?"

"He still hasn't been asked to go on a hunt, but he attends all the council meetings and, well, you know Chase. The world loves Chase."

I still don't hear laughter. "Hello, hello?"

"How about you? Have you made any friends?"

"I've started a Bible study. But I'm having a neighbor dilemma. Chase had this brilliant idea to invite my neighbor, Olya, to Thanksgiving, but she didn't show."

I tell Maggie that, although we couldn't find

turkey, Chase used our abundant supply of venison to sculpt a turkeylike shape and we cooked it in the oven, complete with stuffing and gravy. Even Nathan appreciated it, and the twins gobbled through the house all afternoon. Not a kitty in sight.

The only disappointment was Olya's absence. I invited her—twice—when I purchased my daily *sala*.

We waited for her, steam rising off the deer-turkey.

Finally I fixed a plate and headed over to her house. I still have visions of how she opened the door and stared at the food as if it might be poisonous.

"It's a gift. American dinner," I added. I spied the panic on her face, raw and desperate as she glanced back inside for something to give me.

"I don't want anything, Olya. Please, just take it."

She considered me for a long moment. Then she snaked her hand out and took the plate.

And closed the door on my nose.

"I think I offended her with my Thanksgiving dinner," I say to Maggie, who chuckles.

Now she laughs?

"Maggie!"

"I'm sure your dinner was delicious, Josey. Maybe it's just, you know, sometimes it's hard to receive. I'm sure that's not easy for her. It's not easy for anyone."

I stare at my hands and notice that they are healing. In my own defense, I didn't mention my hands to Chase because, well, I didn't want to complain. Not because of my pride. Really. But now that he's doing the laundry, I feel…indebted.

"Are you saying I shouldn't give her anything?" I ask Maggie.

The line begins to crackle and I fear I'm losing her.

"I'm saying that it's going to be up to you to help her give back."

The line goes dead. Shoot. I have no idea what she means.

I hang up the phone and shuffle out into the snow. The wind is light and the air is crisp. A full moon hangs against the dusky sky. I've always loved the moon and how it reflects the light of the sun.

Humble. Gentle. Patient. Worthy of the calling.

Help her give back. Really? Why can't she simply accept my gift without feeling like she has to repay me?

Lord, help me give peace to Olya, somehow. Help me find a way to reflect You.

In my experience with the Almighty, I've learned that when I ask for something, He doesn't normally give it to me—instead, He gives me the opportunity to discover it. To grow into it.

Unfortunately, it's usually when my husband decides to leave town.

I'm a big girl and I can take care of myself, but when

Chase is away, things begin to unravel. I often wonder if it's God's way of reminding me I'm not invincible.

I get it! I get it!

I should have remembered my prayer about Olya and my hope to reach out to her when Chase left this morning in darkness to take a snowmobile ride to Khabarovsk with Nathan. When I turned on the light to say goodbye, I heard a pop and then saw a trickle of flame travel along the ancient wires strung up outside of our house, exploding in a shower of brilliant sparks when it reached the transformer on the pole.

We stood there in silence in the predawn hour, the cold finding its way under my puffy jacket and through my flimsy jammies. Nathan looked at me. Chase looked at me.

"Do we have candles?" he asked.

I wasn't sure what to say to that, but apparently he had no intention of staying home. I think I nodded.

"I'll be home by dinnertime." Then he kissed me and was gone, slipping into the darkness.

I snuggled back in with the kids until morning lit the room.

Here's a friendly motherhood tip. Don't let your children get up before you. By the time I realized Chloe had risen, she'd gotten hold of the scissors and created a shimmering pool of feather-light blond hair on the floor. I found her half-bald and wet, eating a box of chocolate *padushki*.

At least she knows when to go for the chocolate.

I sat down beside her and joined the party. Justin dragged himself out of bed and stumbled into the kitchen. He took one look at the *padushki* and crumpled into a ball, crying.

"No paddy!"

I simply don't understand a child who won't eat junk food for breakfast.

I fill a pot with water and set it on the furnace to make oatmeal.

By the time we've finished with our morning constitutions, the water is boiling. Justin gets his "meal," as he calls it, and I attire the children in their layers. Chloe's hair is lopsided, so I even her out with the scissors and put on a hat.

Maybe no one at the school will notice the absence of her pigtails.

The sun is high and it must be above freezing, because the water is dripping from the icicles on the house. The snow is crunchy and Justin's foot gets stuck in a drift. I pull him out, leaving behind his sock and boot. After much digging, I retrieve them, but we're late to *detski-sod* and his foot is an ice cube.

On the way back, I stop by the market and buy a piece of *sala,* but Olya doesn't look at me. Perfect.

I return home, pump a bucket of water and watch it heat over the stove. I wash the children's clothes, wring them out and hang them from the line that runs picturesquely through my living room.

It's a lovely garland. Thomas the Tank underwear, Strawberry Shortcake training pants, Chase's thermal underwear and my misshapen yoga pants. My hands burn, so I lather on lotion.

The sting makes my eyes water.

I've never seen a vacuum cleaner in Russia. Even when I lived in Moscow, my cleaning lady wet a towel, wrapped it around an empty mop head and scraped the carpets clean. I've modified her methods by wetting the ends of a bristle broom in a bucket and sweeping the carpet.

It's the hard-knock life for me, it's the hard-knock life…

I shake the throw rugs, change the sheets and finish off the *padushki* for lunch. I don't know what Justin's problem is.

I'm at *detski-sod* early to pick up the kids. Maya is in the yard. I lift my hand in greeting. She considers me for a moment, then turns away.

I don't know what Chase was thinking, but from my perspective, having the kids attend *detski-sod* isn't exactly helping us plow highways into the culture here.

We return home, and I lie down with the kids for a nap.

It's about three when I hear the barking. The door

slams open and I'm yanked out of a sound sleep—
the kind where your body feels submerged in glue.
As I awake, I'm pretty sure I'm back home at
Berglund Acres and Buddy has just returned from
football practice.

"Mommy, doggie!"

Or maybe not. I pry open my eyes. Chloe is
jumping on me, barely missing my gut. I wince and
curl into a ball. Justin sits up, rubbing his eyes.

Lydia leaps onto the bed, barking. She looks like
she dug her way to freedom under the fence, her
body covered in mud and grime. She leans down and
slathers Chloe with her sopping tongue. Justin
screams. Chloe grabs the beast around the neck and
nuzzles it. Of course.

"Lydia!" I'm on my feet. "Lydia, get!"

She's covered the bed with footprints and chunks
of mud, and now jumps to the floor, presses her cheek
to the carpet and runs along my rug in a circle,
cleaning herself.

"Shoo! Shoo!" I grab my multi-use broom. "Get!"

Lydia stops and looks at me, her bottom up, wriggling. She thinks it's a game. Leaping around me, she
grabs Thomas the Tank and pulls down the line.

Chloe cheers from the bed. Justin, the smart
one, is crying.

"Get!"

"Lydia, *Eedi, Syo-dah!*" Olya appears at my door.

She wears what I can only assume is an exact copy of my expression of horror. "Lydia!" She comes in and pounces on the dog, grabbing her by the collar. *"Izvenetye,"* she says over and over as she drags the menace out.

The door shuts with a thud. The house shakes on its foundation.

I slide to the floor. Justin launches himself into my arms. "I scared."

I wrap my arms around him, pulling his trembling body close.

The darkness is hovering, and the heat from the furnace waning. Someone has to find the candles. And feed the children dinner.

I want my mother.

I'm still sitting in the silence when I hear the door creak open. From the shadows of the entryway Olya emerges. She looks tired and wrecked. *"Izvenetye,"* she says again.

"Nu ladna," I say, pushing Justin off my lap. "It's okay."

It's hard to tell in the fading light, but I think relief washes over her face. We stand there a moment, neither of us knowing what to say.

But suddenly—wouldn't you know it?—I start to cry. I put my hand over my mouth, but I can't stifle the sound of my sobbing.

I'm tired.

And cold.

And it's getting a little hard to see.

I think I scare Olya because she abruptly turns and leaves. Probably running for dear life.

I calm myself down, not sure whether I should go after her. I decide to pick up my dirty laundry instead.

Moments later, she reappears with a pot in her arms. She sets the pot on the furnace, opens the door and, taking the tongs, reloads it, stirring the coal brick into the embers.

Then she takes a candle from her pocket.

I watch as she sticks the end into the furnace and lights it. She finds a teacup on the shelf and puts the candle inside, propping it up with a wadded napkin.

Then, turning, she gives me a small nod and starts to leave.

But I grab her and—because I have to, because I can't think of anything else—I pull her into a hug.

She's surprised. But she lets me.

She lets me.

She leaves me with the smell of potato soup, the light from the candle and the wild hope that maybe God can speak even through dumbfounded silence.

It's late and dark when the screaming starts. The soup was delicious—potatoes with chunks of cabbage and dill. And the candle burned long enough for me to read a story to Chloe and Justin.

I go to bed early, of course, which gives me plenty of time to ponder exactly what to do about Olya. Do I go over in the morning with the clean pot, perhaps filled with cookies, and say thank you? Or will that start the cycle of craziness all over again? I think that she might feel we're even, but I know (thanks to the way Justin and Chloe wolfed down the soup) that I'm woefully beholden.

I'm also worried. Where is Chase? He told me he'd be home by dinner.

The screaming is sporadic, followed occasionally by a thump and then yelling. I've never heard them fight before, and everything inside me tightens with the knowledge that I was right about Vasilley.

Please, Lord, tell me what to do.

I close my eyes and pull the covers up to my nose. I hear something crash. What is the number here for 9-1-1? I should know it. Why isn't Chase here? He'd know what to do. I feel nauseated and helpless and angry. And I hate that Ulia was right and I let denial shout the loudest.

Suddenly everything goes quiet. I hear the door slam. I am breathing hard. Should I go over there? I'm still talking myself into it, staring into the filmy darkness, when I hear another thump outside. Our door creaks open.

Please let it be Chase. Please let it be Chase.

"Shh." I hear a voice. "They're sleeping."

My breath escapes. I didn't realize I'd been holding it.

"I'll grab the sofa." It's Nathan's voice.

A second later, Chase appears at the bedroom door. "Hey, GI," he says, climbing into bed beside me. He's cold, his cheeks rough and dry. He pulls me close.

"What took you so long?" I try to keep the panic out of my voice. He nuzzles his cold chin into my neck.

"Halfway home, the snowmobile quit. We couldn't get it to turn over. Had to hitch a ride to the turnoff on the highway, and then hike the rest of the way home."

"The highway is three miles from town."

"I know." His arm tightens around me. "But that's not the worst of it. While we were in Khabarovsk, I ran into Anton."

His beard rubs my cheek as I turn. He props his head on his hand. "He was selling Christmas trees."

I search Chase's face to understand the significance of this.

Chase raises an eyebrow. "The Bursk trees. He cut them down."

"All of them?"

"I don't know. We'll find out in the morning. We stopped by the town hall on the way home. Apparently the trappers in the village are furious. They say it'll upset their traplines."

"Will it?"

Even in the darkness, I can see Chase's concern. "I dunno. I saw Olya's husband at the town hall. He was pretty angry."

I pull in a quick breath. "They just had an awful fight—he and Olya. I just hope he wasn't…hurting her."

Chase stares at me a long time, and I see the old memories from his childhood merge with my information. Then he nods. "I'll check on her in the morning."

I hate that all Chase's dark nightmares have found him in Siberia. And love him even more that he'll refuse to run from them. "Maybe they just had a fight."

"Maybe."

Chase rolls back, throws his arm over his eyes. "I can't believe Anton cut down the trees. And worse, that it was all my idea."

"It was hardly your idea, Chase. You just told him about a childhood memory. He took it from there."

"They'll blame it on me."

"*You're* blaming it on you. Don't. It's not your fault."

He lowers his arm and reaches out to take my hand. "How are your hands today?"

I try to tug them away, but he brings them to his mouth and kisses them. "First your hands, and now I've managed to wipe out the village economy. I'm really making an impact here."

"Shh." I put my finger over his mouth. "We're all going to be fine."

He sighs. "What is it they say about anthropologists? First, do no harm?"

"I think that's for doctors," I whisper. He puts his arms around my neck and pulls me close, kissing me.

"How was your day?" he asks.

"It was more than I expected it to be," I say. Much, much more.

"Josey!"

Maya catches up to me in the hallway just as I'm leaving with Justin and Chloe. The preschool is decked out with paper chains and snowflakes on the windows. Again, I'm impressed with the use of the limited resources.

I'm not as impressed with the use of the town's resources by Anton and his small band of entrepreneurial accomplices who have, indeed, denuded the forest. They've swiped every tree under twelve feet, and the once abundant stand of pine ringing the town is scraggly and sparse with woodchips, pine needles and stripped boughs littering the pristine snow.

Maya stands before me in that tight, black high-waisted skirt and a black jacket. Sad to say I can't shake Ulia's words about Maya from my head. They burn inside me.

This is what gossip does. Keeps you from thinking straight.

"*Prevyet,* Maya," I say.

Her hair is gelled, and with her dark makeup, she looks exotically beautiful. I'm wondering, suddenly, if Ulia's words are born of jealousy.

Maya doesn't smile. I keep a firm grip on Chloe, just in case she does something. Like eat a decoration.

"I heard, in America, you do not have Father Frost." I appreciate her using English, which sounds crisp and British.

"No," I say slowly. "We have…well, Christmas is supposed to be a religious holiday, so we have Baby Jesus, angels and shepherds and the three wise men."

We also have Santa, but I'm not sure what my take on Santa is yet. And I'm glad I'm not stateside where I'd fold under the pressure. Jasmine and I grew up in a Santa-filled world, but she has recently taken a stand against Santa. I realize this sounds a lot like taking a stand against Bambi, but her argument is that she wants her children to grow up without the Big Lie.

Since my kids are only three, and in Russia, I've been able to do an end run around Halloween, Santa and the Easter Bunny. But that doesn't mean I've made my decision.

"Tell that story, about Baby Jesus, to our children. Please," says Maya.

I eye her and speak very clearly. "It's from the Bible."

She stares at me.

"It's religious. And I happen to believe it's true. Are you sure you want me to tell it?"

She nods without smiling. "It's important to understand what other cultures believe."

You can believe, too, honey, because Jesus isn't American, last time I checked. But you don't have to hit a former missionary over the head to wake her up to an opportunity.

"Where and when?"

Three days later I'm sitting cross-legged in front of Justin and Chloe's class, a storybook my mother sent last year for Christmas open on my lap. The kids are cute, dressed for the occasion with bright hair bows the size of their heads on the girls, and bow ties on the boys. I've made frosted Christmas cookies for the event, of course. I now have their undivided attention as I tell them about Mary being visited by an angel, and Joseph, the man who wants to marry her. I tell them about Jesus being born in a manger and field a few questions about what that might look like. I keep it G-rated, although I, too, have wondered just what it might have really been like to give birth in a stable two thousand years before plumbing (although now I have the smallest of glimpses).

And then I talk about the wise men, with their gifts of gold, frankincense and myrrh, riding their camels. This elicits more questions, of course.

To my surprise, the teachers are listening intently also. And they, too, have a few questions, after story time is over, after the cookies have been eaten, and after I've been invited to Maya's office for a private "tea."

"Why did you come to Siberia?"

"Do your children like *detski-sod?*"

"Why does your daughter think she's a cat?" (I love that one.)

"Do you plan on staying?"

As I carefully answer each question, I notice Maya watching me from her perch behind her desk.

The room finally clears out, and I stand to leave, too, but she motions me to sit. She scares me a little. So I stay put.

"I don't believe your story."

I raise an eyebrow. Well, I want to say, get in line with about half the world. But I don't, because I think, deep down, there's more to her statement.

"I don't believe that God would send His son to people who would kill him."

Oh, so she's heard the rest of the story. I nod, listening.

"If He loved him and wanted the best for him—and knew people were going to kill him—why did He do it? A smart God, a loving God, wouldn't do that." She crosses her arms over her chest. "I don't think I could trust that kind of God."

I see the gauntlet thrown down. I lean back on the

sofa. "Why do you think I sent my kids to *detski-sod,* Maya?"

She says nothing.

"I didn't know you. For all I knew, you would hurt my children. But I believed that getting to know you and showing you that I cared was worth the risk. Which is also why Chase and I moved to Siberia."

Something again flickers in her eye. Hope? Curiosity?

I notice her body language—the way she has her arms crossed—and the look on her face, and I remember Ulia's story. Not the sordid gossip, but the part about her husband. Dying. In a fire.

Maybe we should all give the woman a little grace.

"God sent His son Jesus to earth because He loves you, Maya. And He wants to know you. That's the Christmas story."

The flicker is gone, and she gives me a tight smile, pushes her chair away and stands up. "Thank you for your story, Josey."

Chapter Eleven

Open Wide Your Mouth

Russians have a saying: Everyone is an artist. This saying came about during the time of the communists, and communal labor. Rationalization or survival, it was their way of remembering their true identities while being forced into mind-numbing, mindless industrial jobs in the countless factories in Soviet-era Russia.

I have news for you. All the real Russian artists are in Burr, Russia. Did you know that Bursk has one of the most elaborate ice-sculpture festivals on the planet? Didn't think so.

This just might be my favorite Christmas in Russia yet.

"Mommy, cream!"

Chloe is pulling on my hand—have you ever tried to hold on to a preschooler through two layers of wool?—and my only advantage is the fact that the ground is pure ice and she has no traction. But her request has alerted Justin and Nathan to the ice-cream stand nearby. Here's a little-known fact about Siberians: They only eat ice cream in the winter. Because eating it in the summer will cause pneumonia of the throat. Really.

"Wait for Mommy, Justin!"

The sun is high and golden, shining down like a spotlight on the fifty or so ice carvings that decorate the central square. Every town has a central square, and Bursk's has come alive with ice sculptures of characters from every known Russian fairy tale: snow girls and Father Frost, prancing horses pulling a sledge, a Siberian bear with the white half-moon on its chest, and a fierce white tiger. There are also mermaids and dolphins, castles and ogres, and an ice slide. At night, the village turns on red and blue lights and the square becomes magical.

I love Burrrrrsk.

Nathan digs into his pocket to buy Justin an ice-cream cone. The vendor, only her eyes showing under a wool muffler, asks the flavor, and of course Nathan says, "Plumbere." I should have guessed.

Chloe is clapping and meowing, and Nathan feeds the hysteria by handing her a cone, also.

"Want one?" he asks me. I'm scanning the square for Chase. It's Christmas Eve, and he left early this morning on an errand, telling me he'd be back before our celebration tonight.

"No thanks," I say.

Nathan pays the vendor, and we help Chloe and Justin down the slide. They could live in sub-zero temperatures for a week without even a shiver in the layers I've dressed them in. Tights, sweatpants, snowsuits and *shuba*—fur coats that Anton and Ulia dug out of storage—all tied with big belts. They're wearing the requisite *valenkis,* and fur shopkas that tie around their chins, further secured by scarves. The only way I know they're mine is Chloe's constant breaks for freedom. And the meowing helps.

Lest you think I concocted this clothing system on my own, let me disappoint you. I was instructed by Ulia, who has appointed herself Keeper of the Americans. She brought over the clothes and gave me lessons. She also keeps me stocked in home-remedy supplies. Like raspberry jam, which I gather cures any fever.

And it's great on blini.

Which Nathan makes when he stays over.

It has not escaped me that God has provided food everywhere I've lived. There's a verse in the Psalms that says, "Open wide your mouth and I will fill it." I feel like a baby bird.

A happy baby bird.

"Where is Chase?" Nathan asks as we stand at the bottom of the slide, watching Chloe fly down on her tummy.

"Feet first, Chloe!"

Justin follows her on his back. Good boy.

"I don't know. He said he had to do something, but he promised he'd be back tonight. I made soup—"

Nathan looks at me, a smile on his face. He's dressed light for the day—a green military coat, fur boots and his black wool hat. He looks like an undercover Green Beret from a movie.

"Stop. I can cook." Liar, liar. "Okay, I peeled the potatoes. Chase did the rest."

"What kind of soup?"

"Potato."

Nathan claps his hand together, blows on them. "I can't believe it's already Christmas." He jams his hands in his pockets. "It sure is nice to be able to spend it with you."

I glance at him. I know he means *us*. The family. But it warms me, anyway. His friendship is starting to feel comfortable, like the one I have with my brother, Buddy.

The kids finish sliding, and we run into Maya as we take another spin through the displays. She gives me a tight smile, but it breaks open a little when I introduce her to Nathan. Everyone smiles for Nathan.

We finally head for home. "I got you something,"

Nathan says as we near the house. I see the some-thing leaning against our gate, green and bushy.

A Christmas tree.

Since the Great Deforestation, Chase hasn't wanted to think about—let alone purchase—a tree. And frankly, there are none available in Bursk, anyway. Since Russians don't celebrate Christmas on December 25, trees don't go on sale before New Year's Eve. Except, of course, this year, the trees are on sale early—in Khabarovsk, at least.

"Where did you get a tree?"

"I probably shouldn't tell you. I bought it from—"

"Nathan, you didn't—"

"Shh. Let's take it inside." He grabs it and follows Justin and Chloe into the yard. They're jumping up and down, screaming and laughing.

Nathan sets the tree up in the family room and produces a string of lights from his coat pocket. We put them on the tree, relishing the smell of pine.

"Let's make ornaments," Nathan says. We find some white scratch paper and he proceeds to cut out beautiful snowflakes.

Darkness has blanketed the land, but inside we're warm and the light is bright, giving off a magical glow as we sit and eat the potato soup.

"Do you think Chase will be back soon?" Nathan asks. Justin is bouncing on his knee.

I look at the clock. "I really don't know."

Justin climbs down and races into his room.

"Is he gone a lot?"

Is Chase gone a lot?

"Our first year in Russia he was working on an NGO project and practically slept at his office. He's sort of a one-horse guy. When he gets something in his mind, it consumes him. So, when he's here, he's here. But when someone else needs him…"

Nathan smiles. "What if *you* need him?"

"I don't want to burden Chase. He's busy." I get up and retrieve the tea from the stove to pour him a cup. "Chase loves God, and this is his way of making a difference, I think."

I sit back down. "Once upon a time, he mentioned wanting to use his skills as a missionary. But that was years ago."

"Before a wife and kids?"

I look at him, and just like that, it hits me like a sledgehammer to the chest. Paul and his singleness. Have I been holding Chase back? Would he be doing great things for God if I wasn't here? Am I slowing him down?

Wait. Wait. I'm in Siberia. I'm hardly holding the guy back.

The thought, however, has lodged in my mind.

Chase could do so much more if he didn't have me and the kids to worry about. I rub my raw hands together. He could do what Nathan does, going from village to village, spreading hope. "Chase is exceptionally good at what he does," I say softly.

"I don't think he should leave you alone so much, though." I watch as Nathan pours a tablespoon of tea onto his saucer, dips a sugar cube in it and sucks on it.

"Something my landlady taught me," he says when he sees me watching him. "Try it."

So I do. It's tangy and sweet. An unexpected delight.

"Good, huh? Some things just belong together." Nathan picks up the saucer and pours the tea into his mouth. He puts it down. "Have you ever thought about being a pastor's wife?"

I laugh. "I don't think Chase will ever want to be a pastor. He loves helping people, but he's not real comfortable sharing his faith. Besides, I don't think I'd make a good pastor's wife at all." I take another taste of the sugar. "I can't even get my neighbor to talk to me."

Nathan is looking at me strangely, a sort of sadness in his eyes. "But you're willing to try, aren't you?"

I'm picking up my saucer, unsure how to respond, when I hear a thump at the door.

I am in the entryway, all set to open the door, when Nathan stops me with a grip on my arm. "Who is it?" he hollers.

"It's me! Chase! Open the door—my hands are full!"

Nathan opens the door and a snowy, ice-crusted

man who resembles Chase stumbles inside. A trickle of red is frozen in a line down his nose, and his day-old whiskers are covered in frost. He's fashioned a backpack of sorts from twine encircling a box about half the size of our coal furnace. He leans back and lets the box thump to the ground.

"What are you—"

"Ho, ho, ho!" he says, and grabs my face in his snowy hands, giving me a quick kiss.

"What?"

"Merry Christmas, GI." He starts to peel off his layers.

"You're bleeding!"

He frowns at me, and I point to his nose. He touches it and looks at his hand. "I didn't even feel it. Must have been the wind, cracking my skin. It was a long walk from Petrogorsk."

Nathan is helping him off with his snow-encrusted jacket. "Petrogorsk is eight kilometers from here. And you walked it? What were you doing?"

"It's only six through the fields. I didn't know you were going to be here or I would have borrowed your snowmobile. I had to pick up something I ordered from Khabarovsk from the Petrogorsk post office." Chase gestures to the package. "Open it, babe."

I look at the package and then back at Santa. He's all grins.

Justin and Chloe have heard the commotion and barrel out of their bedroom. "Daddy!"

He gathers them in his arms as I attack the package, ripping it open at seams where the staples hold it together.

For a moment, a long moment, I can say nothing. Everything drains out of me, and I reach out to grab Chase's arm. "You carried this home? For six miles?"

"Kilometers," Chase corrects.

"Same thing," I say as my eyes fill.

"What is it, Mommy?" Justin asks, wriggling out of Chase's arms. "Who brought it?"

"Santa, honey," I say, scooping him up, holding him close, smiling at Chase through my watery eyes. "Santa brought me a washing machine."

Merry Christmas from the Kringle Kompany!
Enjoy your specially prepared Almond Crème Kringle.
Now serving eight new flavors to make every day a celebration!
www.kringlekompany.com

Dear Josey,
I'm not sure if this will reach you before Christmas, but I wanted you to have a taste of home for the holidays. I know you're probably

making your own kringle, but I wasn't sure if you could get almond flavoring in Siberia, so here's mine, just in case.

Mom and Dad say hello, and so does your friend H. I saw her working at the Red Rooster Grocery Store.

Only six months until I see you again! By then, maybe our new storefront in Minneapolis will be open! Milton just acquired a warehouse with a commercial kitchen. I can't wait to move to the big city! Don't worry, Mom and Dad have agreed to stay on running Berglund Acres until you and Chase come home. I can't believe we'll be selling the Cape Cod. But with prices skyrocketing in Gull Lake over the past four years, we hope to find a place twice the size in the city. I think Clay and Amelia need their own playroom, and Milton would love to have an office. I'll make sure we get one with at least four bedrooms so you and Chase can have a guest room when you visit.

You're still planning on moving home, right? I know you're doing amazing work in Siberia and all, but maybe it's time, you know?

Sorry there's not more room on the card. I'll send you an e-mail one of these days!

Merry Christmas!

Love, Jasmine

Chase and I are sitting at the table eating kringle, drinking tea and enjoying the smell of pine wafting through our home. Our New Year's Eve dinner—chicken soup—is simmering on the stove. Chloe is on the floor playing with her new herd of stuffed animals (the only gifts we could find in Bursk). She's in the center, speaking in tongues.

Justin is watching *Nu Pagadee* through fuzzy reception on the black-and-white television Anton gave us for Christmas. Evidently, he gave Ulia a new one so she could keep up her *Santa Barbara* habit.

"I can't believe that Jasmine has an online business," I say to Chase, who looks amazing in the red flannel shirt I found in the market. He spent the day hooking up the washing machine while I chopped potatoes for soup.

"Why? It's easy. Set up an eBay account and sell the right merchandise. It's all about having a unique, quality product and decent advertising." He holds up the kringle. "Yum."

I narrow my eyes at him.

"Well, it *is* good." Chase takes a sip of tea. "But I'd take your cookies over it any day."

I'm glad he would, because my confidence took a header when I brought a batch of thank-you sugar cookies to Olya. All she did was stand there silently, not meeting my eyes, as I smiled and handed her the cookies. She took them and again she closed the door in my face.

I thought we were past all that. I'm so confused.

I get up and put our cups in the sink. I stand there a moment, thinking about the cookies and the way the women from the Bible study packed my tiny kitchen. At least *they* seemed to like them.

"Nathan said I'd make a good pastor's wife."

Chase looks up at me. "A pastor's wife?"

See? Even Chase is surprised. "I know. I told him how crazy—"

"Well, you care about people. You always want to help, like wanting to figure out a way to get Olya's daughter back to her. I think you'd be a great pastor's wife. The only problem is, you're already married. To me."

I stare at him to see if he's making some sort of joke. "I think he was suggesting *you* become a pastor."

Chase rolls his eyes. "Like God would ever use me like that." He takes another bite of kringle. "But I have to admit, I sometimes wish I was like Nathan— I'd love to get a glimpse at life in the other villages."

I knew it! I knew it. Paul. Single. I'm trying to figure out how to respond when I hear a knock at the door.

"Hello?"

"Nate!" Chase gets up to let him in.

To be honest, Nathan has been acting strangely ever since Christmas, when he left early, before Christmas dinner.

I hear him stomping his feet and hitting his gloves

together. He follows Chase in, his cheeks rosy, his eyes bright. "Happy New Year!" He pulls out from behind his back what looks like…a turkey!

"Where did you find it?"

"A little international-foods store in Khabarovsk. It was frozen solid when I left this morning. I hope it's okay."

I know nearly nothing about turkey storage and thawing, but I reach out for the bird. "I'll put it in the fridge and let it thaw there." I think I remember my mother doing something like that.

"And there's something else." He holds out one of my plates. On top of it sits a pair of pink mittens and a small box.

"You stole one of my plates."

"No, I found it outside on your stoop. By your door." He hands it to me, and it dawns on me that this is the plate I gave Olya, with the cookies on it.

She's given me back a pair of mittens. Homemade mittens, herringbone it seems. They're soft, made of angora maybe, with a beautiful pattern along the top. "These are gorgeous."

"Take a look at this box." Chase picks it up. It's made of birchbark, overlaid with an intricate design.

"Do you think she made this?"

Nathan takes it from Chase and sits down at the table, turning it over for scrutiny. "I'm sure of it. I've seen these at nearly every house in Bursk. It's one of the crafts the women here do."

"There's more of these?"

"I'll bet that Olya has quite a few more. And if not, she can make them. It's a Nanais skill from long ago, along with making reindeer mittens and hats. I've even seen picture frames made of birchbark."

A unique, quality product…

Olya's house is dark when I go to her door, keeping my eyes peeled for Lydia. I hear someone inside the house as I approach. I knock three times before the door opens just a crack. Olya peers out.

I point to the box. *"Spaceeba."*

She nods.

"It's very pretty," I add, testing the water.

She says nothing, but ducks her head.

"Do you have more of these, Olya? Just like this box? And like the mittens?"

She slowly looks up, frowning at me, and I see she needs some guidance through the labyrinth of my thoughts. "I think I've found a way to get your daughter back from Moscow."

She stands there a long moment, during which I feel the prickle of cold on my nose, weaving through the open collar of my hastily thrown-on jacket, biting at my ears. The sun is low, the late-afternoon shadows creeping into the yard.

As I watch, her eyes slowly start to glisten, filling with tears. She puts a hand over her mouth. Then she starts to nod.

She keeps nodding, even as her other hand covers the first. Finally she steps back, and the door creaks open.

"I have more," she says softly in a voice that speaks of tentative hope. "Many more."

I glance at my house next door. The lights are bright, creating a glow of warmth and happiness. I want her to join us.

But first, perhaps, I need to enter her world.

I stomp the snow off my feet, smile and step into her dark home.

Open wide your mouth, and I will fill it.

Chapter Twelve

Do You Trust Me?

My mother always said I was an entrepreneur at heart. Maybe it was the way I set up the petting zoo by the side of the road, filling it with the ducklings who'd lost their mother, a bunny we'd found in the backyard, my aunt Myrtle's deer lawn art, a cat from my uncle Bert's farm and Sherlock, the dog. I charged admission, and on one hot July day made exactly three dollars and twenty-two cents.

The thing is, you have to believe in the idea to sell it. And not just believe it, but commit to it. Take, for example, the honey-coated peanuts the school forced me to sell in sixth grade in order to send our swim team to Minneapolis for the regionals. I'm all for honey-coated peanuts. But the thought of going door to door to convince my neighbors that a can was worth their hard-earned cash so we could hang out in a hotel room made me want to hide behind the shed.

And eat the peanuts.

I think my parents privately funded my trip after discovering my stash of empty peanut cans.

But my problem wasn't salesmanship. It was lack of vision. (Not to mention the tasty crunch of the peanuts.)

I'm getting the impression that the ladies of Bursk lack vision, too, as I finish unveiling my Great Plan to market their handicrafts. The women huddle around the room, wearing their *shopkas* and knobby wool scarves around their shoulders. January's icy fist is slowly tightening around our village, the sleet and snow isolating us from the world. The fear of wind-chill and frozen appendages keep us shut up in our homes. I see weariness on their pale, lined faces and in their tired eyes, and I know that I look the same. I smell coal smoke on our clothes and feel it in my grubby hair. (Here's a dilemma: heating a second pot of water to bathe in before the first pot cools to the point of uselessness. Sure, Chloe and Justin can take baths in two inches of water, but that ain't gonna cut it with me and my size fourteen—no, ten!—backside).

Yep, winter has come to Bursk, and even the women's spirits have been caught in its iron grip. Granted, marketing their handicrafts is yet a fledg-ling idea, still growing legs, but in my mind, I can see birchbark jewelry cases, picture frames, trivets and even candleholders being bought by craft-hungry Americans. And I'm just getting started. A walk through Olya's dark house revealed sculptures and paintings, tapestries and table linens, knitted scarves and mittens and painted *matrushka* dolls.

A supermarket of Russian goodies just waiting to be shipped to the Mall of America.

And with the new speedy postal rates, which I know about thanks to Jasmine's kringle business, it just might work.

If I can get the ladies to warm up to my idea, that is. Sadly, their faces, like my house, stay rigid and cold.

Although Chase stocked the coal furnace today before heading out with Anton to ice-fish, the behemoth is fighting a losing battle against the below-freezing windchill battering the house and the creep of frost on the inside of the windows. Last night, both Justin and Chloe joined us in bed, and if someone doesn't get night-trained soon, I might move to the sofa. Our sheets hang outside and I'll have to thaw them before I can remake the bed.

Siberia is just like Minnesota? Who said that? Chase? Uh, I don't remember my mother bringing home milk on a stick in the shape of a bucket. And my freshly washed hair solidified into a knot this morning as I took Chloe to the outhouse.

No, I'm sorry, my fellow Minnesotans, but I win the cold-weather war.

I am not going to let the chill in spirit—as well as climate—deter my entrepreneurial passion. After all, I've spent the past few days learning a new Russian vocabulary—words like "marketing" and "advertising." I look around the room and put every ounce of "this is a fabulous idea" into my expression.

"Okay, how many of you have items like this in your home?" I hold up the little birchbark box.

Nearly everyone raises their hand.

Now that's what I'm talkin' 'bout.

"What if I told you that I think we could make money by selling your crafts on eBay?"

The hands go down. I must be speaking Swahili.

"Have you ever thought about selling your products before?"

Ulia raises her hand. I again feel like a teacher. "Yes?"

"Sometimes in the summer, we have tourists. We've sold some crafts to them."

Bingo! "That's right. Only we'd do this year-round. We could use the money to, say—" I cast a look at Olya, who is sitting with her head down, her hands folded on her lap "—buy something you might need. Like a washing machine!"

Yes, I saw the small, intrigued crowd clustered around the newest member of my family before our meeting started. One would think that I'd brought an alien spaceship into the house. Just to set the record straight, it's not a Maytag or anything. In fact, it's just a little bigger than a dorm fridge. It has two compartments—the wash side and the spin side—each roughly the equivalent of a three-gallon bucket.

I add clothes and water to the wash side, and it spins the laundry in a circle. After ten minutes or so, the agitator stops, and I drain the water. Then I lift the sopping laundry out of the wash bin and squeeze it into the spin side. The machine then spins the laundry at warp speed, using centrifugal force to wick out the water. The clothes are nearly dry by the time the spin cycle is finished.

Notice I said "nearly." They're still wet enough to freeze on the line outside.

Each bucket only holds about five items of clothing—less if I'm washing jeans. So I get to repeat this process about five times a day.

All the same, gone are the hours of wringing the laundry manually, and the skin on my hands has actually begun to grow back.

I was feeling like a queen until the village women—after scrutinizing the machine—looked at me as if I had just told the peasants to fetch my scepter.

Does anyone see a mink hat on *my* head? I'd just like to point out that I'm still wearing a puffy down jacket while the rest of the women in Russia wear fur head to toe.

That's all I have to say about that.

"Listen, ladies, I think this will work." I hold up

the birchbark box. "This is beautiful, and with the right marketing, I think we can really make some money here. We can buy food and medicines for your families." And plumbing. Maybe we can even put in plumbing!

Okay, Josey, settle down. But the whole idea has me buzzing. For the first time all day I can feel my toes.

Ulia is looking at me hard, with an expression I can't read. For a moment I can't miss, her gaze settles on my appliance. Then to my astonishment, she stands up, digs into her bag and produces a key chain, braided with what might be deer hide. "Will this sell?"

I take it and look it over. The leather is soft, with a stamped design on the flat surface that holds the ring. "Yes. I think so."

She nods. "*Ladna.* I'll be back."

She glances at the others and without smiling, gives a nod.

Olya looks up and briefly meets my eyes. Again, I get the smile. See, it's all about vision.

And the occasional washing machine.

<Wildflower>: I can't believe I caught you. Every time I go online, I hope you're on, too. How are you?

<GI>: I've been in Mayor Anton's office for six hours now, sitting on a broken stool, setting up an

eBay site for our new business—Secrets of Siberia.
It's a gift store of homemade products by the locals.

<Wildflower>: Are you kidding me? See, that's the
woman I know, the one who deserves to have a
washing machine. I can't believe I am actually
saying that. You know, I can't even think about the
fact you were doing cloth diapers by hand. It's that
sort of thing that makes people scared of missions.
Or motherhood. Or, for that matter, marriage.

<GI>: Marriage? Why?

<Wildflower>: Isn't it because of Chase that
you're in this mess?

<GI>: Mess?

<Wildflower>: Predicament?

<GI>: I like it here.

<Wildflower>: You keep telling yourself that.

<GI>: Seriously. So I don't have hot water. So what?

<Wildflower>: You don't have *running* water.
You have to put on your snow pants to go to the
bathroom.

<GI>: I am here to help people and change lives. But it is cold—so cold that when Chloe sat on her little tin potty yesterday, it stuck to her bottom. But I'm hoping to earn enough through Secrets of Siberia to install a heater in the outhouse.

<Wildflower>: Is there anything I can do to help?

<GI>: With Chloe's potty?

<Wildflower>: Uh…with the business?

<GI>: Really?

<Wildflower>: Sure.

<GI>: Could I send the boxes of gifts to you, labeled with the addresses, and you could send them out from Gull Lake? I think it would be faster and easier to track.

<Wildflower>: Of course. At least until you open your shipping center.

<GI>: You jest, but this is going to be big.

<Wildflower>: I'm not jesting. Look at Jasmine. She and Milton are moving to Minneapolis. Can you believe it?

<GI>: Last time I talked to her, she said you were working at the grocery store.

<Wildflower>: I was wondering—what would you think about me coming to visit you?

<GI>: In Siberia?

<Wildflower>: No, in Hawaii. Of course, Siberia.

<GI>: <><><><><><><> That's supposed to be clapping. Yes, yes, YES! Seriously?

<Wildflower>: I don't know. It's just a thought. But I miss you. And I want to see the outhouse for myself.

<GI>: OK, tell me why you really want to come here.

<Wildflower>: It can't be because I miss you?

<GI>: And?

<Wildflower>: Rex and I have separated. And, well, I'm hoping you can give me advice. I need you.

I hate to say it, but I could give her great advice. Because I'm a wife who submits. Who flings herself into the arms of God with abandon. Who is the most popular woman in Bursk, the entrepreneur of Secrets of Siberia.

<GI>: I'll put clean sheets on the sofa.

We in America have birthday parties backward. At least, according to the Russians, we do. See, in Russia, the birthday girl throws the party—cooking her own dinner and baking her own cake—and invites her friends to celebrate with her. I see a number of positives to this. For one, you get to invite only the people you want. For another, you get to eat only the foods you love.

In the Russian tradition, if you're invited to a birthday party, it's a big deal. You attend.

Even if someone's scary husband is going to be there.

"How do I look?" I ask Chase as I emerge from our bedroom wearing a jean skirt and a sweater. Yes, it might be early-millennium fashion, but anything other than my yoga pants makes me feel like a human again. And the fact that they're two sizes smaller than the clothes I was wearing when I got here, well, you know I'm doing a wild jig. I even wrestled myself into panty hose. I'm not sure why—I won't be taking off the wool leggings I'm wearing over them. Maybe it's simply the knowledge that I'm wearing panty hose. That under the jean skirt and the long johns, I'm dressed up.

Chloe runs out wearing a similar getup—her sweatpants and sweatshirt under a frilly summer party dress.

You have to use your imagination in Siberia.

"You look fabulous," Chase says, leaning over to kiss me. He doesn't look too bad himself in a pair of blue wool dress pants and another red sweater my mother sent him for Christmas. He's a regular elf.

Justin is crawling out of the bedroom, zooming a car along the floor. He's wearing a pair of blue corduroys and a red sweater, looking every inch a miniature replica of his father.

He's going to break hearts from one end of the globe to the other, too.

"Let's go," Chase says, scooping up the kiddos. We don't bother to bundle them for the quick dash to Olya's house.

I check for Lydia as we approach her door. She's penned up in the back and strains at her leash, barking frantically. Good dog, good dog.

Olya opens the door decked out in a black sweater and a gray skirt, *valenki* on her feet. She's swept her raven-black hair back into a clip and has even put on makeup.

Chase gives her a kiss on the cheek. Olya hugs me.

Their house is the mirror image of ours without the fresh coat of paint. Same fraying brown furniture, same black-and-white fuzzy television picture (finally, I get to catch up with *Santa Barbara!*), same gargantuan coal furnace in the middle of the room.

The kitchen has a festival feel. The table has been pushed out from the wall and set with beautiful—albeit chipped—china, and bowls of Russian delights like winter salad, pickles, cutlets, brown bread and, yes, even a cake.

I've seen many a Russian cake. This one looks like it's grown warts. Giant, brown warts.

Uh-oh.

As a general rule, I love cake. But I hate Russian cake. Especially gourmet Russian prune cake. Because Russian prunes taste like they've been soaked in kerosene.

Russians love prunes. They love them in vodka and cognac. They love them in candies, cookies and pies. And they love them in their cake.

I should have known that Olya would have a Kerosene Prune Cake on her table. And this one looks like it's garnished with extra prunes.

I just won't look at it.

Vasilley is sitting at the table. He rises, and I notice he's clean-shaven for this event. He's wearing a brown sweater and black pants and he looks only slightly scary. He takes Chase's hand and glances at me with a nod.

"*Sdyom Rozhdennya,*" I say to Olya, giving her birthday greetings and handing her the gifts we brought—a spray of silk flowers and a can of lilac air freshener.

Before you judge, let me ask you this: Wouldn't you like a blast of spring during the dark days of winter?

That's what I thought.

Besides, I learned long ago in Moscow, during the days when my neighbor gifted me with all manner of personal-hygiene products, that anything goes for gift-giving in Russia. Even panty hose. I kid you not.

As all Russians are wont to do, Olya sets the gifts aside to open later, outside the view of guests. To their way of thinking, it's not polite to pay attention to gifts when you have guests. They might actually have something there.

"*Nu Pagadee!*" Justin says, and wriggles out of Chase's grip to land on the sofa in front of the television. Chloe, however, climbs onto a chair and puts her little paws on the table.

To my shock, Vasilley looks over at her and smiles.

Olya gestures to me and Chase to sit, and I realize we're the only guests.

The only guests.

I'm not sure what to say, think or feel. Especially when Vasilley fills a tiny shot glass in front of my plate with vodka.

And not just any vodka. A prune-enhanced home brew. It's roughly the color of motor oil.

Oh, no.

Even Chase eyes it with some fear.

Before we sit, Vasilley raises his glass and looks at his wife. Is that a shine I see in his eyes?

Or just the vodka?

Oh, I'm so judgmental. I lift my glass, smile and nod as Vasilley toasts his wife. It's something sweet, with lots of loving words. And then, he clicks my glass and downs his drink.

Yikes! I glance at Chase, who is looking a little green, but he closes his eyes and downs his own.

As does Olya.

I put the vodka to my lips, intending only to pretend, when Chloe launches herself at me. "Mommy! Me some juice!"

The vodka spills onto my lips and into my mouth. And sets it on fire.

"Josey, are you okay?" Chase says as I cough and sputter. I'm wondering if I still have lips or if they've been burned off.

Vasilley looks at me with a smile and refills my glass.

I knew I shouldn't trust him.

Olya comes to the rescue with two glasses of prune juice, called *sok,* handing them to Chase and me. At least it isn't spiked. Chase takes a long drink.

"How are the traplines?" Chase asks Vasilley. I know he still longs to go out into the bush, to spend time one-on-one with each of these men, to burrow deep into their souls and discover ways to encourage, to bring light. On top of that is his slim hope that the hunting hasn't been destroyed by the pre-Christmas deforestation.

Vasilley gives him a long look, one I can't interpret. And then he says (in what I consider to be a tone reminiscent of a Mafia hit man), "Why don't you come out and see?"

Gulp.

"I'd like to do that," Chase says just as Olya arrives with a plate of steaming boiled potatoes from her stove.

"Na, zdarovaya!" Vasilley raises his glass to us, looking at Chase. It means "to your health," although I have serious concerns about said health at the moment. Chase considers for a moment, then lifts his glass, taps it against Vasilley's and finishes it off.

I look at him, but he doesn't meet my eyes. Chase doesn't drink, thanks to the legacy of alcoholism bequeathed to him by his father. He chases the vodka with a sip of prune juice probably in an attempt to feel the inside of his mouth again.

I fix plates for the kids. Justin barely looks up from his cartoon as I hand him his.

Chase is piling his plate high with potatoes, cutlets and salad. Olya is smiling and it turns into a full-wattage beam when he starts to make his food noises. Chase is an interactive eater—when he loves something, he "mmms" and "ahhs."

Almost makes a girl want to cook something. Almost.

"To Olya's potatoes!" Vasilley says, grabbing the Nectar of Kerosene and pouring more into Chase's glass, topping off Olya's as well. Mine is still full. He scoops up his glass and raises it high.

Oh, boy.

Chase clinks glasses, winks at me and downs it.

I give him a weak smile, choosing the prune *sok* instead.

Olya finally sits, and I listen to Chase and Vasilley talk about politics, the people in the village and America. Olya keeps glancing at Chloe and smiling.

"Olya tells me that Josey wants to sell her boxes," Vasilley says, filling up Chase's glass for what might be the eighth time. Chase must hold his liquor well, because although he seems to be keeping up with Vasilley, he doesn't have even a hint of Vasilley's shiny eyes or slurred speech. "To Josey!"

To Josey, indeed. Olya has long stopped keeping up and now just gives me a sad smile. Chase downs another drink.

I think I'm going to be ill. Not from Olya's delicious food (aside from the prune cake), but from the change I see in Chase before my very eyes. Has he forgotten the nights he snuck out of the house, having narrowly escaped his father's drunken rampages? Or worse, the days when he didn't escape and showed up on my doorstep a little broken?

Chase always promised me he'd never touch alcohol. And I counted on that, especially during my own high-school rampages.

Now I need that promise even more. He reaches over for my *sok,* takes a drink and moves my glass next to his plate. I don't know why—he has plenty left. But after that last sip, I didn't want mine, anyway.

"Justin and Chloe, I think it's time to go home." I touch Olya's hand. "Thank you for the meal. Happy Birthday."

"I think I'll stay," Chase says, pulling me down and kissing me on the cheek. "Don't worry," he whispers. But I'm past worry and well on my way to an all-out panic attack.

Chloe and Justin are tucked into their beds, the house is warm and quiet, and I'm in my jammies and wool socks under the covers trying to read when Chase steals in. I hear him load the coal stove, stoking it for the night. Then he pumps water and fills up the overhead water storage above the sink.

Finally he locks the door and appears in the doorway to the bedroom. Against the darkness of the rest of the house, the bedroom light illuminates him, showing lines on his face I haven't seen before. I expect his eyes to be bloodshot, but they're remarkably clear. He crosses his arms and leans against the door. Stares at me a long moment.

"Do you trust me?"

I put my hand over the page in my book. I'm not even sure what it's about, having read the same line for roughly the last hour. My heartbeat repeats his question. Do I trust him?

I trust him to love me and the kids to the best of his ability. I trust him to take care of us. I trust him to play with his children and do his best to parent them. I trust him to want to help.

But I don't trust the Chase I saw tonight.

I don't answer. His smile falls and he sighs.

"Vasilley asked me to go hunting with him," he says finally, pulling off his clothes and climbing in beside me. "He says that he wants to show me how they hunt. I think they're not as angry with me about the pine trees as I thought."

Or maybe it's just that in his current woozy perspective, everybody's a friend.

Please, God, don't let Chase get hurt.

He turns his back to me as I turn off the light and lie there in the darkness.

Chapter Thirteen

A Little Bit of Sunshine

"Maybe we can fix up the playground?"

"Or the fountain in the center of the square?"

The conversation is lively and not unlike that of a potluck dinner I might find at the Gull Lake church. The women bring in their supplies, lay them out and go to work. We are in what I'm dubbing the community center, located next door to the *detski-sod*. Old wooden and metal chairs are shoved up against painted propaganda signs and faded pictures of long-gone leaders. A red curtain, worn and ripped, hangs from the ceiling above a small stage.

The wind rattles the windows, and a layer of snow and ice slides in under the door and through the cracks in the windowsill. Everyone still wears their winter coats, although mittens have been discarded for work purposes. I no longer think it odd to see women wearing mink coats with homemade knitted mittens. I tried wearing my leather gloves once and lost all feeling in my pinkies instantly.

I'm still holding out on the Cossack boots, however. There was a vow made about footwear long ago in Moscow, and a girl can only sacrifice so much before she loses herself. I found cute, wide-heel boots lined with fur that lace up the front like something from the sixties. I can mostly feel my toes.

I now wear at least two layers at all times. Turtleneck and sweater, plus jacket. Wool tights, plus jeans. Knitted gloves, plus the mittens Olya gave me.

Olya has finally decided we are friends. Since the birthday dinner, she's been a regular on my doorstep, armed with a hot pot of corn kasha or better yet, *shi,* a cabbage stew made from sauerkraut.

She even showed me a picture of her daughter, Albena, in Moscow on one of these visits. Everything inside me hurt, especially when Chloe came running up and launched herself at Olya. The day we first met Olya and Lydia came back to me, and for a moment, I had a full and vivid understanding of how painful it must have been for her to see my kids.

But to Olya's credit, she picked up Chloe and even gave her a little pat when my daughter purred and made kitty paws. Hey, it's more than I would do. Good thing cats have nine lives.

At the moment, I'm hoping Chase has nine—or even two—lives. I can't bear to think about his upcoming trip with Vasilley. What if it's a ploy to get Chase into the woods alone, with no witnesses, and exact revenge for the years of the Cold War? Or for two months of cold, fruitless trapping? What if Vasilley gets sopping drunk and shoots Chase?

What if they freeze to death?

Do you trust me? I hate that he had to ask me. And that I didn't know how to answer.

I used to trust Chase enough to follow him to the ends of the earth (read: Siberia). Can a girl submit when the one she is "obeying" betrays her?

I'm not ready to answer that.

Instead, I've focused the past three weeks on setting up our eBay account, taking inventory of the gifts, snapping digital pictures and creating descriptions. I've even decided to send Justin and Chloe to preschool for a full day two days a week.

I'm not a bad mom. I'm not a bad mom.

The payoff is that I've learned more about the village and women of Bursk than Chase could ever put in a report.

Like, for example, the women often feel alone and forgotten.

Or, if they had it their way, they might even return

to the life they had years ago—a close-knit, subsistence society. With their television sets, of course. And fur coats.

Boy, do I want a fur coat. I admit it, I'm jealous. Not that I'd give up my washing machine, mind you, but imagine all that fur, all that warmth.

And fur coats don't make noise when you walk. Seriously. Have you ever listened to a person in a puffy parka? She can't go anywhere without making it clear that she's on the way. And that she's fat. I don't care if you're a size two—in a parka, you are never thin.

Just once I'd like to glide into a room in a fancy mink coat.

I don't think, by the way, that the women of Bursk would really like to return to cooking dinner over open fires and sleeping in yurts. But I do think they'd like to feel as if they are contributing.

Hence, the full house at the community center, the excitement, the tentative smiles sent in my direction. See? I knew God sent me here for a reason.

Just as I predicted, we already have orders for products. With Olya's help, we commandeered cardboard from the vendors at the market and have fashioned small boxes. We also have homemade wrapping paper printed with a design one of the ladies whittled into a chunk of wood.

They are a creative bunch, these Siberians.

I'm getting ready to send out our first batch of

orders when I feel a change in the room. The conversation quiets and a few women look up, past me.

I turn, expecting to see Chase. Instead, it's Nathan, standing at the door, thumping his boots and clapping his hands together. His cheeks are red, and he hasn't shaved for a day at least. Frost clings to his eyelashes. He smiles wide. "Hey, Jose. I just came by to see how you're doing."

I hold up a package. "We already have at least ten orders! They're going out today." I motion him over to the table full of packing supplies. "Help me package these."

Nathan pulls off his gloves and shoves them into his jacket pocket. He, too, wears a parka, a black one that makes him look like a puffy mobster, especially with his knitted black stocking cap. He unzips the jacket, and I see the brown scarf that Chase and I gave him for Christmas.

"Ten orders already? That's amazing."

"It's fantastic," I say, looking proudly at the women. "I can hardly believe I'm getting this much participation. I expected maybe two or three women. But the entire town?"

He picks up a wooden box and begins wrapping it in paper. "They're looking beyond their lives, seeing potential. Frankly, I think it's one of the greatest gifts Westerners—and especially Americans—have given to the Russians. A vision of what could be."

I smile at that. Josey Anderson, purveyor of hope. "There's even been talk of redoing the central square and updating the playground."

"If anyone can do it, you can." He looks up and grins at me. "I told you that you'd make a terrific pastor's wife."

Except a pastor's wife has to be married to a pastor.

And last time I checked, pastors didn't drink vodka.

"Nathan, can I ask you a favor?" The request has been tumbling through my mind for the past three weeks. I think it's the only logical answer to my current Chase dilemma. I spot my open door.

I never thought in my wildest imaginations (and I've had many—after all, Chase has always lived with one foot in adventure and the other in reality) that I'd have to worry about him turning into his father.

I wrap a birchbark box in paper, folding the edges down to wedge it into the cardboard container. I can't look at Nathan. "Chase and Vasilley are going hunting next week. Will you..." I look up at him and swallow, aware that my voice has thinned. "Will you finagle a way to go with them?"

He is watching me, and something enters his eyes, something that makes me want to cry. Mistrust of my sweet Chase. "Why?"

"I just...I don't trust...Vasilley." And that's true. "He drinks. And I'm worried about Chase."

Nathan puts down the box and lowers his voice. "Is Chase drinking?"

"I don't… We went to a birthday party. There was vodka." I lift a shoulder, but again I can't look at Nathan. I feel as though I've just plunged a knife between my husband's shoulder blades. "It's not like he even got…" I can't say the word *drunk,* but it's there, hanging, ugly.

Raw. "It's just not like Chase at all. He's a good man. I don't want anything to happen to him." I close the cardboard box, my hand trembling.

Nathan's hand covers mine. It's cold, but when he squeezes my hand, the kindness sends warmth to my heart. "I'll take care of it, Josey. Don't worry."

THE SECRETS OF SIBERIA IN YOUR HOME!

That's right! Straight from Siberia, the land of ice and cold, come handcrafted gifts for the nature lover! Birchbark vases, jewelry boxes and kitchen containers are great for keeping herbs, grain and even milk fresh, longer! The Nanais people are among the few Siberian craftspeople who have preserved the art of carving and pressing birchbark into intricate shapes, designs and unique items for the home. Each piece is handcrafted. Find the perfect gift and take a piece of Siberia home today!

I'm going to have to start paying rent at the government office. I'm also going to have to get a pillow for my backside. I look outside and see that the afternoon has slunk into dusk. If this picture doesn't finish loading, I'm going to be late picking up Justin and Chloe.

We've completely sold out of our initial stock, and I have the ladies working every day at the community center, stockpiling bread boxes and jewelry containers, and making place mats, coffee cups, napkin rings, hairclips and even necklaces.

I wake in the middle of the night with designs in my head.

I am the queen of my empire.

Or at least, I'm frantically trying to keep up with my rapidly expanding empire. At least all this business keeps me from thinking about Chase. Who left yesterday for parts unknown in the middle of Siberia, with Vasilley. And, thank the Lord, Nathan.

C'mon, photo, load. I spy Anton leaning against the door frame. He's frowning. He hasn't asked about my health for a while now. I'm not sure why.

Everything's going to be fine, really. Chase dug out a backpack and packed it full of warm clothes, socks and even a first-aid kit.

I sat on the bed petting Chloe and tried to hold my tongue.

But it wasn't until Nathan showed up with his own stuffed backpack—not until he gave me a smile and the smallest of winks—that I began to breathe.

I hate that I enlisted backup for the man I most believe in. Or at least, want most to believe in. He does deserve my trust, doesn't he? Doesn't he?

Oh, God, please help me to trust Chase!

The picture finishes loading and I shut down the computer. Five more orders today. The post office is sending them out as fast as we can package them, but it's not like they offer delivery confirmation. At least I know H is sending them on to the right locations.

All I can do is pray.

Which I seem to be doing a lot these days, especially since Chase decided to take a jaunt into the nether hills. The good news is that Nathan brought along Secrets of Siberia's first paycheck, wired to a Khabarovsk bank from our online account. I sell on consignment, taking only enough to cover the eBay and mailing expenses. The rest I pay out to the ladies.

I have to admit, I've never seen a woman cry when she got paid before. But when Olya counted her rubles, she put her head into her hands and began to sob. *"Spaceeba,"* she said, over and over.

I'm thinking that it was a good cry.

I decided that it might be good if I cried, too. See, this is why I could be a pastor's wife, if, say, Chase was a pastor. Because I can empathize. This is also why, last week, I had a packed house for my study of the first chapter of John.

It just takes time to win hearts and minds.

I pass Anton in the hall as I leave the government office. I'm sure he recognizes me, despite

the fact that I'm dressed in three thousand layers
with only my eyes showing between my knit cap
and scarf. Still, when I lift my hand in greeting, he
ignores it.

Okay, so I'm not winning *all* the hearts and
minds of Bursk.

The wind picks up trash it has culled from corner
Dumpsters, and an empty bottle rolls across my path.
The late-January winds have pushed snow into drifts
against the swaying fences that line footpaths to
homes. The street is a sheet of thick ice, scarred
here and there by hoof prints or sledge furrows.
Every house I pass has a trickle of gray smoke
curling into the sky, evidence of life in the otherwise
darkened abode, shuttered closed for winter. We
elected to put plastic over our windows, and every
day a hazy sun shines in.

The *detski-sod* yard is well used, even in winter.
The teachers bundle up the children for the Ice Age
so they can spend the requisite hour outside, playing.
To my surprise, Justin and Chloe haven't been ill
once this winter.

We might all need to play outside for an hour a
day, get some sunshine, learn how to get along with
the other kids despite the snow. I think there are some
metaphors for life there.

Justin and Chloe are the only ones on the swing
set when I arrive. Maya is in the yard, wrapped in a

wool coat, looking her Milan-model best. She gives me a small, disapproving shake of her head as I retrieve my children.

"Izvenetya," I say. "Thank you for watching them. I appreciate your time."

She gives me one of those eerie Maya looks and shrugs.

I swing by the corner market, perusing the items on my way home. Olya isn't there today—thanks to her recent payday, I hope—but I spot a vendor with what looks like chocolate chips. I look closer, pulling Chloe to a stop. My daughter is thrilled to begin our daily tug-of-war.

Sure enough, Nestlé's Toll House chocolate chips! I can't believe it. My supply has long run out, and the ladies have been begging for another batch.

I am reaching into my pocket for rubles when I see Ulia down the street, standing beside an abandoned bread kiosk. I recognize her by her *shopka,* which is a sort of swirled, whipped-cream shape made of leather and mink.

And standing very close to her is a man I don't recognize. He leans down and whispers in her ear. She laughs.

She doesn't see me, despite the fuss Chloe is making, and I quickly turn away, feeling as if I've just seen an episode of *Santa Barbara Goes to Siberia.*

Oh.

"Mommy, me seeds!" Justin is pointing to a woman selling sunflower seeds in a little bag.

"No, Justin. You don't know how to eat them." I'm pulling him away as fast as I can. Chloe's decided that she is a turtle and wants to try sliding along the icy path on her back.

"Get up, Chloe," I hiss through my teeth. Please, don't let Ulia see me. I feel suddenly dirty. I haul Chloe up by the back of her fur coat. "Please walk with Mommy."

"Nyet! Nyet!"

Okay, that's about enough of Russian culture for one day. I hike Chloe up by her belt and carry her down the street like a suitcase.

Justin is sliding beside me. "Mommy, where's Daddy?"

He's in the bush, where it's safe. Where people don't see things they ought not to. My stomach burns as we arrive at our house. I let the kids free. Justin runs through the yard, pretending to shoot imaginary wildebeests.

The house is cold. Chase has brought in enough coal to last us while he's away, so I put on my gloves and load a couple of coal chunks into the still-burning furnace and push them around with the poker.

It's a skill I'll bet my mother never learned. But more than likely, one I share with my grandmother.

"Soup!" Justin says, climbing onto his chair. His

cheeks are still rosy from the walk home and his blond curly hair sticks out in odd places. Those blue eyes look at me, sparkling with hope, and I'd give him the world.

"Coming right up."

Nathan, bless him, has left his room-and-board pot of borscht in the fridge, and I serve it up hot with *smytena* and bread.

We read a book, the kids have a warm bath, and then I put them to bed.

The house is quiet and dark as I stare out at the stars. Chase is out there, under them. I imagine him in his sleeping bag, wool hat on, laughing with Nathan. Chase spent much of his high-school years sleeping out under the stars.

I don't need to worry.

I don't need to worry.

Once upon a time, back in Gull Lake, I was the one who caused the worry. I was the one who sometimes forgot her boundaries. I'll never forget the night I went joyriding with Lew and the gang, shortly after we took home the state football title. I'm horrified to admit that I don't remember how, exactly, I got home.

Except to say that it had to do with Chase and his attention to detail. He noticed that I wasn't in the parking lot waiting for him after the team bus arrived home and all the other football players had showered and moved on to victory events.

Chase spent half the night looking for me and finally found me, apparently, on Lew's porch furniture.

I woke up on the beach of Berglund Acres, wrapped in a stadium blanket. Chase was sitting beside me.

He said nothing.

I said nothing.

And he covered for me when my father found us. He said we'd come out to watch the sunrise.

I can trust Chase.

I turn off the light, climb into our cold bed and shiver.

Don't you think there should be some warning, especially from God, when you are going to have to pull out your spiritual arsenal? I know that the Bible says, "Be ready in all seasons," but really, just like a race or a boxing match, there should be a designated warm-up period.

It's somewhere around two in the morning. I've been asleep for at least four hours—long enough to have bad breath and matted hair. And it's greasy hair, too, because Chase has been away for three days, and Chloe and Justin aren't tall enough to pour water over my head to rinse out the suds.

I realize too late that I'm still half-asleep—a girl with all her faculties wouldn't open the door to crazed pounding in the middle of the night.

I don't recognize the snowy person wrapped in layers and a scarf, only eyes showing, who stumbles into my foyer, bringing in the frigid night air. I gasp as the air climbs up my nightgown, despite the coat I've wrapped around me.

"Hello?"

I know those eyes, but it takes a moment for me to place them. And when I do, I'm speechless. Frozen in place.

Why would Maya be at my door in the middle of the night?

"Can I stay here?" she asks, and as I nod, I see that her mascara has run and her face is blotched from the chill. I close the door behind her as she sheds her scarf, turning her back to me.

"Yes. Are you okay?"

She is trying to nod, but it's not working and she puts a hand over her face, probably to hide the fact that she's crying, but I'm pretty savvy—I can spot sobbing with the best of them. Even in the wee hours. I ease off her jacket and hang it on a hook over mine. I open the inner door and take her elbow to move her inside.

When I spot her swollen and bloody mouth, the slightest trickle of blood from her upper lip, I pull in a cry of horror, not wanting to scare her. I motion to a chair. "Would you like some tea?"

She nods and moves somewhat stiffly to the chair, taking out a handkerchief and pressing it to her eyes and her mouth. She looks down at the blood on it.

"Are you okay?" I ask again. "Do you need some ice?"

She shakes her head, but her hand is trembling. The furnace needs stoking so I open it and push around some blocks. The coal supply is dwindling, but Chase will be back tomorrow, in plenty of time to bring in more coal from the pile outside. I put the teapot on the stove and sit down opposite her, taking her hand. It's ice cold. "What happened?"

She glances up at me, and now I see, truly see what is behind those beautiful, deadened eyes.

Pain. Brokenness.

"What is it, Maya?" I ask softly.

She sighs. "I can stay here tonight?"

"Of course. Are you afraid to go home?" It occurs to me that I don't even know where Maya lives. Which is odd, because now I know where nearly everyone in town lives.

She looks again at the blood on her handkerchief and nods.

"Who hurt you, Maya?"

She closes her eyes and takes a long, deep breath. And then she says, "I was born in this village. My father was an elder."

The teapot's lid starts to jiggle against the steam, but I ignore it.

"He committed suicide when I was thirteen." She stares at her fingernails. Her nail polish is a deep red.

"My mother couldn't take care of me, and she didn't have money to send me back to boarding school, so," she says, shrugging, "she gave me to a man in the village to marry."

Oh.

Maya glances up at me with a flicker of a sad smile. "He might have loved me. But mostly he drank, and I kept his house." She shakes her head. "He wasn't always mean."

I imagine her, a young girl, afraid, trying to keep everything in order. No wonder she runs a tight ship over at the kindergarten.

I get up, turn off the stove and bring the pot of water to the table. I'm reaching for the cups when she puts her hand on my arm. "He would have killed us both that night."

I sit back down.

"I know it. He was drunk, and he barricaded my door. I woke up and smelled the smoke. I knew he'd fallen asleep with his cigarette. I tried to get into the room, I tried to save him, but by the time I got out the window, the house was engulfed." She shakes her head as if to erase the memory. "The council called it an accident. They gave me a room at the community center, in the back, behind the stage."

So that's where she lives. Right next door to the *detski-sod*. No wonder she's always there.

I retrieve the cups and set them in front of her. "You're safe here, Maya. Whatever happened tonight, you're safe here. And when Chase gets back, he'll find out—"

"Nyet!" Her eyes widen. "No, it's not…I can't…"

"Calm down. I just want to help—"

"He will kill me if anyone finds out."

The clock on the wall ticks behind me as I let her words sink in. Who will kill her? If anyone finds out what?

I take her hand. "You're safe here, Maya. I promise. And we don't have to know anything. Except, if my children are in danger…" I raise an eyebrow, and she shakes her head.

"He wouldn't come here."

I get up and bolt the inside door just the same.

Maya fixes herself a cup of tea. Her hand shakes a little as she sips it.

"Thank you," she says softly.

I nod. "Maya, why did you come to me?"

She takes another sip, measuring me with her eyes. "Because I've been watching you, and I think I want to believe you."

Believe me? Is anyone else lost?

"He loves me, you said. And I want to believe that. But I'm not sure I can."

Oh. He. As in God, He.

"Why not?"

She shakes her head and looks away. And I recognize a look I've seen way too many times on my own face. Guilt. Shame. The morning-after dread on the shores of Gull Lake.

I touch her trembling hand. "I learned long ago that God doesn't keep score. It's all one big lump of sin to Him. And His one big remedy is forgiveness. Just like that. He doesn't promise to make all our problems go away. But He does promise to forgive us and to walk with us here on earth, give us wisdom and hope, and give us life after we die. One of my favorite verses says that God knows the plans He has for us, and they're good plans. But we need to seek Him to find those plans."

Her dark eyes examine mine as if testing my words, my resolve. And then, just like that, as if the sunshine has found Siberia, she smiles. It's small. But enough. "I think, maybe, I can do that."

Chapter Fourteen

The Hot and Cold

I think my marrow has frozen. For sure, every cell in my body is turning to ice. I move like a ninety-year-old woman, and it hurts. I've lost all feeling in my fingers, and I've taken to holding my hands over the steam off the potato soup, hoping to thaw them.

Outside, the wind has turned into a snarl, and a blizzard white-outs the yard. I can't even see the street. My coal supply is buried under the snow—I keep praying over the furnace, but if Chase doesn't get home soon, I'm going to have to get out there and dig.

Chase is out there. A day late, already.

Maya left early yesterday morning before the kids woke up, and I cleaned the house and waited for

Chase, nearly bursting with the need to tell him about what happened to Maya.

I waited and waited…

I'm not going to worry. I'm not.

I stand at the window, staring at a swirl of snow, and everything inside me is tight.

"This is not what I signed up for, Lord." My voice sounds thin against the wind rattling the windowpanes. Chloe and Justin are still asleep, bundled in layers of comforters and wool blankets. I pull my sleeves down over my fists and fold my arms across my chest for warmth. "I'm not ready to be a single mom."

I go over to the coal bucket and stare into its emptiness as if God might suddenly fill it. But it stays empty.

It only takes a second for me to succumb to the temptation of the warm Cossack boots. I pull them on, along with a jacket, a hat and Chase's work gloves, then grab the bucket.

The wind nearly takes me down. My nose immediately hurts, and snow is in my eyes. The blizzard isn't a peaceful drift of thick snowflakes, but a torrent of ice crystals hitting my face—the fury of Siberia, unleashed.

I bend my head and trudge over to the pile, pick up a shovel and work out a few rocks. I'm not sure what coal in America looks like, but in Russia, coal is grimy and black and comes in boulders. A dirty chunk tumbles down from the pile, landing at my feet. I pick it up and drop it into the bucket.

Coal is also heavy. I only fill the bucket halfway and trudge inside. No, this is not what I signed up for at all.

Humble. Gentle. Patient. Peaceful.

Be worthy of the calling.

I was worthy yesterday. I just hope to survive today.

I dump the bucket into the fire. A blaze of heat begins to fill the house.

I stand back, pry off my layers. Warm my hands. Hmm. Wow, I did that. All by myself.

We might survive living in Siberia, after all. Perhaps we'll even help people solve the problems that have plagued this village for years. And help Olya reunite her family. And show Maya the way to hope. And even help Nathan start a church. Maybe Siberia isn't as difficult as I thought.

I start a pot of hot water for cocoa and again stare out the window. It's getting darker, even though it's supposed to be early morning.

We are in for a doozy of a storm.

Please, God, keep Chase safe.

I climb back into bed, warmed by the bodies of my two little Chase replicas.

"Josey! Josey, wake up!"

I am warm, so warm. I take a deep breath.

And smell smoke. I sit up and whack something, hard.

"Ow!"

A Chase-like form pulls back, his hand on his forehead.

"Chase!" I reach up to put my arms around him, but I can barely see him through the fog of gray smoke.

"Grab Chloe!" He scoops up Justin, along with a blanket. Panic ignites me as I throw off the covers and drag my daughter from the bed. I follow Chase through the house, putting my hand over my mouth, clutching Chloe to my chest. "Are we on fire?"

Chase grabs a jacket and throws it over me, and I slip on my boots as we dash out into the snow. "What's happening?"

Justin is awake now, blinking at Chase. Chloe is just starting to stir. The snow hits my face with a bite.

"What did you do?" Chase rounds on me now that we're outside. The blizzard roars in my ears, and he looks a little wild with all that snow caked on his *shopka* and his four-day beard growth.

"We're all clear," Nathan says coming out of the house, holding the plastic sheeting that used to cover our windows. "It was just the coal furnace smoldering."

Chase's eyes are red-rimmed, and he closes them as he turns away from me. I see him pull Justin tight against him and lean his face into his son's neck.

"What happened?" I ask.

Nathan pulls off his jacket and puts it around Chloe. "Your coal fire was smothered. The entire house is filled with smoke."

I stand there a long moment as the truth sinks in and cuts off my breathing. "We could have died."

Nathan looks at me and then turns to Chase. "Buddy, you okay?"

Chase glances at me, and for a second, I think I see his eyes glistening. He nods. "Yup." But his tone makes me believe the opposite.

He was scared. I haven't scared Chase in years—not counting the jellyfish. "I'm sorry," I say, my voice barely functioning. Chase reaches out and wraps his arm around my neck, pulling me to his cold, puffy jacket. I feel him tremble as he holds me.

"I'm sorry," he says. "So, so sorry."

I'm not sure what he's apologizing for, but I've learned never to turn down an apology from a man. I hold on.

We're a little family package of gratefulness as Nathan walks around the house, opening windows to air out the smoke.

"How did it happen?" Chase asks finally.

"I dumped the bucket of coal in to stoke the fire?" I prop Chloe on my hip, pulling the coat over her even as she fusses with it.

"You dumped the bucket?"

"Yeessss…"

"You can't dump coal dust on a fire—it'll smother it. Just put the pieces in by hand."

Oh, I'll be sure and file that away in my Coal Furnace Maintenance Manual. I sigh.

"I'm just thankful we got here in time."

I'm not able to address that.

"Dzhozhy! Dzhozhy!" Olya is running across the yard calling my name, Lydia behind her, barking. *"Deem edyot!"*

Yeah, I know about the smoke. But I'm heartened to see Olya in her housedress, her *valenki*, her *shopka* and a ragged coat wrapped around her, running next door to save our lives.

She wraps me in a hug. *"Vwe Spequeny?"*

"Yes, we're safe," I answer.

I notice Vasilley is also here. He looks like Chase and Nathan—icy eyebrows and beard, his fur hat covered in snow. "Was there a fire?"

Chase shakes his head, briefs him.

I don't look at Vasilley because I know I'm getting one of those "stupid American woman" looks.

Let's be nice to the foreign girl who didn't grow up with a coal stove.

"Why didn't you wait for me?" Chase asks in English, his voice low.

"Wait for you? You were supposed to be home yesterday! I had no idea when you were coming back!" Or *if* he was coming back. Or what condition he'd be in when he came back. "It was getting cold in the house!"

Chase looks stricken. "I never should have brought you here. I never should have left you alone. This is all my fault."

Everything inside me begins to burn.

"Piedyom," Olya says, gesturing for me to follow her and taking Justin from Chase's arms.

I'm not sure where we're going, but anywhere is better than here. "Welcome home," I snap as I follow Olya to her house.

Coal smoke is black. I know this because it is now embedded in my curtains, my bedsheets, my walls, my carpet and my pores. And because it's about negative two hundred outside, I can't wash anything.

Including myself. Because even my pots are covered in coal smoke, and I can't get the water hot enough to wash the pots off without also taking off my skin.

Yeah, it's been a cold, silent and sooty week.

Nathan has brought new plastic sheeting from Khabarovsk, and Chase is out trying to locate nails with Vasilley.

Now, raise your hand if you would have known *not* to put coal dust in the stove. Yeah, I thought so. Which means I don't deserve to be treated like a two-year-old. However, I do take back that comment about surviving Siberia. It is harder than I thought.

I put the pot of hot water down on the center of the table with a thud.

"He blames himself, you know." Nathan picks up the teapot and pours water into a cup already armed with a teabag. "Not only for being late, but for bringing you here in the first place."

I really have nothing to say to that. Because, in a way, Chase is right to blame himself. But more than that, those words irritate me. I'm not exactly helpless.

"But in truth, it's my fault," Nathan continues.

I raise an eyebrow at him. How could it be his fault? Did he bring us here? If we're going to blame someone, maybe we should blame God. Nathan has his angelic moments, but I'm pretty sure he's not God.

"How's that?" I pour water into my cup and sit down. Chloe and Justin are at *detski-sod,* a fact I now welcome, knowing they'll be warm and fed.

"When we were camping, Vasilley wanted to know why I was here, which led to a discussion about spiritual beliefs. We talked late into the night and overslept a bit the next morning. When we awoke, the storm was closing in. We had to wait until it passed before we could pack up. Chase drove us crazy—he made us leave at the first sign that we could travel."

Oh.

"Did Chase mention that Vasilley gave his life to Jesus? He became a Christian out there on our hunting trip."

Nathan is smiling, giving me a look I've never seen before. "He's the first man in Bursk to get saved." He touches my forearm. "And that, Josey, I blame on you."

His words make me feel warm, right to the center of my cold soul. Because I'm feeling pretty unworthy—unhumble, ungentle and impatient— these days. "Why?" I ask, needing more.

I'm such a glutton for words of affirmation.

"Because if you hadn't said yes to Chase, he never would have come here. And it's because he came and told Anton to sell the trees—"

"He didn't tell—"

"—and then humbly drank vodka with Vasilley and was willing to shoulder the blame for the trees, that he got invited hunting. And because you were afraid of Chase getting hurt, you made me invite myself." He shrugs. "See? Your fault."

My fault. There are certain things I'm willing to take the blame for. Vasilley's redemption is definitely in that category.

Not forgetting, of course, that it is God who draws people to Himself. But I got to be a part of it. I'm on the team.

"By the way, you might want to ask Chase about that night at Vasilley's. He wasn't drinking."

I eye Nathan. "I saw the vodka go down. Shot glass after shot glass."

"Not to disgust you or anything, but did you also see him spit it back out into his juice?"

Okay, I'm a little disgusted. But as I rewind those events in my memory, I see Chase taking a drink of *sok* after every shot.

Ew. But yay, Chase!

"How do you know that?"

Nathan takes a sip of his tea. "I had to level with him to get him to invite me on the trip."

Oh, no. "Nathan, then he knows that I—"

"Didn't trust me?" Chase is standing at the door, holding a hammer and a handful of nails. I look up, meet his eyes and swallow.

"Chase—"

"Save it." He comes inside and grabs the plastic. Nathan squeezes my arm and gets up to help him.

I watch them struggle to put up the plastic as they pound in the nails, creating a barrier between us and the cold.

Or perhaps, locking in the cold that's seeped into our lives.

"I'm going next door," I say, hoping for a reaction.

Nathan nods. Chase the Ice Cube says nothing.

I garb up, hurry over to Olya's, wave to Lydia, tied to the outhouse who is instantly hysterical, and knock on the door. The smell of something delicious filters through, pulling me inside.

"Yum," I say. A word that translates easily. "What are you making?"

"Perogue," Olya says. Pie.

Actually, it's more of a bread with stuffing inside, like eggs or salmon. *"Kakoi?"* I ask. What kind?

"Potato pie—Vasilley's favorite."

Olya looks good today—her hair is back in a high bun and she's wearing a sweater and pants, instead of her usual housecoat. And is that a touch of makeup?

"Where's Vasilley?"

"At the post office. Sending a letter." She doesn't mention who it's for, but I can guess.

Her daughter.

I shed my coat and boots. I don't care that Chase is hurt. Okay, maybe a little, but how was I supposed to know about his ploy?

Shoot. I didn't mean to hurt him.

But what about him trusting *me?* Why didn't he tell me that he wasn't getting snockered with Vasilley and that he had a plan? He could have even told me at the table—it's not like our hosts would have understood English all of a sudden. Then again, Chase is very aware how rude it is to speak English in front of non-English speakers.

Personally, I think we need all the help we can get.

Olya pulls the *perogue* from the oven and sets it on the table, covering it with a towel. Then she comes over and touches my hair.

That is my personal space, there, Olya. Russians really aren't into personal space—not in Siberia, or Moscow, or anywhere else.

"Pidyom K Banaye," she says.

It's not until she grabs a couple of towels and shampoo that I get it. She's noticed the buildup of grease and coal dust that's glued my hair to my head.

"Oh, no, Olya, I can't—"

But she's got me in a Russian armlock.

And what am I going to do, anyway—go home?

I'm not a girl who likes to get naked in front of other people. Yes, okay, there was that skinny-dipping incident as a senior, but that was a dare.

And we all know what happens when I'm dared to do something.

Which is probably how Olya gets me into a steam room, naked, with twelve other women.

I did put up a fight, however. I sort of had a flash-back to when I was twelve and forced to change clothes in front of the girls on the swim team. Needless to say, I became the master of dressing underneath a towel.

I should have recognized the public bathhouse by the word *Banya* (as in Bath) written across the door, but of course, I was looking for something like a Japanese spa, not a log cabin resembling the town hall. Once inside, we veered appropriately into the *zhenshina,* or women's, section. Inside, a locker room made of cement and lined with rough benches managed to capture every gulag nightmare and trap the Siberian deep freeze, as well as a latent impression of prison.

"You don't seriously expect me to take my clothes off," I said, hoping to add levity to the moment. Apparently, Olya didn't appreciate my attempt at humor. She proceeded to strip.

I wanted to yell, "Stop, stop, my eyes aren't ready!" But before I could get the words out, she'd turned me around and started shucking off my clothes.

Again. Personal space.

"You have to get naked if you want to get clean." Okay, Dalai Lama, I got it.

I took over and utilized my dormant locker-room abilities, showing only a small amount of skin before I was completely naked under the towel wrapped around me.

Alas, it would not be around me very long. Nevertheless, I clung to hope as I hung my belongings on a hook and then followed Olya.

There is a *banya* process, not unlike that of washing clothes. First comes the steam room, where a gal sweats off the grime of the day (or last five months). Then, the cold plunge and, finally, the showers.

I wondered, couldn't I just skip straight to the showers?

I entered the steam room to find…well, naked

women. I was so, *so* not ready for this. Where to look? Horror rose inside me when Olya reached over and yanked off my towel.

I was twelve again as I frantically tried to cover places.

And then I realized…I've had babies.

In Russia.

This is about a billion times less humiliating.

Besides, the sauna room is dark, and hot. Really hot. I stood there, the heat seeping into my pores, warming those frozen bones. I found a spot on a bench and sat, keeping my head down.

Now, ten minutes later, I think I just might be in heaven. Heat—precious, delicious heat. I'm starting to listen to the chatter of the women around me.

Someone greets Olya.

And then me. I raise my hand in greeting and close my eyes to focus on the heat.

"Can you believe that Sophia was going to betray Ken with that guy CC?"

Ah, the update on *Santa Barbara*. I sigh, breathing in the hot air, nearly crying with joy over the warmth of it.

"Ken deserves it. He is terrible to her! He ignores her, and now that he's left, I'll bet he cheats on her again. Too bad she feels too guilty to go with CC."

"I wouldn't feel guilty. I'd leave Ken."

I glance up, surprised at the venom in the voice.

My eyes have adjusted, and through the haze and the curtain of my hair, I see…Ulia.

Oh, no.

"Sophia loves Ken, even if he is bad to her," another voice says. "She should stay with him. They have history."

"Sophia could be happy with CC. He listens to her. Especially after everything she's been through. He wants her to be happy," Ulia says angrily.

Uh-oh. Methinks we're not talking about Ken and Sophia anymore.

"Ken needs to appreciate her. Maybe he needs to see that he's losing her."

Ulia's words sink in. Yeah. Maybe Ken needs to appreciate her and all she does. Maybe Ken is a big lout.

"I think Sophia should leave him and be happy with CC. She needs to think about what's best for her." Ulia opens the door to leave and a whoosh of cold air rushes in.

I climb to the highest bench in the back. Sweat pours down my face and drips off my chin. It's getting hard to breathe, so I head toward the door.

Olya meets me there. "Time for the cold plunge," she says. I am instantly afraid. (C'mon, wouldn't you be, too? "Cold plunge"?)

The cold plunge is exactly as advertised—it involves jumping into a pool of freezing water. Olya grabs my hand and pulls me in with her.

My breath is yanked from my lungs and a thousand icicles pierce my skin. "Yow!" I scream, and Olya laughs as she climbs out.

"Now the shower."

Ah, the shower. I lather my hair, three times. I use conditioner. I feel like singing. I love the *ban-ya*. I love the *ban-ya*.

Why didn't I do this sooner?

"Ready for round two?" Olya asks.

If it includes more heat, I'm all over it.

We do four rounds, and by the time we're finished, I'm a noodle. A really clean, happy, bursting-with-Bursk-secrets noodle.

I've just discovered the Russian version of Bunko night.

And I think Ulia is going to leave Anton.

Chapter Fifteen

When I first moved to Russia, the desserts enthralled me. Beautiful creations drizzled with chocolate or frosted with glaze that tantalized from kiosk windows. I remember the day I succumbed to the call of these delicate confections, purchasing a sugar cookie with a floral design, almost too pretty to eat. The air was fragrant with autumn, the wind swirling leaves at my feet. I bit into the cookie…

…and it was tasteless, like sand. It morphed into glue as I chewed, sucking every bit of moisture from my mouth, turning it into the Sahara. Apparently, the sugar-cookie factory had run out of sugar and made cookies, anyway. I stumbled to a nearby beverage kiosk and purchased the first liquid I found, which turned out to be a glass of Kvas, a non-alcoholic beer-like drink made from fermented black bread.

Yes, I said fermented black bread.

I'm still in recovery. Thus, when Olya appears at my door with a metal mold and a can of sweetened condensed milk, announcing that we're going to make Russian cookies, I'm leery.

Lately, Olya's been in spirits before unseen, and I'm wanting to get to the bottom of all this, so I let her in.

She takes down a pot from the shelf, fills it with water and puts it on the stove. Then she peels the label off the can of sweetened condensed milk and puts the can in the pot, the water covering the top.

"What are you doing?"

She gives me a cryptic smile and turns the burner on high.

"That's going to…" I search for the word *explode* but come up blank. "Boom!" I accentuate with the appropriate accompanying hand gestures.

She laughs and shakes her head.

O-kay.

We make a dough that resembles a tea cake—butter, flour, walnuts and honey. She forms it into balls and pushes them into the mold. I check the can. It's boiling nicely, although its texture still seems hard. (One needs to have a sense of humor in Russia. Especially when you're cooking potentially explosive materials.)

She turns on a burner and holds the mold over the flame like she's roasting marshmallows. Clearly I'm the only one afraid of burning the house down.

"What are we making?"

"*Arehki.*"

Nuts. Nuts? I take a pot out, fill it and put on water for tea. I check the can. Still boiling.

I reach for two cups on the shelf and notice that the bucket under the sink needs emptying. At least the cold doesn't take my breath away when I go outside. Instead, it just finds the nooks and crannies where I'm not quite warm and bites. I'm starting to wonder if I'll ever see spring again.

Maybe I'm just overreacting to the cold chill from Chase's side of the bed.

I did, after all, apologize. And I saw the old Chase in the way his eyes softened, the way he reached out and caressed my cheek. "There's nothing to forgive," he said. "You were trying to help."

I was trying to help. We all know that, right?

But something is still not right.

When I come back in, Olya is taking the mold off the burner and laying it aside to cool. The teapot whistles and I pour water into our mugs. I hand her a sugar cube and she surprises me by filling her saucer and dredging the cube in the tea. Apparently she knows that trick, too.

I'm saturating my own cube when she says, "What did Chase do to Vasilley?" She puts down her cup, and I know she means this in a positive way, because she's smiling.

"What do you mean?"

"He's better. Calmer. Doesn't drink as much." She leans back, and I notice that her smile touches her eyes. Her haunted look is starting to vanish. I still haven't found the courage to ask her about her black eye so many months ago, but the fact that, except for the day of the great deforestation, I haven't heard a fight or seen any bruises makes my hope that I was wrong take a firm hold. Even stronger is the hope of a better future. I didn't expect their problems to change overnight with the news of Vasilley's salvation, but maybe my expectations were too low.

"What did he tell you?"

Olya grows a little red at this and looks down at her cup. Oh, Olya, we've come so far, don't retreat now. I wait for it.

"He said he realized what a terrible man he'd been. And that he found forgiveness." I cover her hand with mine. She looks up at me, and her eyes glisten. "He is a better man every day. Nathan gave him a Bible. And he visits us. He is teaching Vasilley about Jesus."

I didn't know that, but warmth swells inside me at the thought of Nathan teaching Vasilley, and Chase persevering and even tasting vodka so he could earn Vasilley's trust. I should have trusted Chase—I know that now.

"Is this why Vasilley is different?" Olya asks.

"Yes. Imagine you are Vasilley. He knows he's hurt you and others. If God were to judge Vasilley based on his past, do you think he'd let Vasilley into heaven?"

She makes a face, shaking her head.

"But Vasilley's been forgiven by God. He's been given a second chance to live this life on earth, and because of God's forgiveness, he'll live forever in eternity. I suppose that's what is making the difference in his life."

The can starts to bang against the pot. I get up to turn down the heat, but she stops me. "Let it boil. It needs to boil to become a sweet filling."

She takes a towel, lays it out on the table and then takes the hot pads and dumps the shells from the mold. Golden brown, they look like hollow walnut halves.

"I want to be a better wife, too," Olya says as she sits down, and this time she meets my eyes. "Can you tell me how?"

While there have been days that I thought I had that job nailed, now I'm not so sure.

"I know that being a wife is about more than just following your husband across Russia," I say, more to myself than Olya. "It's about forgiving, and being patient and gentle and learning how to make peace. But I know that I can't do that without help—God's help."

She's looking at me hard, struggling to understand, and I'm trying to find the right words. "I know life hasn't been kind to you, Olya. And I know this is going to sound too easy, but God loves you. You know how you feel about being apart from Albena? That's how God feels about being apart from you. But you can have a second chance, too, just like Vasilley."

She says nothing, and we watch as steam rises from the boiling pot, gathers on the ceiling and dissipates. The room is warm, almost too hot.

Finally she gets up and takes the can from the pot with tongs. She sets it on the counter to cool.

"Vasilley and I have been married ten years," she says, her back to me. She takes a can opener and pries the lid off the can. "I think it's time for a second chance."

The milk has thickened into a light-brown caramel and smells sweet, like boiled sugar. She takes a walnut half and, using a spoon, fills the hollow with caramel. She fills another half and then puts the two halves together.

"Boiled sweetened condensed milk makes caramel?" I hand her a plate, and she puts the cookie on it before handing me the spoon.

I take it and fill my own cookies, delighted by the sweetness inside the hard crust.

"Do you want me to take these to the post office?" Olya has a box full of orders ready to go. The Secrets of Siberia ladies are barely keeping up with the demand, but our happy group has full coffers and is trying to decide what to do with their cash.

Most importantly, Olya nearly has enough for her tickets to and from Moscow.

"Yes, thank you," I say. Olya is smiling as she leaves the community center, her arms full of goodies.

I leave right behind her, heading for the house to change clothes before the afternoon Women's Day program at the *detski-sod*. The smell of chicken soup cooling on the stove is evidence that Nathan has been here. He must be over at Olya's for his weekly Bible study with Vasilley. I have to say, I've noticed the change in Olya's husband—I saw him helping her milk the cow. I know, but still, nothing says "I love you" like holding old Bessie while your wife milks her and then carrying the milk inside.

As for me, I am looking forward to Nathan's visits more and more these days.

At least he talks to me.

Chase just drinks his tea and listens to us.

I've always loved Chase's ability to fit in, to listen before he talks, to analyze his role in an unfamiliar society, to blend in. Many people actually think Chase is Russian.

But it is exactly this ability that plagues me. I know that Chase managed to do an end-run around Vasilley and his birthday imbibing, but that trick can only work so many times. And worse, what if Chase blends in so well that he starts to adopt the Bursk male mind-set?

It certainly feels like he's turned into Ken. Not Barbie's Ken, but Santa Barbie Ken, the One Who Ignores His Woman.

By the way, Sophia was right. Ken *was* cheating on her and she should have left him, because she can be happy with CC (who adores her), but no, she has to pack her bags and fly off to surprise Ken. And she's going to be bitterly disappointed because he doesn't love her. Maybe he never did! He doesn't see how she feels betrayed, how he's losing her....

Yes, I'm getting my weekly updates at the *Banya*. And not just about *Santa Barbara*. Ulia hasn't left Anton yet. Although I've never been so clean in my life, I feel like a dirty little spy. A naked, double-crossing secret agent. All this information I hold would be invaluable to Chase and his study, not to mention his friendships. I think a guy would like to know if his wife was about to leave so he could fix things, don't you?

Or maybe that's meddling.

I get so confused about these things.

By the way, Chase sailed right through Valentine's Day without a nod.

Okay, yes, I forgot it, too—it's not like they celebrate it here in Russia. Everyone's too busy trying to keep warm. (Although one would think Valentine's Day would be a mandatory holiday for exactly that reason.)

So I'll cut Chase some slack.

Especially because I notice a bouquet of flowers sitting on the table as I enter the house. Roses of all colors, surrounded by baby's breath. Oh, Chase! He remembered International Women's Day!

I'm not sure where Chase tracked those down, but then again, this is the man who brought home a washing machine for Christmas.

I breathe in the smell, letting it fill my cold, nearly iced-over senses. I touch one of the flowers. It's smooth and soft, and silly tears prick my eyes. Chase and I are going to be just fine. I don't know why I worried. Even though I jumped to conclusions, he knows I'm on his side.

After all, I am here in Siberia.

And right now, Siberia seems to be in the clutches of a deep freeze. I thought the ice would break at the beginning of March. Instead, we got a blizzard. What is the saying about March—in like a lion, out like a lamb? What about in like a wildebeest?

Thankfully, life doesn't stop in Siberia no matter how cold it gets. The people trudge on and find celebration in every moment. I change into a skirt, keeping on my wool tights, then bundle up again, smell the flowers one more time and head out to the community center.

I'm wearing my parka and, yes, finally, the Cossack boots. I can't believe I've been cold-pressed into wearing the furry boots out in public. On Women's Day, no less. Hence the skirt—my attempt at femininity.

I can't help but feel I'm an embarrassment to fashionable females around the globe.

I suppose it should cheer me that under all this padding, no one would really know that I'm a woman—I'm more of a thing. A blue, puffy thing in fuzzy footwear.

Now I'm depressed.

The community center is humming with conversation. Olya and I spent most of the morning packing away our supplies and hauling chairs for the afternoon program by the kindergarten and grade school. I find a seat.

"Oh, look at that Chloe," Nathan says as he sits down next to me.

"I know, isn't she adorable?" I wave to my daughter, who is wearing the traditional brightly colored dress of a Nanais native. Under her costume, she's also wearing three layers of snow clothes, but the costumes are designed to be large.

And her hair has grown enough for tiny, high pigtails to sprout above her headband.

She waves at me as the teachers line the students up to do a little dance. Maya sees her wave and follows with a wave of her own. She seems different lately. She smiles when I greet her in the yard.

Justin is also in line, fiddling with his shirt—a silver-and-blue pullover that of course goes over his own snow attire. He isn't smiling. He told me yesterday that boys aren't supposed to dance. Thank you for that, Chase.

"Where's Chase?" Nathan asks.

Yeah, good question. I scan the room. I don't see Olya or Vasilley, but there's Ulia sitting in the front row, and a number of the other ladies from Bible study. I can't look at Ulia without feeling like I'm an accomplice in her crime.

"Chase?" He's probably out skinning fish with his teeth or something.

Uh-oh. Did I say that out loud? Nathan is looking at me strangely.

"He'll be here," I say.

The music starts, and my little Nanais children skip in a circle, clapping and singing with their classmates.

"What are they saying?" I ask Nathan.

"I don't know. It's traditional Nanais. But probably something about Mom, and spring and fertility."

Perfect.

Justin isn't smiling, and he keeps kicking the boy in front of him. Apparently Chase—and Justin—are correct about the nondancing thing.

Chloe, however, is twirling, watching her skirt fly out. Oops. She falls. Oy, there goes the entire circle…

Just when should a mother get involved?

"You want me to get them?" Nathan asks as other mothers rise.

I sit there in silence, grimacing. See, this is part of motherhood—dealing with your child's foibles.

"By the way, I stopped by the house," Nathan says. "I went ahead and put your flowers in water."

I glance at him. He's giving me the strangest look. Almost…embarrassed. And pleased.

Like a man might look if he gave a girl flowers.

Oh. No.

"Did you… Are the roses from…"

"They were on sale in Khabarovsk. I had to wrap them inside my coat to keep them from freezing on the snowmobile ride north. I thought you needed something cheery to put a dent in these gray days. I wanted to thank you for letting me sleep on your sofa and invade your kitchen."

I dredge up a smile.

But inside, everything turns just a little colder.

"What's the matter, Josey?" Nathan's smile is gone, and he's frowning.

"Nothing," I say, but the catch in my voice gives me away. I try to turn up the wattage on my smile.

I probably look like a hyena.

Nathan isn't buying it.

I've got to come up with something. So I blurt out the first thing that comes to my mind.

"I think Ulia is going to leave Anton."

See, I'd make a horrible spy. At the first hint of bright lights, I'd spill everything.

Nathan lowers his voice (apparently he'd make a better spy than me). "What?"

"I'm not sure, but the way she's been talking…"

Now I feel sick, like the time I ratted out H for breaking the window at the high school during our Girl Scout meeting.

"Maybe I'm wrong."

Nathan scoots his arm around me, turns toward me, his face tight with concern. "What makes you think this?"

Um…okay, the way she thinks that Sophia should leave Ken for CC and, oh, boy, never mind.

"I'm probably jumping to conclusions. The *Banya* does make a girl a little thickheaded."

Nathan isn't appeased, though. "The last thing this village needs is the mayor's wife leaving him. Who knows what that kind of behavior will start?"

Oh.

"You'll tell me if you hear anything. I could talk to Ulia or Anton—"

"No, are you kidding?" My shrill voice, laced with panic, makes him wince. I lower it to a stage whisper. "Let's wait until we know for sure, and then we'll talk to him." Hey, not only is the *Banya* at stake, but let's remember that I'm dependent on

Anton's benevolence to keep our little village business running. No need to rush things or make a mountain out of a molehill.

Besides, Sophia is staying with Ken for now. Maybe things will turn out all right.

And really, I'm not sure any of this is our business anyway.

On stage, Chloe has untangled herself, and the teachers are helping the children down from the stage. Justin, however, is still wrestling with one of the boys.

Chloe is streaking toward us. I hold out my arms.

"Daddy!" she yells and barrels past me.

I turn.

Chase is sitting behind us. He doesn't look at me as he scoops up Chloe. But as he holds her tight, he closes his eyes.

As if he might be in pain.

I love this Siberian village at night. Did I actually say that? Did I use the word *love?* Okay, I did. I've fallen for Bursk the way one might fall for a mangy puppy with sad eyes or a worn-out teddy bear. Bursk does have charm. Take, for example, the stars blinking against a velvet black sky, undimmed by city lights. Or the pastoral elegance of snow piled up along a faded blue fence.

A husky trots out from a yard, looks at me and

heads down the street. Snow falls lazily from the sky and blankets the roofs and yards.

The village is quiet at this time of day, right before dinner, when light from the houses pushes through the cracks in the shutters, and the air smells of coal smoke from stoked furnaces. A cow lows, waiting for relief. I relish the walk home from the community center, alive with the excitement of our flourishing business. We have stayed late three nights in a row now to complete orders for Mother's Day, which is still nearly six weeks away. My eBay early reminders are paying off.

My feet crunch on the freshly fallen snow, and I stick my mittened hands in my pockets and burrow my nose into my wool scarf. I'm warm, despite the winds, because I now dress like an Arctic explorer.

Warm, of course, in body, rather than heart and soul because Chase is avoiding me like I've cut out his heart. Am not sure why—is he mad because of Ulia's secret? He said nothing when he left the community center, and nearly nothing since.

I open the door and am greeted by the smell of soup—perhaps chicken—simmering on the stove. Hanging my coat on the hook and unlacing my boots, I slip into wool slippers and enter the house.

I'm not surprised to see Nathan sitting at the table with Chase.

I am, however, taken aback by what they're up to.

They have a bowl of dough before them, and flour covers the table. Chase has a small rolling pin and is rolling out little circles the size of a biscuit. Nathan is filling them with meat and then gathering the edges and pinching them together to form a sort of dumpling.

They are works of art.

"What are you doing, and please tell me those are edible."

"Making *palmeni* for the soup," Nathan says, as if that should have been obvious. He looks up and smiles, though. "It's something else I just learned in Khabarovsk from my Russian landlady. *Palmeni* is delicious in chicken soup."

Chase's reception isn't as warm. "You're late. I was getting worried."

I'm going to translate that as, "I missed you, and didn't want anything bad to happen to you. Which makes me sort of irritable, and is a disguise for how much I love you."

I think every marriage could use some creative translation now and again.

"Can I help?" I ask as Chloe runs to me and hugs my leg. Justin rolls off the sofa, where he's watching a Russian cartoon, and jumps at me.

"Sure. You can roll out dough," Chase says as he scoots over. "I'll help Nathan make the *palmeni*."

I can do that, probably. My first few are misshapen disks, but after a while, I start to get the hang of it.

I'm mesmerized watching Chase. He takes the circle, plops in the meat, closes it with the other hand and deftly twists it into a ball. I always knew he was magic in the kitchen.

Only, it's not just his form I'm marveling at. It's his speed.

And the fact that Nathan has picked up his pace to match Chase's.

Chase is now twisting dumplings nearly as fast as I am rolling out the dough. Nathan grabs one from my hand and Chase gives him a dark look.

"That was mine."

"She handed it to me."

"No, she didn't. You reached over me to get it. It's not yours."

"Why would I do that?"

Chase says nothing, but I see his jaw grinding.

"I'll go faster," I say. "I can keep up with both of you."

"No!" they both bark.

O-kay.

"Maybe I'll just add this to the soup," Chase says, picking up the tray of dumplings.

"It's not ready yet. It has to be boiling. Don't rush it."

"It's ready. Don't worry, it'll be fine."

"You're going to turn them to mush and wreck the entire supper."

Chase dumps the *palmeni* into the pot. "It's my soup. Make your own."

He chucks the board into the sink and walks away.

Nathan looks at me, something on his face I can't read. Then he puts down the piece of dough he's been folding. "I'm going to go," he says, and gives me a tight smile.

I'm left alone in the kitchen with flour, half a bowl of dough and raw, ground chicken.

Perfect.

My *palmeni* don't exactly look like Chase's or Nathan's, but I finish half an hour later and put the board of little dumplings out in the entryway (aka our second freezer).

I ladle out the soup for the kids. Nathan was right—the dumplings are mushy.

Chase is sitting on the bed in the dark, peeling flour and dough off his hands.

"Hey," I say, sitting down next to him. "Good soup." (Liar, liar, but I'm using the adjective *good* in the sense that he is taking care of and providing for us, which is good. Thus, good soup. So, I'm not lying, if you take a step back and work with me here.)

He leans his head back against the wall and sighs. In the darkness, I see the fatigue on his face. "I think I'm beginning to understand why Siberian men feel overwhelmed."

I hear disappointment and frustration in his voice.

"I totally forgot Women's Day," he says, his eyes now cutting to mine. "I'm sorry."

My smile comes easily. "I forgive you."

"You shouldn't. You should be really angry. You should probably not talk to me, for at least a month or two."

Uh…okay. I reach out to take his hand, but he pulls it away.

"What are we doing here, anyway, GI?"

I'm sitting in the dark, brushing dough off my sheets. But perhaps he meant something bigger. "Helping?"

"Yeah, but how?" He leans forward. "How?"

I open my mouth to speak, but I can't find the right words. I have all sorts of cosmic platitudes, but none of them fit. Because we're improving their economic base? Teaching them how to use eBay? Putting a dent in their collective social depression?

"Nathan has had more of an impact than I could ever hope to." Chase is looking at me now, something strange in his eyes. "Maybe he's right. Maybe you *would* make a good pastor's wife."

Except, Chase, you're not a pastor.

I'm frowning at his words when he smiles. I see it's forced, and it makes my stomach hurt.

"I have to go to Moscow next week for a six-month recap for Voices International."

Bagels. I get bagels! I get to see Maggie! Okay,

maybe my priorities need a little adjusting. But…I get bagels! I flip on the light.

Chase is wearing a familiar grimace. The last time I saw it was when I confronted him about the ambush he and Marc planned. The one that brought me to Siberia.

Yeah, *that* look.

"What?"

"They only sent one ticket."

Of course they did. "That's okay."

"No it's not." He stares at me, then suddenly gets up, pulling me off the bed with him.

"Is Nathan still here?"

I shake my head.

"I'll be right back."

He yanks off his apron, wads it into a ball and chucks it into the kitchen on his way out. In a moment, he's back with Olya, who's grinning.

What's going on?

Chase kisses me, grabbing my hands and pulling me through the house. "Come with me. I want to show you something."

I glance at the kids, but Olya is already sitting with them, singing them a little song. Practicing for when Albena returns, I hope.

We bundle up and head outside. Night has fallen. Chase turns toward the river.

"Where are we going?"

He takes my hand, or rather, my lump, because it's hard to hold hands in mittens. But we shuffle and slide together down the street. It is getting warmer out, the days almost above freezing. Spring could be fighting for purchase.

I hear a sound in the distance, something like wind chimes. Overhead, the sky is perfect and clear, a million stars winking at us. There is little wind, and in the distance, a village dog howls.

The tinkling sound continues, a crackling, almost. I glance at Chase, and he's wearing a tiny grin but refuses to look at me.

"What is that?"

"Don't rush it," he says, but pulls me faster.

We reach the dip in the land the village calls the harbor. The snow is caked along the shore, and the moon glints off a thousand pieces of ice that move with the rhythm of the awakening water. The noise is louder now and I have to raise my voice to be heard above it. "What is that?"

"Close your eyes." Chase turns to me. "Close them, GI."

I do, and his arms go around my waist, his hands in the pockets of my coat, pulling me to him. His breath is in my ear. "What do you hear?"

"I don't know."

"Think. What does it sound like?"

I lean my head against his chest and let the sound

envelop me, slide through me. It's like raindrops on glass, or maybe glasses at a party, clinking.

"How about the railroad? Cars going past—click, click, click."

I listen, and yes, I hear it now. The railroad tracks, like the ones near his house in Gull Lake. I nod, and open my eyes. "Yes."

"It's the ice, flowing over itself, banging against each other like pieces of chandelier glass. The first time I heard it, you know what I thought of?"

I haven't a clue how to answer.

"That time we walked home from school. Remember? I wanted to walk home on the railroad tracks and you were scared, but I talked you into it?"

I start to smile. Yes, I would have done anything for Chase in fourth grade. And fifth. And sixth…

"And then the train started to come, and I got scared." He is holding my scarf now, his face close to mine. "You grabbed my hand and pulled me off the tracks, and we hid on the side until it passed."

"I didn't know you were scared."

"I was terrified. But I couldn't tell you that." He grins. "But I knew that day that I couldn't ever let you go. I held on to your hand and knew I loved you."

The wind burns my eyes, and they water a little. "It only took you fifteen years to tell me."

He shakes his head. "I've been trying to tell you ever since."

Oh. Well.

He brushes away a tear that escapes down my cheek. "But I'm not doing a very good job lately."

"Chase—"

"No, listen. I'm so sorry I missed Women's Day. And Valentine's Day. And that I scared you with Vasilley and my hunting trip. I'm sorry that I put you in the middle of nowhere without plumbing."

"I really don't care about the plumbing anymore." I smile up at him.

He doesn't smile back. "I do. And I know you miss Gull Lake." He looks out at the river.

I lean my head against his chest and his arms go around me. "It really does sound like the tracks. Like home."

We stand there a long while, as the moon and stars light up the ice, making it glitter like a river of gems.

"I did something. I hope it's okay."

I lean back and see a glint in his eyes. I'm almost afraid to ask.

"I asked H to come and visit you. You said she wanted to, so I e-mailed her. She's going to keep you company while I'm in Moscow. I can't take you to Gull Lake. But maybe I can bring Gull Lake to you."

He's grinning now, and it's shy, cute and perfect. "Happy ValeWomen's Day."

Oh, Chase. I stand on my toes and kiss him. Really kiss him.

He's smiling when I pull away. "I did a good thing?"

"You did." I pat his chest, right over his thumping heart. "You did real good."

Chapter Sixteen

H

H and I became friends in sixth grade when her father took over as head coach of the Gull Lake Gulls. She was determined never to date a football player.

I, however, lived for the whole sports enchilada.

Okay, I admit it, I was a football groupie. I sat on the sidelines, watched practice and memorized numbers (as in jerseys, not plays).

Mostly, however, I watched Chase. He started at halfback, moved to fullback, and when he began catching the ball on a regular basis, became an all-state wide receiver.

H, on the other hand, was a musician. She spent her time after school in band practice, and I'm not talking marching band. She put together her first garage band at the age of ten, by thirteen was writing her own songs, and by fifteen had gone on the road twice for summer gigs at local fairs.

H lives to play music. And not just the punk music she loves (and I don't understand), but nearly anything. Case in point—she accompanied our classical choir on the piano, punk hairstyle and all.

So I understand as she sits at my kitchen table, talking about Rex and his decree that she should hang up her guitar and "start acting like a married woman."

"Jon Bon Jovi is married. Does he have to give up his life?"

I still can't wrap my mind around the fact that my friend is here, in the middle of Siberia. Chase left two days ago, and Nathan met H yesterday in Khabarovsk and ferried her up to Bursk on the now-running boats.

She looks good, too. I can't believe I haven't seen her for three years. Last time, she had purple hair and was walking down the aisle with said oppressing husband. I had just given birth to the twins and was hoping my pregnancy weight might mysteriously vanish.

Things haven't changed much. She still has purple hair (although now the ends are tinged with a fetching midnight black, and she's gotten another piercing, right above her eye), and let's not talk about that pregnancy weight, shall we?

"He can't expect me to just surrender everything I am for him, can he?"

I'm probably not the best person to answer that, given that I'm pumping water to add to my above-the-sink holding chamber. "Does he want you to stop playing all together?"

"No, but he has a job teaching band at the high school and wants us to limit our gigs to the week-ends—in town."

I expected Chloe and Justin, having never seen anyone with purple hair, to shrink behind me when they met H. But that thing they say about children seeing past outside appearances to the heart must be true because Chloe went right up to her with kitty paws and purred.

Justin waved and said, *"Nu Pagadee!"*

I translated that very loosely to "He's really glad to meet you."

"So I moved out," H finishes, pouring herself more tea. She's tired, her droopy eyelids evidence of serious jet lag.

"Don't fall asleep," I say, sliding the sugar cubes toward her. "Let me teach you a Siberian trick Nathan showed me." I show her the cube-in-the-saucer treat, and the sugar rush revives her.

"I can't believe you came all the way to Siberia to see me." This is an understatement. It's like when Jasmine came to Moscow, only this is better because

I was in labor when Jasmine arrived and couldn't take time to show her how well I surfed the subway or bartered for food at the market. Finally, I get to show someone from back home that I really do have this Russia thing well in hand. Sort of.

"I can't believe you actually have an outhouse and a water pump." H leans back just in time for Chloe to climb into her lap. She twirls one of Chloe's pigtails around her finger. "Tell me about this guy who picked me up."

"Nathan? He's a friend of Chase's. He's from South Dakota and is planting a church here in town. I hold the weekly women's Bible study at my house."

"Still doing that Bible thing, huh?"

"Still doing it." I get up and pour water into the bucket above the sink. I splash myself as I pour and it's so cold it snags my breath. "The truth is, H, I'd never make it here without God's help."

"He'd *better* help. He got you into this mess."

Ah, yes, H—my lovable agnostic.

"There's a verse in James that says that when we go through trials, our faith is refined. Everything fake is burned off. I've heard that Siberia brings out the best—and the worst—in people. I'd like to hope it's made me a better person. And if that's the case, then yes, I'll be happy to blame God for that."

H is staring at me, an expression on her face I've never seen before.

"I don't get you, Josey. Your husband drags you all the way to the ends of the earth, and you're happy about it?"

Happy? Let's take a moment to define that. Happy is…what? Seeing Olya and Vasilley walk hand in hand down the street? Smelling soup on the stove when I tromp in from a blizzard? Listening to the crunch of snow as I walk through the village on a crisp, sparkly night?

Hearing Justin and Chloe laugh as they slide down the street on their sled. Snuggling in close to Chase's warm body as the frigid wind buffets our windows.

"Yeah, maybe I'm happy."

"Unca Nate!" Justin springs across the room as I see the door open. Nathan grabs him up and puts him on his hip.

"Hope I'm not too late to help with dinner." He holds up a bag of frozen chicken thighs and leg quarters.

Oh, yeah, right. Still, I appreciate his implication that I have something to do with food preparation in the house. "No, you're right on time. In fact, why don't you take on the cooking for tonight?"

He winks and moves past me as I sit down at the table again.

"Bush legs," he says as he pulls them out of the bag. "Named after President Bush One when he started sending humanitarian aid to Russia."

I'm assuming the trivia is for H, who is watching

Nathan with some interest. He pours water into a pot, sets it on the stove to boil and adds a bouillon cube.

Now, just for the record, I *have* started to do more cooking. All this watching Chase and Nathan over the past few months has taught me much in the way of culinary skills. I'm now a whiz at peeling potatoes. And opening a can of tomato sauce? I'm a master.

Nathan disappears into the entryway and I hear him rustling around in the potato bin. When we arrived and Chase informed me we had two fifty-kilogram bags of potatoes, I thought, what, are we feeding the Vikings' defensive line?

Yeah, we're on our third bag. Ask me how to prepare potatoes and I have flashbacks to Bubba Gump Shrimp—baked, boiled, fried, mashed… I'll be happy if I never see another potato.

Nathan returns, potatoes cradled in his arms. He dumps them on the table. "Start peeling, soldier."

I laugh, grabbing a bowl and a potato peeler.

If Russia holds the market on anything, it's potato peelers. This one molds perfectly into my palm. And I have developed the hand strength of a sixty-year-old babushka. If I *was* planning to eat potatoes again once I got stateside, I would bring this back to America with me.

Nathan sits down and grabs his own potato. Soon we're racing and have piled up naked potatoes on the table.

"When I was a kid," Nathan says, "my mother would make potato pancakes on Sundays. I would peel all Saturday afternoon. I think she did it on purpose, to make my hands sore for Sunday, so they'd stay folded." He laughs. I love Nathan's laugh. It's warm and deep.

H is watching me, holding her teacup. "I remember Josey hiding out on Saturdays, when Jasmine and her mom rolled out three billion pecan buns." She quirks an eyebrow.

"I would have rather mowed the lawn than bake." I finish the potatoes and dump them back into the pot for Nathan to wash. "I was never a chef."

"Although you make a mean chocolate-chip cookie," Nathan says, picking up the pot. He releases water from the upper chamber and lets it run into the sink. "And you're pretty good at everything else."

His compliment turns my face warm. He's so sweet.

Justin drapes himself over my lap. "I need to go out."

Right. I bundle him into a jacket and we tromp out to the outhouse. The sun is low, but the smell of spring hangs in the air. No longer do my ears hurt or my sinuses sting when I leave the house. The streets are getting muddy. And I smell a freshness, a new life, in the breeze.

Out like a lamb.

H is outside when we finish, leaning against the

house, smoking a cigarette. I nudge Justin inside and stay with her while she finishes.

She is wrapped in an army jacket, a purple scarf and black boots that lace up to her knees—hey, I have a pair of those!

"Nathan come here a lot?" she asks, watching the sky.

"About once a week," I say. "He's a great cook."

"Mmm-hmm," she says. She takes another pull on her cigarette. The wind suddenly lifts my hair and whistles in my ears. Maybe I was wrong about that spring thing.

"I'm not sure I should be taking marriage advice from you," she says, blowing out smoke through her nose.

Her words hurt and I'm too stunned to respond.

She drops her cigarette, smashing it with her boot. "I think I understand, now, exactly why you're happy in the middle of Siberia."

"What?" I stare at her, something sour in my chest. She raises a spike eyebrow and says nothing. "Nathan? Oh, please. H. He's Chase's friend—"

"He seems to be your friend, too."

"He stays here—cooks for us."

She shakes her head. "You never cease to surprise me." Her tone suggests that's not in a good way.

"Or you, me," I say and tramp inside to be with my true friends.

* * *

I'm not sure what I did to make H angry, but she's treating me like the time I asked her if she was still going out with Jeff, and if not, would she mind if I took a shot at him? Offended. Betrayed.

Okay, yes, I broke the universal girlfriend code with that smooth move. But why she acts now like I've sold her out for a song… Her concern about Nathan is ridiculous—she'll see that soon enough.

More than that, I've done everything I can to show her a good time. Nathan and I taught her to make *palmeni,* and we showed her around the village, stopping in at Olya's for some of her delicious plum *perogue.* Yes, I opted out of *banya* (c'mon—it's one thing to get naked with a bunch of Russians, but I'm definitely not going there with my own kind!), but I did spend the afternoon making birchbark boxes with her and *introducing* her to the Banya Girls. Nathan had a delicious pot of tomato borscht waiting when we got home. And one night, we invited Maya over for potato soup, and we spent the night laughing over stories of the munchkins at the preschool. I know we don't live the high life here in Siberia, but we're keeping her warm and fed.

So there's no need for the pout fest as we sit outside *detski-sod,* waiting for the twins to finish for the morning.

"How's Lew?"

My party friend, turned football coach, used to be one of H's pals, too.

"He left his wife for the secretary at the school." Oh.

"And Jasmine? Do you talk to her much?"

"Not since she moved to Minneapolis. She left your parents to run Berglund Acres. There's talk of them selling."

This news grabs me by the throat and I'm trying to breathe. Apparently H has the heart of an executioner, because she says nothing to soften that blow.

She throws her cigarette down, grinding it into the mud. Spring has arrived in the span of five days. I can even see the smallest of buds on the trees. Birds occasionally sing. And, I've gone back to my lace-up Italian boots.

"Sell Berglund Acres?" My voice is barely more than a whisper.

H crosses her arms over her chest, watching the kids, her face hard. "Yep. I guess you can't count on anything lasting anymore."

I frown at her, but at that moment, Chloe runs over. "Mommy!" She hugs my legs and I swoop her up and set her on my lap.

Oh, Chloe. "Honey, what happened?" She's wearing her leggings and a pair of winter snow pants, but she's soaked through.

"I go *ah ah!*" She covers her mouth with her

hands, her eyes wide, the little drama queen. But this is not good.

"What is '*ah ah*'?" H asks, eyeing my expression.

"It's Russian for she wet her pants." I put her down, take her hand and walk over to Maya. Sometimes we chat long enough for me to walk her home to the community center.

Or occasionally she comes over for tea. She's even hinted that she might be seeing someone, and by her blush, I know it's not the man who left her bleeding three months ago.

"Chloe had an accident," I say in Russian.

Maya nods. "She doesn't have a change of clothes here."

Of course not, because my daughter hasn't wet her pants in months. "Okay, time to go home." I turn and see H coming toward me.

She, by the way, hasn't let Siberia stand in the way of fashion. She's wearing her high-top boots, a leather jacket that looks like it might be from some 1960s vintage rack and has painted her lips black.

Yes, we got quite a few looks the first day out on the town.

"Can you hold on to Chloe while I get Justin?" I hand over Chloe.

H smiles down at her. "Did you make naughty in your pants?"

"H! We don't call it 'naughty.' We don't want her

to get a complex. She made a mistake, an error, a misjudgment."

"Right." H's smile dims. "Sorry." But I can tell by her tone she doesn't mean it. "Did you 'error' in your pants, sweetie?"

I roll my eyes, turn and scan the yard. "Do you see Justin anywhere?"

"Mmm-hmm."

I glance at H. "Where?"

"Oh, he's the one making a 'misjudgment' with his middle finger at the teacher." She nods toward a group of kids.

Sure enough, in the center is my darling three-year-old. Giving one of the elderly teachers the bird.

Lovely.

"Now." H turns to me, a sweet smile on her face. "Would we call that making naughty?"

"Justin!"

My voice scares every kid on the playground. Maya stares at me, wide-eyed, as I stalk over and grab Justin's hand.

He looks up, terrified, having no idea what he did wrong. Fortunately no one else does, either, except H and me, since the Russians have different sign language. Still, I'm horrified, and wondering where he learned that. Not from me.

Perfect. I have a wet daughter, a hoodlum son and now I'm the Hulk of the play yard.

I walk past H, who regards me with a raised eyebrow.

It's a long, quiet trek home through the mud. The streets are swamps, and the sidewalks, if you can call them that, are brown-slush trails through patches of matted grass. Every previously hidden empty vodka bottle and newspaper wrapper is now exposed by the receding dirty snow.

Chloe falls and plasters herself with mud. I haul her up by the arm with H following, and drag my two delinquents home.

Where I find Chase in the yard, just getting in from the ferry. He looks refreshed, clean-shaven, his hair soft and conditioned as if he's just spent a week in…civilization. Without crabby children and a grumpy what's-her-problem houseguest.

He has a life.

I have a village.

Still, despite my simmering sense of injustice, I want to cry with relief. I trudge toward him and lay my head on his chest. He throws one arm around me, still holding his satchel.

"Hey, GI." He kisses the top of my head. I still have a firm grip on the hooligans, who are jumping up and down. "Miss me?"

Desperately. I didn't realize just how much until this moment.

"Hey, H. How are we doing?"

H trudges by, shooting me a look. "Naughty. We're all very naughty."

Dear Jasmine,

Hello from Siberia! I hope you're liking your new home in Minneapolis. H was here for a week and she caught me up on the Gull Lake happenings. Sounds like you and Milton are making quite a go at this kringle business.

I never thought I'd say this, but I'm glad H is gone. She spent the whole week angry at me—and I don't even know what I did!

Chase had a great week at Voices International. Apparently, they're thinking of renewing our term.

Please, God, save me from Siberia.

It's not that I don't like it. There are times when I know, without a doubt, that I am supposed to be here. Like yesterday, when Olya came over with a plate of raspberry *blini*. (By the way, you'd love *blini*—little flat pancakes rolled up and filled with jelly, not unlike crepes, but yummier.) She sat down at the table, her brown eyes glowing. And then she fished out of her pocket…airplane tickets. Three of them—two round trips and one from Moscow to Khabarovsk.

She's going to get Albena, thanks to the

money she made from Secrets of Siberia. Maybe helping Olya was the reason I was sent to Russia, I don't know. But as we sat in the kitchen and cried, something went through me, a deep *whoosh* of joy. I wanted to capture that feeling and hold on tight.

I love seeing lives changed.

Nathan—I know I've mentioned him—said that I'd be a great pastor's wife. I can't get the words out of my head. Sometimes I think I'd like to be a pastor's wife. Except for the fact that Chase isn't a pastor.

But I am hoping that at least I'm exhibiting pastor's wife qualities—humility, gentleness, patience, peace. Even, perhaps, submission.

Chase has been different since returning from Moscow. For one, he's keeping a journal. I think he must have started it before Moscow, because he's already halfway through it, but still, every night I see him scribbling in it, his brow furrowed. It reminds me of when we shared study hall, and he'd scratch out his English papers. I would normally go through and fix all his spelling errors, but he won't let me near the journal. Okay, yes, I tried. It was lying on the bed and I was just going to move it, but Chase came up behind me and snatched it out of my hand.

"Not quite ready yet," he said. As if perhaps someday he would be?

Chloe is back to wetting her pants every day. I'm not sure why. Did Amelia ever have a relapse? I'm not even going to tell you what Justin did last week in the playground. Let me just say that it involved obscene sign language. Where he picked that up from, I have no idea.

Only three more months. Three.

Tell Mom and Dad not to sell Berglund Acres. I'm coming home.

I just hope Chase is with me.

Love, Josey

Chapter Seventeen

Matchmaker

Oh, Sophia, you're so stupid! Don't you see that Ken doesn't really love you? And that woman who just hired you—that's his mistress! Run, run as fast as you can, back to CC!

I'm squinting through the static, trying to translate the Russian, and barely notice the knock on my door over the noise of the washing machine churning.

Run, Sophia! Follow your heart!

The knock comes again.

Shoot, not now!

Okay, yes, I might be a little addicted to the goings-on of *Santa Barbara*, but it's not my fault.

The Banya Girls started it. And a gal has to keep

up her side of the conversation. Especially to get her mind off the nakedness.

I am relieved to report, also, that Ulia seems to have dropped her complaints about Anton. So I might have been overreacting. Like I said, I blame the steam.

It's not like my to-do list is overflowing out here in Mudville. H isn't responding to my e-mail, and we have a full stock of birchbark crafts, now catalogued and stored at the community center. Olya has gone to Moscow and Chase has commandeered my computer to write his analysis on the Nanais for Voices International.

Justin and Chloe are still attending *detski-sod,* but I've taken to sending extra clothes with Chloe.

"Dzhozhy?" Olya says, now inside and standing at my door.

"Olya!" Except… Oh, no, Sophia don't go in there if you don't want your heart broken. Ken is there, with—

Olya clears her throat.

I look over.

And standing behind my friend's legs, peeking out with giant, luminous brown eyes, is a little girl. She has short brown hair and is wearing a white hand-knitted sweater and a black skirt over a pair of tights. She's all dressed up to meet the neighbor.

"Albena?"

Olya grins and turns to sweep up her five-year-old. "Say hello, *lapichka*."

The little girl turns and hides her face in her mother's shoulder. I'm consumed with emotion, words completely gone as I take in Olya's face.

She looks transformed. Gone, without a trace, is the woman I met six months ago, broken, afraid, despairing. This woman is full of life, full of hope.

I can do nothing else but come close and hug her. "Your daughter is beautiful," I say, when I'm finally able.

"I know," Olya says, pride in her eyes. "We just got back."

I turn off the television and put on a pot of water for tea.

Tea, by the way, has become one of my specialties. I'm very, very good at pouring a cup of water and dunking in a little baggie.

We sit at my table, and my eyes are on Albena, this formerly missing chunk of Olya's heart, as Olya tells me about her trip.

She's never been to Moscow, but as she talks, old memories churn in me, and I miss it—the Gray Pony, a karaoke place where I sang "Stand by your Man" to Chase. And the subway, where I got my traveling legs. The bagel shop, where God continually reminded me that He cares about the little things, and my friends Sveta and Thug, who took care of me, even if I said I didn't need it.

The tea water whistles, and I can't believe that I've made a new life here in Siberia. And that, despite my desperate moments, it's starting to feel like home.

I pour the water into cups, and Olya and I sip together. I laugh as Olya gives Albena a sugar cube dipped in tea.

"Did Chase have a good meeting in Moscow?" Olya asks.

"I think so." I'm not sure—he's been pretty quiet since his return. Writing in his notebook, which calls to me to read it. But I'm not going to. Even if it should, say, accidentally fall into my hands, open, while I was, perhaps, dusting. Under the bed. "He's trying to figure out a way for the men in the village to create an economic future."

Olya kisses the top of Albena's head. "Maybe it's not from the outside that change will happen." Her eyes are shining. "But from the inside. Vasilley hunts for me, not for money. And now, Albena."

She presses her hand over mine. "You gave us our future, Dzhozhy."

Her words inflate my ego too much, but they warm me all the same. "I'm really going to miss you when I leave."

She withdraws her hand. Her expression turns hollow. "You're leaving?"

Uh, well… "Our project is over at the end of May. I think we're going back to America."

She swallows, a panicked expression on her face.

Albena spills tea down her sweater and starts to cry. Olya grabs a napkin and tries to dab it. But it's too late, there's already a growing stain on the shirt.

Olya gets up, tears in her eyes. "I should have expected that."

I am not sure if she's referring to Albena and the tea…or me.

Suddenly my eyes are filling, too. "I don't want to leave," I hear myself saying.

Before I can qualify those words, however, I hear the front door open and heavy feet coming inside.

I get up just as Chase opens the kitchen door and stands on the threshold. His expression is dark, and for a second, I'm scared something terrible has happened.

"What?"

He glances at Olya and opts to speak English. "Ulia left Anton." Then he lowers his voice and says, "And Anton is saying it's all your fault."

Does anyone think that's fair? Just because a woman leaves her neglectful, sullen husband, I don't think it's right to blame it on the first forward-thinking foreigner that happens by.

Even if said foreigner did somehow manage, inadvertently, to arm the woman with her own supply of cash with which to leave.

But that's not Chase's biggest issue at the moment. As he ushers Olya and Albena from the house and closes the door behind them, I see something darker in his eyes.

"Ulia said, and I quote Anton, 'If Josey can leave her husband for someone else, I can too.'"

There's more than anger in his eyes. There's hurt. As if he believes her?

"What on earth are you talking about?"

Chase shucks his jacket and hangs it on the chair, then runs a hand through his hair. His jaw is tight. He turns his back to me.

"Please tell me it's not true."

What's not true? I'm on my feet and I touch his back, but he shrugs me off and stalks away from me.

"Chase, I don't know what you're talking about." Besides, I thought he already knew about Ulia after overhearing my conversation with Nathan. Or… maybe not.

He rounds on me. "You and Nathan. Apparently he spent most of his time here when I was in Moscow."

"H was here—"

His stricken look, as if he's seen into another realm and is horrified by his vision, cuts off my words.

"Naughty. That's what H meant—"

"She was talking about the fact that our son made a rude gesture to the teacher at *detski-sod!*"

"Really, Josey? And why would he do that? Maybe

because he's stressed out? Maybe because he's thinking his mother and father are going to split up?"

"He's three, Chase! He didn't even know what he was doing." But his words have broadsided me. Split up?

I press my hand to my stomach and reach out for a chair. "There is nothing going on between Nathan and me."

"I heard you talking on International Women's Day. I thought, no, it can't be me. They aren't talking about me—"

"What? What?" I'm thinking back to the event, trying to figure out… Uh-oh. I remember my stage-whispered, panicked words to Nathan. *Wait until we know for sure, and then we'll talk to him.* Maybe he had heard our conversation. But not enough.

"I was talking about Ulia. And Anton."

But Chase isn't listening. He's got his hands over his face, shaking his head. "I'm so blind. I'm so stupid."

"Stop it, Chase. Nathan and I are just friends."

But he's beyond listening. In fact, I'm not even a part of the conversation anymore. "I let it happen. I invited him into my house. I saw the way he talked to you, listened to you and paid attention to you."

I'm starting to see his point. Nathan *did* pay attention to me. Like bringing a turkey for New Year's. And flowers on Women's Day.

Making soup on a regular basis.

The increasingly frequent visits.

You'd make the perfect pastor's wife.

My mouth feels as if a hedgehog has climbed inside, all muddy and thick.

"Chase, I—"

He turns, his eyes red-rimmed. "I can't trust you, can I?"

"That's not fair, Chase."

"Apparently, I've done exactly what the elders warned me against. Here I was, fighting for your business, telling the elders to let the women have their *hobby*—"

"Hobby? You're calling it a hobby? I'd say that the several thousand dollars we've brought into this community is more than a hobby."

"But Anton is right. It's more than that. Maybe you are exactly what he says—a bad influence on this community. And thanks a lot for proving to everyone that I'm an idiot. So much for them ever listening to *my* ideas."

I'm speechless, every thought wiped clean out of my mind as I watch him snatch up his jacket and throw it on. He breathes hard and I'm still trying to conjure up a coherent thought in response to his tirade when he rounds on me one last time.

"I'll tell you one thing, Josey. Your little home business stops. Today."

He's out the door before I finally find the right words.

Not on your life, pal.

* * *

I live in Santa Barbara.

So maybe we don't have swimming pools and breathtaking vistas of the Pacific Ocean, but the river is free-flowing, the lilac trees are budding and the Banya Girls know how to blow off steam.

Or at least create it.

It's a hotbed of gossip and chaos in Burrrsk, and apparently, I'm exactly what Chase accuses me of being: the ringleader.

Just because a girl sits naked in a sauna and occasionally nods at the conversation around her—mostly to keep her head from filling with fog—doesn't mean she endorses the torrid affairs of others.

Apparently, that's exactly what Ulia was having. One version of the story is that a tall, handsome ferryboat captain from Khabarovsk whisked her away at the first sign of spring. Another story says she's upriver, sailing to the mouth of the Amur with a salmon fisherman.

The only thing we know for sure is that no one has seen her. And that she took off with her all the cash she'd earned from the sale of her birchbark crafts.

I'm sitting in the steam room, listening to the women assail their husbands, sure that I shouldn't say a word.

"Misha says I can't go to the community center anymore," says tall, thin Anya.

"So does my husband," says another woman. "And I was planning on remodeling our kitchen."

I wonder what that looks like without plumbing…

"Igor took all my money and hid it."

I purse my lips at the words.

"What should we do, Dzhozhy?"

You're asking me? I shake my head. I'm the last person who has answers, given my own crumbling marriage. Chase has practically moved in with Anton, although he slinks in every night like a jackal. I haven't seen Nathan in two weeks, and I'm dearly hoping that he didn't rap on the door looking for shelter and get a coal shovel to the head.

No, Chase wouldn't do that. Would he?

"I don't know," I finally mumble, because everyone has fallen silent.

"Are you going to leave Chase?" a voice pipes up from the back.

"Of course not!" My tone is stronger than the question deserves, but I wouldn't think of leaving Chase.

Or running home to Berglund Acres, where I'm loved.

Accepted.

And where there are flushing toilets.

"I'm not leaving Chase," I repeat quietly. But I wish the words didn't feel so far away, so outside my body.

"But you love Nathan, don't you?"

These words, from Olya, shock me.

"Of course not," I say with surprise. I mean, I love him like a brother or a friend. I breathe in the thick air, turning over my memories. It's true that Nathan makes me laugh. And he listens to me. And compliments me. And he's smart and full of wisdom and knowledge. Of *course* I like him.

"We saw the way he looked at you at the Women's Day celebration. He had his arm around you," Anya says.

"He picks up your kids at *detski-sod.*"

"And he's here more than he's ever been since you showed up."

"I think he's cute."

Oh, that's helpful. But as I listen, I see their point. From all outward appearances, it does seem as if Nathan and I have a little…something. I close my eyes, and the truth rushes in. Maybe I did enjoy his visits more than I should have. Maybe I enjoyed his attention, appreciated that he saw me, listened to me, enjoyed my children. I let him open a door that should have stayed locked. Maybe that's what H was trying to tell me.

Oh, Chase.

I wince, remembering the hurt in his voice and eyes.

"I think you need to be like Sophia and follow your heart," Anya says.

I am not Sophia and I don't live in a soap opera. Anymore.

"I'm not leaving Chase," I say again, and this time the words come from clarity and settle inside.

"What about the business? They can't just take

that away from us, can they? It's our future," Olya says, sounding panicked.

I glance at her through the curtain of my wet hair. I feel like I'm in grade school. Boys against girls.

Except, somehow, we all have to win.

I get up, step out, take the cold plunge before I lose my nerve and then hit the showers.

Lord, please help me fix this.

God must be on Chase's side. (After careful examination, I wouldn't blame Him. I do look guilty. But He knows my heart, right? I just had a little issue with boundaries.) It's so utterly unfair that I find Nathan on my doorstep when I get home, his duffel slung over his shoulder.

"What are you doing here?" I hiss, looking around to see who might be watching. Suddenly I feel like I'm naked and running down the center of the street screaming, "Adulterer! Adulterer!" I feel dirty. And sneaky. "Chase is going to be here any minute!"

Josey, you are making it worse. Please, mouth, stop.

"So?" Nathan smiles at me.

Perhaps I imagined his feelings for me. Or maybe he's just a giant faker. I narrow my eyes at him.

"You don't care that Chase is about to come home…and…" What, interrupt us? There is nothing to interrupt!

"Is this a game? Is it Chase's birthday? Did I forget a surprise party?" Nathan asks, confused.

Oh, good grief. "Where have you been for the last two weeks? I thought you'd been buried in a potato field."

"Huh?" Nathan slides the duffel down off his shoulder. "Are you okay?" He peers at me like he can see deep inside my soul and identify the alien that has taken possession of my body. Josey, are you in there?

"Stop it. Don't pretend like you have no idea what's going on."

He raises his hands, as if in surrender. "Okay, you got me. I'll stop pretending and say it right out. I have no idea what you're talking about." He lowers his hands and shrugs.

Now it's my turn to peer deep inside.

"What is it, Josey?"

I shake my head in disgust. "You haven't a clue that the entire town thinks we've been having an affair and that Ulia left Anton because of it?"

He actually turns a little white.

Clearly he didn't have that clue.

"What?" he says, and there's something wrong with his voice. He takes a step back from me, like I'm emanating some toxic gas.

"Oh, stop. Like you haven't been super nice to me, complimenting me, and bringing me flowers and a turkey and making me dinner—"

"I'm staying on your sofa, for crying out loud. What's a guy supposed to do to show his thanks?" But his color hasn't returned.

"And what's with the 'you'd make a great pastor's wife' line? I'm not married to a pastor!"

"But you should be!"

His frustrated tone stops me in my tracks. He shakes his head, dialing his voice back to normal. "I mean Chase. *Chase* should be a pastor. He has it in him—the desire to help and to change lives—and I think all this frustration over the past year is telling him exactly that."

I blink at him.

"And it's not every man who has a woman like you who would be willing to sacrifice and minister to people who live way out in places like Siberia."

See, it's statements like these that get us in trouble. I don't know whether to strangle Nathan or thank him.

"And I should know," he says, looking away from me. "My fiancée broke it off with me when she found out God had called me to be a missionary in Siberia." His voice is tight, and when he looks back at me, I see pain in his eyes. "Chase is a lucky man. I would be the last guy in the world to mess that up."

Oh.

"In fact, the reason I've been up here so much is… well, I've been seeing someone."

He's turning red now, and I can't help an instant flare of annoyance. I *live* to play matchmaker, and here he found someone right under my nose? Without my help? "Who?"

"It doesn't matter. What *does* matter is that I'm

sorry I…damaged our friendship. And put you and
Chase on the skids. And made you feel uncomfort-
able. And made the whole town believe a lie. I was
just trying to encourage." He picks up his duffel and
slings it back over his shoulder.

Oh, Nathan.

But I don't stop him as he walks past me, and I
stand there in the mud long after he's gone.

Chapter Eighteen

A Blank Slate

The house is quiet when I enter. Chase agreed to pick up the kids from *detski-sod,* and I only hope he hasn't forgotten.

The hum of the furnace fills the house. Chloe's kitties are taking a nap on the sofa. Justin has left a toy car on the television set. I go into my bedroom, pull up a pillow and lie on the bed, staring at the ceiling.

Now what, Lord?

Humble, gentle, patience, peace.

Yeah, I'm real pastor's-wife material. Brought real peace to this little community. I'm just a stellar example of tranquillity and homemaking.

I put the pillow over my mouth to stifle the scream I feel building inside.

But what were my choices, exactly? Throw myself over the threshold and demand we return to Gull Lake? Or follow my Vagabond Hero to the far reaches of the world for yet another adventure?

Can you fix this, Lord?

I roll over, and there it is, evidence that I have it all together. My Bible, with the bookmark in Ephesians where it's been for, oh, say, four months?

I sit up and open it to where I left off.

My eyes fall on Ephesians 5. You know what I'm talking about. The Submission chapter.

Perfect. Submission is what got me into this mess. It was Chase's idea to invite Nathan into our lives.

Chase's idea to let him cook.

And Chase gave his thumbs-up to me helping Nathan with the women's Bible study.

So I was a willing accomplice. Another perspective might say I was submitting.

I'm starting to think that perhaps I've misunderstood all this submission stuff. Maybe it's not about going along with everything that enters my beloved husband's head.

I track back to the Humble verse and read Ephesians 5:1-2. "Be imitators of God, therefore, as dearly loved children and live a life of love, just as Christ loved us and gave himself up for us as a fragrant offering and sacrifice to God."

I stare at the verse for a moment and suddenly I see. *Live a life of love, just as Christ loved us.*

The win-win.

Because maybe this isn't about who will surrender and who will dominate, but rather about finishing the race together, side by side.

I must be on to something because I flip back to the submission verse and discover that the amplified words say, "Adapt yourself to your husbands, as a service to the Lord."

As a service to the Lord.

Don't know why I missed that earlier.

But I see it now and I realize what I have to do.

I slip to the floor, kneeling beside the bed. It's not often I find myself here, and perhaps that's part of the problem.

"Lord, I've made a mess of things here, but you know I didn't mean to. However, I want to serve you. And if that means serving Chase, then I'll do it." I take a breath. "Help me to see Chase and love him the way you do."

I hear the door opening, someone calling my name.

I meet Olya at my bedroom door. She's sweaty and breathing hard. She doubles over and clutches her knees. "Dzhozhy, come quickly!" She stands up and grabs my hand. "The community center is on fire!"

* * *

As we run up to the community center, the fire practically growls as it licks up the sides of the building and rolls over the top. Sparks spit from the flames and fly over the heads of the onlookers. The gray dusk of the night is lit up like high noon as flames pour out of windows and twine into the sky.

"Where are my kids?" I look over to the *detski-sod* yard, but it's empty. I see others—Misha and Anya's two children are huddled in fear around their legs. Where's Maya? What if she's inside?

"Have you seen Maya or Chase?" I direct my question to Vasilley, who is standing near me in the crowd. He looks at me with incomprehension, but I see relief wash over him when he realizes Olya is right behind me.

Anton is standing away from the crowd, in the street, his hands in his pockets. Watching.

I turn back to the fire, a sick feeling in my gut. All our hard work in cinders. All the hopes and dreams of the women, of the village, turned to ash.

I stalk over to Anton. "How did this happen?"

He lifts a shoulder and I suddenly want to send my fist into his face. This is no time for humble. Or gentle.

"Anton, I swear, if you know anything—"

"Josey!"

I turn and see a blackened-faced Chase running toward me. Tears, probably from the smoke in his eyes, run down his face. His jacket is smoky black, and he's covered in mud. "I can't find Chloe!"

I stare at him for what seems like a long moment. I can't seem to process his statement. "You… Where did you last see her?"

He is wild-eyed. "We came out of the community center, and I told her and Justin to stay by the fence—"

"You didn't stay with her? She's three!" I take off, running toward the blaze, but it's so hot it pushes me back.

Chase catches me around the waist. "Maya was with her! But she ran away from her—"

I hit his shoulder and yank his arm off my waist. "Maya!"

I see her, holding Justin by the hand, tears running down her face, mesmerized by the flames. "Maya! Where's Chloe?"

She looks at me, but her eyes are vacant. I remember that this isn't the first fire she's been through in her life.

Oh, God, help us all.

"Chloe!" I scoop up Justin as I run toward the *detski-sod.*

Please, God, just keep her safe, wherever she is.

The blaze is burning bright as I hurdle the knee-high fence encircling the play-yard. I hear breath behind me and then Chase passes me. "Chloe!"

Where would she go when she's afraid? My mind spins…

Lord?

The playhouse. She loves the playhouse. I turn toward it and see that Chase is already there. He's on his hands and knees, crawling inside.

I hear her voice and it turns my knees weak. "Daddy!"

Chloe.

Chase pulls her out, and her arms are tight around his neck, her legs around his waist. His face is buried in her soft blond curls.

I've reached them now, and Chase looks up, grabbing me and Justin and pulling us to him.

For a second, we just breathe relief. Then we move apart. We both look closely at Chloe, scanning up and down as if assessing for damage. "Are you okay?" Chase asks her.

Chloe nods.

He's the one who looks like he's walked through Hades. "What happened to you?"

He shakes his head, wraps one arm around me and Justin and holds me close again. He's still shaking a little. "I'm really sorry, GI."

I nod, but can't find any words. He takes my hand in a death grip and we walk back to the crowd watching the blazing community center. The fire takes down the front wall with an explosion of flame and sparks. "Why isn't anyone putting it out?"

"They don't have a fire department."

I stare at him. "So if something catches fire, it just burns down?"

"You found her!" Maya runs up and takes Chloe from Chase, hugging her tight.

Chase gives me a grim look. "I tried to rescue some of the crafts."

I blink at him, trying to wrap my mind around his words. He must see my confusion.

"After I got the kids out, I went in and tried to save a few boxes." I see now the sweat on his face and realize he wasn't crying but perspiring from the fierce heat. "I'm so sorry. All your hard work, destroyed."

In the face of that huge fire, he tried to salvage the village livelihood. Maybe, in fact, the man does have the heart of a pastor.

And when he thought Chloe was gone, he had the heart of a father.

Just like that, I see it. The long hours spent listening to the elders talk about their lives. The disgusting vodka he consumed (or not) so Vasilley would invite him hunting. The days he picked up the kids at *detski-sod* and made me soup. Even my beautiful, sweet-smelling outhouse. All Chase, trying to love me, to love others.

"It's okay about the crafts, Chase," I say quietly. "I was going to close the business, anyway."

He looks down at me, pain on his face. "Because of my stupidity?"

"No. I mean, I wouldn't call it—"

I'm interrupted by Anton. "There she is! Arrest her!"

For a second, the voice yanks me back to a place in my past and I stiffen. Me? I didn't do it!

But Anton strides past me and grabs Maya's arm. "She set the fire!"

Behind him are the locally appointed militia officers, looking at one another, not sure what to do.

Maya yanks her arm free, rage and fear in her voice. "What? I didn't set this!"

"Where were you this afternoon when the fire started? I checked with your preschool—they said you left early." Anton's voice is low, and it contains enough hatred to prickle my skin.

The memory of the night Maya showed up at my house, bloodied and afraid, rushes at me and I stare at Anton, horror creeping up my spine.

Who, really, was having the affair—Ulia or Anton? Something dark grips my stomach, twists it.

It's not my place to make accusations, but I do know who is innocent here. "Maya didn't do this." I glance at her, stepping closer. She meets my eyes with surprise. "Maya *wouldn't* do this." That much I know.

"What do you know about this?" He refers to Maya with a bad word, one that even I know. I feel slapped. "She probably killed her husband, too."

I hear myself gasp, and all possible retorts vanish from my open, speechless mouth. Maya goes pale and shakes her head.

"She didn't do it, Anton." The voice comes from behind Maya, and it's one I know, one I've come to recognize without looking.

Ulia shoves her hands into the pockets of a green army coat. I barely recognize her in a scarf and jeans. "You know she didn't set this."

Anton's face hardens. "How would you know?"

"Because she was at Sasha's house, bringing her food."

Sasha, Sasha. I'm scanning my brain— Oh, Sasha, their widowed daughter-in-law with two little children. I look at Maya and see the truth on her face. Maya's been bringing food to someone in need. Reaching out beyond herself, her pain. Pride and affection surge through me, and I can barely stop myself from throwing my arms around her.

"She does it nearly every day. I see it because I'm staying next door, at Leonid's house."

From behind her, a man who could be the Other Man puts his hand on Ulia's shoulder. Oh, that's bold.

Except that Anton looks up at him and nods, as if to say, "Hey, it's okay that you stole my wife, let's all be friends."

I'm so confused.

"I thought you left me," he says quietly.

Uh, me, too! Me, too!

Ulia's voice softens. "I wanted to. I was tired of us. Tired of wishing for something better. But I love

you, Anton, and I don't want to leave you. I know
about your mistakes…but I miss you, and it only
took a couple of weeks staying with my brother to
figure that out."

Oh, brother. Oh. *Brother.*

Again, I feel like I'm in the middle of a *Santa
Barbara* episode, because Anton's eyes actually get
glassy. And he takes a step toward his wife. "I'm so
sorry. I didn't mean to cause all this. I thought you'd
left me because…" His gaze cuts to Maya.

Maya shrinks back a bit, and I get it.

He thought Maya told Ulia about their affair.
Okay, that was a leap, but when you're in the
middle of a soap opera, those kinds of leaps are
easy. Expected, even. In fact, here's another easy
one—Anton burned down the community center,
which is also the home of his former mistress, to
destroy his wife's livelihood and maybe even
enacting revenge and killing his mistress in the
process. How am I doing? I probably could write
an episode of *Santa*—

"You did this?"

Obviously I'm not the only one doing the math
here, because Chase, in a total soap-opera response,
lets go of me and launches himself at Anton.

He grabs Anton up by the shirt. "You set this fire?"

Anton has his hands on Chase's wrists.

They go down in the mud. Chase is speaking half-

Russian, half-English, and it's not pretty. Much of it sounds like it's coming from a place inside Chase I don't know.

"Is this how you treat people who have worked hard for Bursk, to help you build new lives? Don't you care about anyone but yourself? No wonder Ulia left you!"

Chase dodges a punch, and I scream, pushing Justin's face into my jacket.

And then Nathan appears, grabbing Chase, yanking him off Anton.

But Anton isn't finished. He finds his feet and takes another swing at Chase. Vasilley nabs him by the arm. There's a lot more power in Mr. Skin and Bones than I thought.

Chase rounds on Nathan, and for a second I think he's going to take a swing at *him,* but he shakes himself free.

Nathan steps back, hands up. "It's not worth it, Chase."

Chase gives him a long look. Then he turns, and the despair on his face makes me want to weep.

My man is down for the count.

Without a word, Chase walks away.

The militia guys finally decide to pick sides. They drag Anton away from the crowd. I notice that Ulia follows.

Behind me, the rest of the building caves in with a thunderous roar.

"Mommy!" I turn to see Chloe tugging at Maya's hand. She's wide-eyed and afraid.

I scoop her up and hold both my children tight. Chloe wraps her legs around me. Justin is shaking.

"Shh," I say, watching the fire begin to smolder. It's going to burn long into the night, however. "Everything's going to be okay."

I see Nathan standing at a distance. But he's not looking at me. His eyes are on Maya. He crosses to her and pulls her close, wrapping his arms around her.

Oh.

She looks at me, and I see tears spilling down her cheeks. *Spaceeba*, she mouths.

Now I have tears, too.

Slowly I turn and walk home, my children clinging to me.

The house is dark when we enter, and Chase's jacket, a puddle of soot on the floor, confirms that he made it home. His boots, caked with mud, lie on their sides as if he flung them off.

I put the kids down, de-layer them and dump their clothes in a pile. Wash day will be fun tomorrow.

The fire is dying. I open the furnace and throw in a chunk of coal. I set Chloe and Justin on the sofa, pile toys around them and turn on a cartoon.

Then I look for Chase.

He's sitting on the bed, his head in his hands. His shoulders are shaking.

I get scared when I see Chase's shoulders shake. "Chase?"

"I meant to do this right."

His words still me. Meant to do *what* right? I hold my breath.

He looks up at me. His eyes are red. "I'm sorry about that, back there. I— Anton probably did set the fire, but I shouldn't have done that. If anyone is to blame for you losing everything, it's me."

He shakes his head. "I shouldn't have followed my ambition to Siberia. I should have taken you home."

I blink at him, and the verse I read—was it only an hour ago?—flashes through my mind. *Live a life of love, just as Christ loved us.* And love speaks the truth.

"Babe, listen. I *do* feel as though I've been running around Siberia a little bit unprotected. I needed to know that you were still the guy who would ride in on his motorcycle in the dead of night and rescue me, and I wasn't always sure that was true. However, I'm *not* sorry we came to Siberia. I'm not thrilled about having an outhouse, or about letting Nathan so far into our lives that you thought we were having an affair—and don't look at me like that, because we're not, and didn't, and that's all I'm going to say about that—but I'm not sorry about the rest. I'm not sorry for giving these women a sense of accomplishment, or for helping Olya get back her daughter, or for holding down the fort while you went hunting with Vasilley so he could find Jesus. And I'm especially not sorry about being stretched so far I thought I might break, and discovering I had more in me than I realized. So you don't get to take the blame for all the bad or the good stuff. God gets that."

I sit down and lean against him. "And He's bigger than you. He can take it."

Chase doesn't smile, but he puts his arm around me and closes his eyes. "Oh, GI. I just wanted to do more here. Something that would really change their lives. Do good." He sighs deeply and I can practically feel his exhaustion. "Would you read something?"

Would I read something? Like the Secret Journal of Chase Anderson? Oh, I suppose, if you insist. I school my voice. "Um, sure."

He pulls his journal from under the bed and hands it to me.

I feel like I'm being given access to his heart. The Chase I don't know. Yet.

He leans back on the bed as I open the book. "Where do I start?"

"Anywhere. But don't stop until you read the part where I say that I know you and Nathan didn't have an affair but I wouldn't blame you if you did. And be sure not to skip over the section where I realize that everything I've done over the past five years is a failure."

What?

I close the journal without reading it. "I'm not going to read that, because it's not true."

His eyes are still closed as if he doesn't want to hear what I'm saying. And now I'm angry.

"Hey, we have two adorable, incredible kids who love their daddy. And unless I'm mistaken, we have the nicest outhouse in all of Siberia. So don't tell me that you're a failure."

I get a little smile. But it quickly vanishes.

I put the journal down on his chest. "Could it be, though, that you were supposed to see that God has something bigger for you?"

He opens an eye.

"Could it be that God brought you out to Siberia, not so we could change the economic future of the people of Bursk, but their spiritual future? Maybe Nathan is right—I *would* make a fabulous pastor's wife, because *you* were meant to be a pastor."

"Nathan said that to you?"

"Yes. And he feels sick about putting us in this position. He wasn't after me, Chase. But he knows he can't be our friend anymore. Or at least not our roommate."

Chase looks at me. "He told me that you'd make a fabulous pastor's wife, too. He also told me that maybe God was doing more in my life than I was willing to see."

Well, that could apply to all of us, couldn't it?

"The thing is, GI, I…uh…" Chase clenches his jaw, as if the words have to be wrestled out. "I came here because I was selfish. I saw my life spiraling down to nothing in Gull Lake, and I panicked. And when you were so supportive, and enduring, it just made me feel worse, and then I couldn't talk to you, and then Nathan could, and I got jealous." He attempts a smile. "You wanted the guy who would show up on his motorcycle. I wanted to know that you'd still jump on the back and ride with me anywhere."

Oh, is there any doubt? I lean over and kiss him, and his arms go around me.

"Forgive me, babe?" he whispers.

I love forgiveness. Especially when it includes Chase holding me, his lips on mine, making me remember just why I went to all those high-school football practices in the Minnesota cold. I suppose it was just a warm-up to the real thing.

He finally sighs and leans back. "Nathan asked me how long I was willing to wait to become the man God plans me to be."

I touch Chase's hair and smile. "And?"

"Not a day longer." He sits up and takes my hand. "Maybe I could be more." Something gathers in his eyes, something that fills my heart, and I see the Chase I knew years ago, when he first dreamed of following God into the hinterlands. "Maybe I want to start over," he says softly. "Be a blank slate for God to write on."

A blank slate. I love that. A do-over, except with everything we know now.

"Except, I'm not sure how to get there, Jose."

I take his hand, run my fingers over the calluses. "Olya told me not long ago that you have to get naked to get clean. Seems like a good place to start, huh?"

So for the second time today, I find myself praying. And beside me is the man I'd happily follow anywhere.

Chapter Nineteen

Already Home

Dear H,

I owe you an apology. Because I get it now. *Really* get it.

Nathan and I weren't having an affair. But I let him inside my heart, and you saw that. It wasn't on purpose, and it happened one day at a time, without my awareness but definitely with my consent. I suppose if I had let myself, it could have been something more, but well… because of you, and God and even my beloved Banya Girls, it wasn't.

In fact, what I didn't know is that Nathan has been seeing Maya—you remember her? The pretty woman who came to dinner?

Did I tell you that the community center burned down? Anton, the mayor, set it on fire. He blamed Maya, but I knew she couldn't do that—not after the way her husband died. And when Anton's wife showed up, apologizing for leaving him, and then confronted him, he admitted what he'd done. Apparently not long after her husband's death, Maya and Anton had a brief affair—something she cut off, but he kept pushing for. Eventually he hated her for not giving in. Maya felt so guilty, she started taking meals to Anton and Ulia's widowed daughter-in-law, Sasha, and her children. But I think that was more about redemption and restitution. Ulia got that part, thankfully. But Anton was afraid of losing his wife, and he thought maybe Secrets of Siberia gave her too much freedom, so in desperation, he burned our business down, hoping to scare Maya with the fire, too. He claims he wasn't trying to kill her, and maybe that's the truth. He's in the town jail, awaiting trial.

I know. I'm telling you, there's more drama in frozen Bursk than a Saturday night in Gull Lake!

Forgiveness is contagious, and the entire village is going through a sort of revival. Nathan has started a church, and even the men are attending.

Anyway, I wanted to tell you that there *are*

things you can count on. Like, it doesn't matter where you live, just who you live with. And submission doesn't mean that you have to surrender your brain, just your heart. I think the best relationships are the ones where everybody wins. Marriage is a partnership, not a division of labor. A life carrying burdens and joys, together. Helping each other. At least that's what I've learned living in Siberia.

I believe you and Rex are going to make it, H. Talk to him and trust in his love for you. I know you can work it out. Even in Gull Lake. Most importantly, don't be afraid to give up what you think is most important, because God has a way of making your surrender feel like a reward and giving you back even more than you gave up.

Forgive me, please, for letting you down?

Rock on,

Josey

I shouldn't be surprised that the news of the fire made it all the way to Moscow. After all, it's not every day that a man burns down the biggest building in town in a jealous rage.

And, of course, Chase had to include this cheery event in his analysis of Bursk for Voices International.

I am surprised, nonetheless, when Dalton and Maggie appear at my gate nearly two weeks later. "I like what you've done with the place," Maggie says as she crosses the threshold.

Maggie is walking elegance, even in a Siberian village. She's wearing a jacket lined with rabbit fur, and of course, I notice the boots—supple brown leather, obviously imported.

"I especially love the outhouse," she says with a smile.

I've decorated it for spring with a spray of lilacs, and it's hard not to come out woozy from the smell. The fragrant floral smell, I mean.

I drop my shovel where I've been digging rows for a garden. I'm not sure why I'm doing this—we leave in just a few weeks—but I figure that Misha and Anya will appreciate having seeds in the ground. It's the least I can do for the people who gave up their home for us.

The sun is high, and we've set our clocks forward. I am thrilled that the days are lengthening.

I embrace Maggie, and then little Steven, who runs into the house looking for Justin and Chloe. Dalton wraps me in a one-arm hug. "I hear you have a decent sofa." He smiles, and I'm trying to figure out how it will hold two.

Not that I'm complaining.

"What are you doing here?"

"Chase told us about your little village home, and I just had to see it for myself," Maggie says. Her brown eyes are twinkling.

I should mention here that it was Maggie and her State Department connections that really got Chase's peanut-butter cottage industry off the ground. And I have a feeling she's not just here to share a cup of tea.

I find out the reason for their visit at dinner— we've graduated from soup and moved onto mashed potatoes and cutlets.

"Chase told us about your business, Josey. And we want to help." Dalton spears another cutlet and puts it on his plate. "In fact, we'd like to start similar businesses in native villages all over Russia."

I stare at Chase, and he looks as surprised as I am. But I win this contest because behind my surprise, is shock that he was talking about Secrets of Siberia in Moscow.

Chase smiles at me. "Want more potatoes, Chloe?"

"No tatoes!" Chloe says, and pushes herself away from the table. As she gets down, she paws the ground and lets out a neigh.

Oh, we're moving on to larger animals. My little pony.

Maggie doesn't notice the equine in the family room—she's intently focused on Chase and me. "And the best part is, we want you and Chase to move back to Moscow and run the business. You will have offices in WorldMar, and we'll fund your first year, just to get you off the ground."

"Are you saying it'll become an NGO project?" Chase asks.

"No, no. It'll be a business. But one that we'll both have equal stakes in," Dalton glances at Maggie, his eyes betraying his excitement.

"We can have investors lined up in no time," Maggie adds as Steven pushes off her lap and gallops in a circle with Chloe. Maggie is pregnant again, and has the smallest, cutest bulge. I wonder what it's like to have them one at a time.

"Listen, with Maggie's State Department connections, we can figure out how to fast-track shipments out of the country. It'll streamline everything. We could even set up a warehouse in New York City. Think of it—you and Chase can travel to the villages and help people develop their crafts. With Chase's experience working with the elders, I'm sure he can bring them to agreement, especially when he shows how the proceeds can benefit the village—medicines and vaccinations, new structures, anything the village needs, basically. Chloe and Justin can attend the best schools in Moscow," Dalton says, leaning forward and giving me a sly smile, "and Josey can have indoor plumbing!"

But I'm starting to like my outhouse.

Okay, not that much.

"What do you think?" Dalton says, wiping his mouth with his napkin. "Can we lure you back to Moscow?"

* * *

It's late by the time we clean up, get the kids in bed, pull out the sofa bed and finally climb into our own bed. We keep our voices low because Maggie and Dalton are in the next room.

Chase's hand finds mine in the darkness. "So, GI, what do you want to do? Move to Moscow? Or," he says, rolling over, his whiskers brushing my cheek, "should we go home?"

Oh, boy. What is it they say about history repeating itself?

"Me, cake!" Justin is sitting at the table, his grubby little fingers just itching to take a swipe out of the chocolate frosting I'm layering on the twins' birthday cake. I can't believe they're four.

Or that I made a cake from scratch. It's not unlike cookies, despite what I previously thought.

Most of all, I can't believe that four years ago today, I learned that God loves me in ways I never imagined. And it seems He hasn't slacked off, either.

The plastic is off our windows and they're open, allowing in a breeze smelling of jasmine and lilac, overturned garden dirt and the fresh start that spring brings. Chloe is dressed all in pink, in short sleeves, her hair in high curly pigtails. She's trotting around the yard whinnying. I think I miss the kitty.

"Olya sent over a salmon pie," Chase says, walking into the house with a plate covered by a towel. He's looking cute and American in a pair of faded jeans and a long-sleeve pullover that makes his blue eyes shine. Yeah, I'm still crazy about the man who stole my heart in the sandbox. "She said she'll send Vasilley over in a bit with *sok*."

Because a party is not a party without prune *sok*.

But I *am* glad for the help with Chloe and Justin's birthday party. Besides the cake, I've baked eight-dozen peanut-butter cookies (thanks to Maggie and Dalton's re-supply gift), pretty much exhausting my kitchen repertoire.

Chase sets down the pie. "I invited Nathan." He looks at me, gauging my response.

I give him a nod. "I hope he brings Maya." I'm proud of Chase, seeking out Nathan and apologizing. The fact is, Nathan asked the right questions and made Chase see his potential losses, as well as his hidden gifts—every guy needs a friend like that.

Even if the friend needs to work on his boundaries. Like not giving flowers to other people's wives.

I finish the cake, put it in the center of the table and go outside. Chase has set up a long picnic table with benches. I cover the table with a sheet and decorate it with orange flowers I find growing along my fence.

Already, the potatoes are sprouting through the dirt we furrowed. Hopefully, when Anya and Misha move back in, they'll be pleased by the garden. Not to mention Chase's award-winning outhouse.

Chase comes up beside me, puts his arm around

my waist and kisses me. "Just think of the garden you'll have in Gull Lake."

I touch his hand and then turn, twining my arms around his neck and laying my head on his chest. We've decided to turn down Maggie's offer. The last thing the twins need is more time away from Mom. I've taught Olya the ins and outs of the Internet, and she's taken over most of the eBay responsibilities of Secrets of Siberia. Chloe and Justin are back to half days at *detski-sod,* and both of them are "error"-free and keeping their sign language to themselves.

Even Vasilley and some of the elders have joined the business, making bread boxes and cutting boards. I'm amazed at their skill. And their new willingness to be partners.

As for Maya, she lost everything in the fire. The town has banded together and not only furnished a room for her at *detski-sod,* but also given her clothing. I'm not sure she likes the clothes, but I know she loves the grace she's been given.

I'm also able to spot the grace I've been given. I like life in this village. The crow of the rooster in the morning, the low of the cows, the smell of coal smoke. I love that when I go to the post office, I always see someone I know.

In fact, perhaps Bursk isn't so different from Gull Lake.

"Hey there, lovebirds, none of that in front of the young'uns." Nathan's voice makes me smile, and I give Chase a quick kiss before I greet him. Nathan is holding Maya's hand, and I recognize a smile on her face that I know comes from healing.

"Want a cookie?" I loop my arm through hers as she laughs.

Before we can go into the house, more people come through the gate—Ulia and her brother, Misha and Anya and the Banya Girls, who I now have begun to recognize fully dressed. Olya and Vasilley arrive with little Albena, who breaks away and runs to find Justin and Chloe.

All the commotion attracts Lydia's attention, and she tries to force her body through the fence, barking her hellos. I toss her a cookie as I turn and greet our guests.

Everyone's brought goodies—sauerkraut, pickles, *sala,* salad and bread.

"Congratulations!" Olya says as she gives me a kiss on the cheek.

"Why congratulations?" I receive a kiss from Vasilley.

"We congratulate the mother on the birthday of her children," Olya says. She's still glowing, as if Albena just arrived home yesterday. Or maybe it's because in about six months, she'll be accepting congratulations for number two.

I hear a shriek followed by pounding feet, and Justin flies out of the house, followed by Albena.

"Mommy! Chloe ate the cake!"

Of course she did. But I can see that Justin's far from innocent, because he's wearing a beard of chocolate frosting.

I roll my eyes and turn, but Chase stops me. "I'll handle it." He gives me a wink.

"So have you guys decided what you're going to do?" Nathan asks as Olya and Maya lay out the treats on the table. I frown at him, and he looks confused. "Apparently Chase hasn't mentioned it to you."

Uh-oh, here we go again. "Hasn't mentioned what?"

"I'm headed stateside to finish seminary." He lowers his voice. "I'm going to put it off just a bit longer." His gaze flashes to Maya, and I see tenderness cross his face. "But eventually I'll need someone to take up the reins of this ministry. Someone with a heart and understanding for the people of Siberia."

My throat is tight. And not because Chase has kept this question from me but because I suddenly realize how much he loves me. Chase knows how much I miss Gull Lake. And he wants to give me my home.

I'm wondering, though, if I'd miss Bursk as much as I've missed Gull Lake. Because maybe it's not *where* I live, but how. And with whom.

And *I* want Chase to be everything God intends for him.

"You told me once, Nathan, that I'd make a good pastor's wife. But all I've ever wanted to be is a good wife. One who loves her husband. And if God wants to do this amazing work through Chase, I'm going to help…by not standing in the way."

Before Nathan can say anything, Chase appears. He's clutching Justin under one arm and Chloe under the other. They're both covered in chocolate and giggling.

Because Chase is also covered in chocolate. When he tries to give me a kiss, I laugh and dodge him.

But he'll catch me. He always does.

And as I watch him chase the other kids around the yard, our little weapons of chocolate destruction under his arms, I know in my heart that it doesn't really matter where we live.

Because, together, we're already home.

Epilogue

Ready, Set…Go!

"Are you ready?" I'm crammed into a Radio Flyer wagon, perched atop Bloomquist Mountain. Below, Gull Lake sparkles under a perfect summer sky.

"Josey, really, this is crazy. I'm going to win, and you're going to get hurt." Chase is sitting in a matching wagon, all grins. He looks just as cute as he did twenty-some years ago, in his cut-off T-shirt and faded jeans. And here I am again, poised to race him down a gravel hill. I might turn over into the ditch. And yes, I might even get hurt.

But I know I'm going to win.

"I can't believe it's our last day here." I'm stalling for time as I eye the descent.

Chase has his legs over the side and is rocking his

wagon back and forth. The sun has browned his face and arms. He's been working at Berglund Acres over the past year with Dad, getting it ready for the new ownership, namely my brother, Buddy, who is moving with his fiancée back to Gull Lake.

Has it already been a year since we left Bursk? I can still see them—Olya, Vasilley and Albena, waving to us from the dock, along with the clothed Banya Girls. And Ulia, standing with Sasha and her children. Last I heard Ulia was living with her daughter-in-law while Anton serves his sentence for arson. And I can still see Maya and Nathan at the Khabarovsk airport as we *fly* out, thank you very much, courtesy of Chase's insisting that Voices International treat us to plane tickets.

It's been a contemplative but busy year, ending with our commissioning service last week at the church.

Buddy is already manning the coals for the big Berglund Acres barbecue. Aunt Myrtle and Uncle Bert have probably arrived, along with H, who is already starting to show, a cute lump under her hot-pink maternity shirt. (It's hard to tell which is glowing more—her shirt, her hair, or her face.) I knew she could do it.

So they're all here. One family ready to send us back to the other.

"Caleb and Daphne called this morning," Chase tells me. "They'll meet us at the airport in New York. Apparently Caleb wants to show her Central Park."

"It's the last glimpse of mowed grass they're going to have for four years," I say. "But I have a feeling that Daphne is going to love Bursk."

I reach over and grip his arm. "Say it again."

"Indoor plumbing, I promise." He grins. "I've already contacted Vasilley, and he says they're working on it. And not just for us—they're contracting for plumbing for the whole town. He makes a great mayor, if you ask me."

I finally dredged up the courage to ask Olya about her black eye—and she looked at me a long time, dumbfounded, until she burst into laughter. "Lydia!" she said, and explained how Lydia had taken out the fence, and Olya had wrestled her back to their side of the yard. "And Olya is fine. She and the kids send their love. You were smart to put her in charge of Secrets of Siberia. She has to fight for dial-up time with Maya, however, who spends all her free time online, chatting with Nathan. Apparently, Maya's coming stateside for Thanksgiving this year. Nathan told me last time we talked that he might pop the question."

I'm so glad Chase still has Nathan in his life. I wonder what else they talk about. Like, the Bible classes Chase has been taking? Or perhaps the way he is devouring God's word? He went through Ephesians in just a week! It took me…oh, never mind.

The breeze stirs the pine and poplar trees, reaping the last smells of summer. I can't believe it's nearly over.

"Your parents are probably back from the pool with Justin and Chloe. I know they've loved all this grand-parenting time. They're starting to get the hang of instant messaging, and I already installed the webcam. I tried it on Jasmine last night. She and Milton said they'd leave for the barbecue right after church."

"She'd better be bringing kringle."

"She mentioned that, and bagels."

I laugh. See, the people who love me won't forget, regardless of how far I roam.

"We'd better get going if we hope to get any ribs."

I stare down the hill again. It's not as steep as I remember—more of an incline, really.

"Are you sure about this?" Chase says, also looking down the hill. His smile dims, and I see the same un-certainty in his eyes that I saw the day we received our acceptance letter from Mission to the World.

Dear Chase and Josey Anderson,
    We're pleased to inform you that you have been accepted as career missionaries…

"I'm sure about this," I say, grasping the handle of the wagon. "But can you keep up?"

His smile is back, part danger, part challenge. My stomach does a small roll of delight.

"Ready…set…"
"Go!" I yell, and push off.
Chase is behind me, laughing.
And my face is to the eastern wind.

* * * * *

QUESTIONS FOR DISCUSSION

1. Josey has been married for a few years when the book opens. Her plan is to go camping with her husband so he'll be willing to move back to Gull Lake. Do you think spouses "bargain" like this? How effective is it?

2. Why do you think Josey agrees to go to Bursk? Would you have gone?

3. Josey takes the train across Siberia. What is the longest trip you've ever taken as an adult? Did you have children with you? Did you have any crazy moments? What were they?

4. Chase promised Josey a house. Have you ever moved someplace, sight unseen? What would you have done if you'd discovered you had no indoor plumbing?

5. Do any of Chloe and Justin's antics remind you of children you know? Who, and how?

6. Josey thinks that Olya is being abused by her husband. Have you ever been in a situation

where you suspected something like this? What did you do about it?

7. Why does Josey enroll her children in *detski-sod?* Do you think that was a good idea? Why or why not?

8. Josey struggles with her sister's success, despite her happiness for her. Have you ever had someone close to you experience success? Were you jealous? How did you deal with those emotions?

9. What was your reaction when Chase brought his Christmas present for Josey?

10. In Russia, it is quite common for guests to drop in and stay for a while, as Nathan does, with Josey and Chase. Do you have a friend that drops in the way Nathan does? What do you think Josey should have done, given that Chase invited him?

11. Have you traveled or lived abroad? What is your favorite foreign dessert or delicacy?

12. Why do you think that H could see Nathan's effect on Josey, but Josey couldn't? Do you think Josey would have cheated on Chase if Nathan had been after her heart?

13. What is Josey's epiphany in the story? How does she change and grow? If you've read either of the two previous novels (*Everything's Coming Up Josey* and *Chill Out, Josey!*), how has she matured?

14. Have you ever wanted to have a blank slate and start over again? What would you do with your life?

15. Why don't Chase and Josey take the job Maggie and Dalton offer them? Do you think they'll live happily ever after? Why, or why not?